"Who are you?" Wentworth snapped. He was a man used to command.

"A *venator*."

"And that is?" he demanded impatiently.

She sighed. "Your judge. Your jury." She unsheathed her sword and swung it. One officer's head fell off and rolled toward the dead soldier. "Your executioner."

Another officer pulled out his pistol and shot her. The bullet passed through her with a stinging pain. Before she said her next words, the wound had closed. "Have you learned nothing about what you have become?" She tried not to let the lingering pain show. She hated when people shot at her.

"What do you know?" The general's interest was piqued.

"Since I'm over a hundred years old, much more than you."

"You're nothing but a woman," he scoffed, and she could see in his eyes that what he really meant was 'black woman.'

Mignon studied him. "I will save you for last."

BLOOD LUST

J.M. JEFFRIES

Genesis Press Inc.

Indigo Love Stories

An imprint of Genesis Press Inc.
Publishing Company

Genesis Press, Inc.
P.O. Box 101
Columbus, MS 39703

Copyright© 2005 by J.M. Jeffries

ISBN: 1-58571-138-1
Manufactured in the United States of America

First Edition

Visit us at www.genesis-press.com
or call at 1-888-Indigo-1

DEDICATION

From Jackie: For my Omi, my mother and Aunt Bobbie, like Mignon, you survived the worst the world has to offer. Thank you for your sacrifice, your strength, your wisdom, your love and kick-ass DNA.

From Miriam: For my husband, my daughter and my son, thank you for your patience and love even in the most difficult of days. For my brother and sisters, your belief in me sustains me. For my mom who shared her own dreams. For all the Wild Women Writers who have hopes and dreams. May they all come true.

ACKNOWLEDGMENTS

For Sidney: a vital part of the J.M. Jeffries team, who whipped this story into shape. We could never have done this without you, your eagle eye, tenacious grasp of the story and incredible mind. Thank you so very, very much.

And for Niani and Angelique: you are both more important to the J.M. Jeffries team than you will ever know. Thank you both for your keen intelligence, imagination and willingness to let us stretch our wings a little bit.

PROLOGUE

Martinique — 1745

"You sold my children!" Mignon curled her hands around the edge of the blanket covering her nakedness, fighting the impotent fury inside her. Candles lit the opulent bedroom, casting flickers of flames over his face, highlighting the evil twist of his lips and the shadow of his eyes.

Charles Rabelais seemed to gloat. "Your brats were mine to dispose of as I chose." He stroked her cheek with long, pale fingers.

She tried not to turn away as he traced her bottom lip with his thumb. Instead, she concentrated on his white skin showing stark against her duskiness. "Please give them back."

Because he was her children's father, she had hoped they'd be safe from the slave blocks. Charles felt had no kinship despite the fact his seed, planted deep within her, had given them life.

"*Non,*" he said.

Agonizing pain knifed through her as his chilled fingers slid across her light brown cheek. She steeled herself not to draw away no matter how she loathed his touch. Once before, she'd been foolish enough to defy him. The bite of the whip still echoed in her mind, as well as the piercing pain that had raced across her back. His amused laughter had frightened her most of all.

"Why?" she asked, dreading his answer. Lace curtains billowed in the breeze, bringing a hint of fragrant wisteria inside the room.

Leaning over, he kissed her earlobe. "So that you will be mine for eternity."

She trembled as he slid his hand down the side of her throat to the curve of her breast. "Master, they are so little." Her darlings were gone. Helplessness filled her. They had been the only reason she had not taken her own life as her mother had. She would not leave her babies at his mercy.

Charles chuckled. "I brokered a deal with the devil and your whelps were the price."

Her lips trembled. A tear slid down her cheek. "Angeline is only eleven years old and Simon is but seven. They are your children, too."

Charles waved his hand. The soft light of the candles illuminated his pale skin. "Be happy I didn't kill them. My love for you is what kept them alive. What should concern you now is an appropriate means of showing your gratitude." He moved over her, parting her knees with his leg.

Gratitude for what? For her living hell? For her children's lives? What were her choices? She was a woman. A slave with no recourse.

If she complied with his demands, she might find out who he'd sold the children to. Perhaps then she could...she couldn't finish the thought. She had no means of finding them or obtaining their freedom. Mignon closed her eyes and forced out the words he wanted to hear. "Thank you for letting them live."

"Very pretty." He kissed her lips. "Now I must finish what I started."

He had talked about that before. What did he mean? "I don't understand."

"Do you want to live forever? By my side? Warming my bed?"

What choice did she have? He already owned her flesh, her blood, everything but her soul. "What are you saying?"

He scraped his thumbnail along the throbbing pulse in her neck. "Say yes and I will give you eternal life. Eternal beauty. My heart forever. Everything any woman could ever want."

She only wanted her children back. A dark pit formed in her heart, and an icy shell seemed to surround it. "What must I do to please you?"

"Say yes." He kissed her again, forcing his tongue between her lips.

Whatever Charles wanted, he had only to take. He'd already taken her virtue. Her mother, once a household servant, had been put to work in the cane fields when she'd objected to him taking Mignon as his whore. She had died soon after. Of her own father, Mignon had no knowledge, only that her mother had warmed the bed of another planter before being sold to Charles. Now Charles had sold her children. Nothing was left for him to take. The years stretched out before her bleak and dismal, all joy removed. "Yes."

"I knew you would." His hand tightened around her neck. He forced her head to one side.

Squeezing her eyes tight, she willed the pain rippling through her to end. Endless years, endless nothing. With her children gone, what did she have to live for?

"Look at me," Charles commanded in a guttural tone.

Mignon opened her eyes and stared at his mouth. Was she mistaken, or were his teeth growing? The pearly white tips rested on his colorless bottom lip. Fear surged through her. She wanted to pull back, but his grip was so strong, she feared he might snap her neck.

Charles licked her neck, starting at her ear and slowly moving down toward the beating pulse. The seconds, measured by the ticking of the clock on the mantle, passed slowly.

She couldn't look away from the evil in his face. Suddenly his mouth opened. Sharp fangs gleamed at her. No sound came out of her mouth as she tried to scream. He gripped her hair in a tight fist, pulling, bringing tears to her eyes.

He smiled at her, enjoying her distress, her fear. He sniffed at her mouth as though her fear were a palpable object to be fondled and enjoyed.

Her body froze. She couldn't close her eyes.

His mouth neared her neck. After a long moment, he bit and sighed, as though savoring the trembling of her body. Pain seared into her flesh. Her blood seemed to run like fire in her veins. Death, she hoped, she prayed. Let him give her death.

CHAPTER ONE

Present Day — New Orleans

Detective Ryan Lattimore's stomach convulsed into a painful knot. The stench of decaying bodies no disinfectant could mask filled the darkened room. A faucet dripped endless drops of water into a metal sink.

Who had thought up this lame-assed idea to set up a stakeout in the morgue? Oh, that's right—his boss. Score one for the brass.

Although the dead couldn't get much deader, someone had been sneaking into the morgue after hours to hack the heads off the stiffs in the morgue cooler. That someone had been dubbed the "Vampire Slayer" by the newspapers.

Ryan lifted a mug of steaming, hot coffee to his lips and breathed in the bitter aroma, hoping to mask the stench of decomposition. The sludge brewed at the morgue was toxic enough to eat holes in the soles of his Timberlands. But he couldn't complain; at least the caffeine kept him awake. Night shifts sucked. He craved a cigarette, but knew he couldn't indulge at the moment. With all the chemicals in the air, he might just blow the place up. And that would be bad. Then again, if he were dead, he wouldn't have to worry about finding the killer. He chuckled to himself. Macabre humor seemed to be the trademark for his current assignment. New Orleans did that to a person.

He forced air into his lungs, and an eerie calm descended on him. The stakeout would have been easier to tolerate with his partner, Mary Sanders. He could have used her objectivity on this case. She had a talent for details that Ryan's big picture mentality never could grasp.

Mary had been sidelined to desk duty while the rat squad investigated her for allegedly shaking down drug dealers. Like that was a really bad thing. He didn't believe for a minute she was guilty, but the Public Integrity Bureau, as Internal Affairs was now called, needed a home run to show the city they were keeping cops honest.

Numbing cold penetrated his bones. He flexed his fingers, trying to keep them nimble. The morgue was creepy dead at midnight, no pun intended. When on a stakeout, hoping to catch a serial killer, a person appreciated the bizarre.

Ryan's boss, Lieutenant Barton, had come to the conclusion that the person beheading the dead was also the killer, who was returning to complete some grotesque sort of ritual. Ryan wasn't certain how that conclusion had evolved out of the evidence. But his job was to catch the hacker and make the Big Easy safe for hookers, drug dealers, gang bangers again. Why couldn't some drunk guy shoot another jerk in a bar on his shift? Nope, he got the crazies.

Ryan blew on his icy fingers. He could just hear his neighbor's sons asking what he'd done last night. Babysat corpses. That should keep the kiddies entertained for a few weeks, though they'd probably have night-mares. Or not, considering some of the gruesome practical jokes the kids had played on him.

The murders in and of themselves hadn't aroused much interest in New Orleans since the victims were known to be on the wrong side of the law to begin with. What did one less lowlife matter? But the recent decapitations had the whole city whipped into a frenzy. There was even talk about bringing in an FBI profiler. The last thing Ryan wanted or needed was to work with the "Freakin' Bunch of Idiots" as he liked to call them.

Ryan had seen some sick and kinky crap during his six years with the police and eight years as a Special Forces commando before that, but he could say without batting an eyelash that beheading corpses in the morgue took the chocolate cake. And then some. His suspect was not a garden variety freak. This boy was slick as cat poop on the kitchen floor for getting away every time. This was the kind of case that built a career. And it had landed right in his ungrateful lap.

The constant buzzing of the one flourescent light left on over the cooler door made him edgy. Muted light glinted off stainless steel counters arranged around the walls. A large drain in the center of the white tiled floor looked like a hole to hell. He didn't want to know what had been washed down that drain. A large gunmetal gray desk, which sat perpendicular to the double door entry, was stacked with files and toe tags. A row of brown file cabinets ran along one wall. Floor to ceiling metal shelves, containing bottles of human organs and other peculiar things Ryan didn't want to investigate too closely, hugged the leftover wall space.

Ryan huddled in the shadowed corner, wedged in between the water cooler and a stainless steel cart. Ten minutes ago, his boss outside in the corridor, pretending to be a janitor, had radioed him to check the five bodies locked inside.

Ryan didn't know what Lieutenant Barton thought the bodies were going to do. Get up and do the electric slide out the doors? No other way into the cooler existed except through the door Ryan watched. If the serial killer wanted those corpses tonight, he'd have to pull a Houdini. No one was getting past Ryan or Milos Reed, who was masquerading as the night clerk, or Barton, who was pretending to wipe down the floor with a dry mop.

Missing persons reports of the city's degenerate population had been stacking up. Indignant mothers, angry girlfriends, and confused parole officers had flooded the precincts with calls demanding action. Some of the missing had been found residing in the morgue's cooler. Others had been found out in the street minus their heads, while others were still missing. Ryan could only hope they'd moved on to be another city's headache.

Most cops didn't give a flying flip when a bunch of losers wound up dead. The crime rate was way down in N'awlins—always a good thing. Why anyone would get all worked up if someone decided to lend a helping hand in ridding the city of gangbangers, drug dealers, and low-life criminals was the question *du jour.*

Okay, Ryan cared. He had this odd idea that justice belonged to everyone. And when the heads starting rolling across New Orleans's lawns, the department began to pay attention, especially when one serial rapist's noggin had the bad luck to end up next to the mayor's prize-winning wisteria.

Ryan wasn't a philosophical kind of guy. The implications of a headless corpse on the mayor's lawn didn't require a lot of thought. The shit had started sliding downhill until it plopped right on top of his little shotgun house on the edge of the Garden District.

Spending the night in the morgue smacked a bit too much of final destination for Ryan. Bad enough he'd end up here some day, flat on his back, but being around the dead bodies while he was still alive set his nerves on edge.

The entry door swung open on squeaky hinges.

Ryan came to full alert, every muscle tensing. He peered through the gloomy shadows. For a second, he saw nothing but shimmering waves that distorted the air and made the hair on the back of his neck stand up. Disorientation settled over him, and he shook his head trying to fight his way through the odd fogginess. He tried to move his hand toward his Smith & Wesson, but he felt frozen in place, as though he were battling his way through ten layers of lead.

Primal fear radiated through him. What the hell was happening? He tried to clear his head. Suddenly, his mind broke free of the suction that held him in a tight fist. The shimmering waves cleared, revealing a tall, slender sister with skin the color of his favorite iced mocha blend.

Hello gorgeous!

She paused inside the room, her lithe body a delicate balance of grace and strength. Except for the huge axe that looked like the grim reaper's scythe in her hands, she was a goddess. From the shoulder length, midnight hair to the body-hugging, black leather outfit embracing every curve of her luscious body, she was a vision. But with the axe in her hands, he figured she was a dangerous one.

Ryan's pulse started to race and his palms started to sweat He wasn't even going to speculate on what was going on south of his belt buckle.

The babe slid further into the room, the axe held out in front of her with an ease that just screamed she knew what she was about.

This was his headhunter! Damn, he should be dating her, not busting her. God was a cruel master to make a sister that fine into a psycho serial killer. Whoever had tripped her switch needed to be hurt bad.

This just couldn't be true. He tilted his head, wondering if she was some sort of long-repressed fantasy come to life. Hell, he needed to get laid.

His fingers inched toward his gun as he fought through the strange lethargy that tried to keep his arms glued in place. What the hell was going on? Time had come to a total standstill. Even the minute hand on the clock was functioning oddly, going forward one second and back the next. Ryan wondered how the hell she'd gotten past the cops in the hall.

She moved across the room with the controlled elegance of a dancer, perfectly in tune with her body. For a few seconds Ryan worried about Barton and Reed in the hall outside. Had she attacked them? Were they dead? He saw no blood on the blade.

The woman stopped at the door to the cooler and opened the latch with a loud click.

Ryan struggled to release himself. He opened his mouth to yell at her, but no sound came out. His feet felt stuck to the floor. When he tried to stand, the air seemed to close around him, binding him with invisible fingers. He wrestled against the denseness, pushing his hand through the thick, resisting air closer toward his gun. Move, he commanded his arm. Move. But every inch was a battle against the strange lethargy that held him imprisoned.

The woman swung the door open with ease. Inside, Ryan saw the five bodies on wheeled stainless steel tables covered by white sheets.

This honey couldn't be his killer. Women weren't serial killers, especially not beautiful sisters with cinnamon-colored skin and a behind that could stop time itself. His mouth went dry just staring at the proud lift of her breasts and the firm muscles of that butt. She was hot.

Suddenly, the dense air dissipated and he broke free to stumble forward onto his knees. He caught himself on the edge of a desk and pushed himself to his feet. "Yo! Axe-wielding babe!" Good, his voice worked again.

The woman turned to gaze at him, her aristocratic face calm and serene. She smiled at him and raised one hand. "Forget." Her voice was a caressing whisper that circled him like a cloud.

The word hung in the air as though her very voice had given it life. The word reverberated through his mind like a mountain echo. Something in his head begged him to obey her, to lie down on the cold tile floor and go to sleep. Instead, his fingers slid around the handle of his Smith & Wesson and he drew it out of the holster. "Forget what?"

The woman paused, her calm beautiful face registering surprise. Her eyes widened and then she frowned at him.

Gun raised, he approached her, determined to stop her rampage. "Drop the axe and step away from the door."

A shadow of alarm flickered in the depths of her attractive eyes, but quickly disappeared. "I can't." Her honeyed voice was soft and lilting, promising languid nights on a beach in some Caribbean paradise.

His fingers tightened on the grip of his gun. "I'm N.O.P.D. *I* have the badge. I make the rules. 'Can't' isn't part of your vocabulary. Put the axe down."

"Do not attempt to stop me, officer." Her voice rippled like silk across his hot skin. "You're not ready to face the consequences." Fine words from Ms. Double-Digit Serial Killer.

"That's Detective." A movement in the cooler distracted him. One of the sheets had fallen off a body. A dead man pushed himself into a sitting position, pale blue eyes gazing vacantly at the woman. He mouthed words, but no sound came out. Then he swung around and slid to the floor and started walking in a jerky motion toward her.

Ryan's mouth fell open. His mind went numb. Dead bodies did not suddenly get up and start walking. "Oh shit."

Another body sat up, pushing away the white covering. He slid off the table and started for the door. Both men met at the door and pushed against each other to get out of the cooler.

"Sweet Jesus." Ryan pointed his weapon at one of the men. The vacant blue eyes stared back at him. These men were dead! They couldn't be walking toward him. He was hallucinating! Axe-wielding babe was messing with his mind. How, he didn't know, but she was. The woman whirled toward the first body, and with a swift motion of her axe, cut off the head. The head sailed into the air. The body crumpled to the floor. She whirled and attacked the second man, whacking off his head.

The head ricocheted off Ryan's shoulder and thudded to the floor. A third body stood in the doorway of the cooler, stared at Ryan, then the woman.

"Get out!" the woman hissed at Ryan. She swung the axe again, but the third undead man dodged away, and the axe hit the wall with a thud that rang hollowly through the morgue.

What was happening? The dead didn't come back to life. Right? Yet inside the cooler more bodies were sitting up and opening their eyes. He hated to admit it but panic filled him. His instructors at the police academy hadn't covered this situation.

Another body suddenly lumbered out of the cooler. Ryan raised his gun and aimed. He recognized the guy as a biker they'd found outside a waterfront bar. The dude was huge, with tattoos inked on every surface of his pale skin, and his hair was wild and frizzy about his face.

Ryan fired. The bullet hit center mass. The biker staggered and clutched his chest, but didn't stop. Stone-dead eyes focused on Ryan as he kept on coming. Then he opened his mouth and Ryan saw fangs. Big, long, nasty fangs with Ryan's name written all over them.

Ryan fired again. The biker didn't even falter as the bullet hit him in the heart. *Fight or flight, buddy. Make a decision.*

He rushed forward, preparing to mix it up with a little hand-to-hand action.

The biker grabbed Ryan by the neck and snapped his head back. Ryan tried to fire again, but the biker grabbed his hand, twisted the gun away and tossed it on the floor. Unarmed, Ryan hit the biker directly in the solar plexus, but nothing happened. The scent of rotting flesh surrounded him.

Ryan saw the glint of steel as the woman swung the axe. The biker's grip suddenly relaxed and his head tilted, then just slid off the massive shoulders to bounce a couple of times on the floor and come to rest near the drain, the eyes closing, the jaws going slack.

Figuring the time for some help had arrived, Ryan backed toward the door. The last body hit the ground with the head sliding across the tile floor. The woman twirled the axe a couple of times then glanced Ryan. "Almost done."

Yeah right. He was done and intended to get his ass outta here. He shoved a table at her. Smiling, she leaped over the table, grabbed him by the arm, pulled him out of the morgue, and down the long hall toward the double glass doors leading outside.

Lieutenant Barton stood in the hall, caught in the act of pretending to be a janitor, frozen with his mop held in mid-air. Reed sat at the check-in desk, a game of solitaire spread out in front of him. Like the lieutenant, Reed's hands were frozen, hovering in the air over the cards. Ryan stared at them, wondering why they weren't moving. Or why they hadn't seen him.

The woman yanked him down the hall as though he were no heavier than a feather. When he attempted to free himself, her grasp tightened until he thought the circulation in his arm was cut off. Pain radiated through his fingers and up his arm. The woman kicked opened the double doors and they burst outside into thick, humid night air.

Distantly, Ryan heard chanting. Chanting! Okay, this was living nightmare time. Ryan struggled against the woman, wanting his freedom and his sanity back.

She stopped and looked around. "Charles, face me. Now!"

The weird chanting ceased, replaced by haunting laughter.

Ryan jerked his arm free and psycho babe turned to glare at him. Her eyes were like the sparkling depths of a faceted topaz. He wisely kept silent, hoping he hadn't pushed her to the edge already.

"Damn you!" She pushed him away from her, and he collided with the fender of a black Lexus SUV parked on the grass. She flipped open the side door of the Lexus and tossed the axe inside with a casual flip of her wrist as though the weapon were little more than a matchstick.

Now that ticked him off all over again. He was willing to let a thing or two slide especially since she'd saved his ass, but now she was acting like this was all his fault. "What do you mean, 'damn me'?"

"Do not interfere in things you don't understand," she hissed. Her voice was filled with such menace the hair on the back of Ryan's neck stood up.

He grabbed her arm. Her bare skin was soft and smooth, yet he felt the steel core of muscles beneath. "What the hell went on in there?"

She shook him off and gave him a look of disdain.

He stepped back from her, reaching for his gun. The holster was empty. Dammit! He'd lost his Smith & Wesson.

"I have no time to waste on you." She slid into the car and started the motor. In seconds, she was wheeling away while Ryan stood next to a lamp post feeling like an idiot.

As the car squealed down the street, Ryan realized he'd just let the headhunter get away.

He raced down the street after her. She hit the brakes to let another car have the right of way. Beneath the glare of a street light, he was able to see the license plate number. As the Lexus sped away, Ryan pulled a notebook out of his pocket and wrote the number down. Then he trudged back to the morgue, just knowing he was gonna get a big spanking from his boss over this one.

As he approached, the doors crashed open and Lieutenant Barton ran out. By the twisted set of his boss's lips, Ryan could tell he was not a happy man.

He glared at Ryan, confusion in his eyes. "Lattimore, how the hell did you get past me?"

Ryan took a deep breath. How the hell was he going to explain about the dangerous superbabe and the five chopped-off heads in the morgue? But he had to give it a shot. His boss would never believe a woman had dragged Ryan outside, tossed him around like a bag of potato chips, and then driven off in a fancy car that would cost him a year's salary.

Oh yeah! That sounded real believable. His next stop would be a straightjacket and a Thorazine cocktail at the county loony bin. He shrugged. "Bathroom break."

Barton rubbed his forehead. "While you were out here draining the lizard, the serial killer did his number on the bodies again. We have heads everywhere. It's the biggest mess yet."

Ryan glanced over his shoulder into the dark night. Yellow street lamps lit the pavement at intervals. A car sped past and Ryan heard laughter from the open windows. Two women, probably students at Tulane from the piles of books in their arms, walked down the other side of the street. If the students who peopled Tulane University during the day knew what was happening in their midst, they'd probably form a conga line and charge admission to the slaughter.

As if that would top the last fifteen minutes of his life. "Well, what do you know about that?"

❧

Mignon du Plessis entered the courtyard behind her house and parked beneath the thick branches of a two-hundred-year-old live oak. She pushed the button on the remote clipped to the sun visor and the gates swung closed behind her, sealing the world outside. The white marble of a fountain sparkled in the moonlight, as water sluiced down a playful mermaid's breasts.

Mignon sat back and closed her eyes, resisting the urge to pound the steering wheel and vent her rage on the hapless leather.

What the hell had that cop been doing hiding in the morgue? He could have easily ended up as a vampire appetizer, turned to the blood, and then she would have had to behead him, too.

She got out, slamming the car door to ease her frustration. The sound echoed through the darkness. Somewhere on the other side of the courtyard, a dog barked frantically and then stopped. Her neighbor, Mrs. Gibson, looked out the yellowed square of her upstairs window. Apparently, Mrs. Gibson was having trouble sleeping again. Mignon would have to brew some more herbal tea to help the elderly woman sleep.

Mignon walked rapidly across the courtyard, up the steps of the veranda toward the kitchen door that led into the old French Quarter mansion. She had bought the place for a song just after World War One when the owner had died of influenza and no heirs could be located.

She stalked through the wild tangle of garden. The sweet scent of night-blooming jasmine swirled around her. An old magnolia, branches loaded with blooms, dangled over the edge of a fence separating her house from Mrs. Gibson's. Mignon paused a moment to take stock of the situation before she walked into the house.

She had been so close. If the detective hadn't interfered, she might have tracked Charles to his lair. Eighty years had passed since she'd been this close to Charles. With the fate of humanity resting on her shoulders, she couldn't afford another fiasco like tonight.

Charles was growing stronger. His power roared in the wind, polluting the night air. Soon, he would be strong enough to put his plans into motion and then nothing she could do would stop him. How their roles had reversed. Charles had become the hunted and she the hunter.

She should have left the foolish detective to his fate. Instead, she had saved him, and now he knew about her. She slammed her fist against the white painted bannister. The wood shattered under her hand, and a trickle of blood escaped down her fist. Taking a deep breath, she concentrated on healing. The blood backtracked up her skin as she walked up the steps. The wound healed in seconds.

What was she going to do now? That man had meddled in her business, and Charles had managed to elude her once more.

Her enchantment hadn't worked on the detective either. Mortals shouldn't be immune to the high-frequency sound waves vampires used to project a barrier to keep mortals unaware of them. Why couldn't she enchant him?

Once in the far past, she'd heard that some humans were immune to vampire enchantment, but like most of the brethren, she had thought the rumor to be little more than a myth, a silly story told to newly-created vampires to keep them cautious. And now she'd come up against one and he had seen what she was forbidden to reveal.

She would have to eliminate the detective, robbing her of the time needed to hunt Charles, and giving Charles more time to hide from her and the rest of the *venators* sent to execute him. No, she would have to hunt Charles first. The detective wasn't going anywhere and once she'd disposed of Charles, the detective would meet with an untimely but easily explainable accident. The existence of the brethren had to remain hidden at all costs—even at the expense of one mortal's life. She reached for the knob and opened the door to the kitchen.

Lucas, her great-great-whatever grandson, leaned against a kitchen counter watching the coffee maker. He ran a hand through silken brown hair. Lucas was one of the youngest of her many descendants and ran the family banking business.

"You're back early." Lucas lifted an eyebrow. "And not very happy." Lucas was tall and slender with just of hint of Mignon's features in his face. His skin was several shades lighter than Mignon's, a testament to his father who had married a white woman.

"I'm not upset," Mignon snapped. "I'm never upset." She prided herself on her ability to control her emotions. So why was she ready to smash everything in sight?

His lips quirked at her white lie. "I assume your meeting with Charles didn't end as you had hoped."

She put the bloody axe on the tiled kitchen counter. "Charles gets to live another night because some interfering cop saw one too many episodes of Adam 12."

"Adam 12!" Lucas laughed. "That was way before my time."

Mignon drummed her fingers on the counter, seething. "Just about everything worthwhile was before your time, young one."

"Such as?"

They always played this game. She thought for a moment. "Bessie Smith."

He shook his head, grinning. "You really had to reach back in time for that one."

"So far back, I believe I might have strained something." She put a hand in the small of her back and grinned. She never could stay angry at anything when around Lucas. He had a way of drawing out the anger and replacing it with humor. Of all her descendants, he was her favorite, though she was careful to never let him know.

"It's time for the litter box, Granny. You're being very catty tonight." The coffee had finished brewing and he poured himself a cup, adding a generous spoonful of sugar and half and half.

Mignon glared at her grinning grandson. "I'm not amused, Lucas," she said even as she felt her mood lightening and her humor returning.

He laughed again. "You always say that when you don't have a good answer."

A little chuckle escaped her before she could contain it. She kissed him on the cheek. His skin was warm beneath her cool lips. "I'm an old woman. I'm allowed to be difficult."

He smelled of life, of blood pulsing through his veins, of his wife's subtle vanilla-scented perfume. A touch of jealousy slid through Mignon. Lucas knew love, life and passion. He could afford to make plans. He knew his time was finite while vampires lived an almost endless stretch of nothing. One night melted into the other, one existence into the next. Though she would eventually die, that was a millennia or more in the future.

"What happened with Charles?" he asked.

BLOOD LUST

Mignon ran a hand through her hair, releasing the strands from the barrette she'd used to contain the wild tangle of curls. "The *Praetorium* should have taken his head eighty years ago. But they had to prove to themselves that they still retained a bit of their mortal sense of justice." When the vampire tribes had united under a single governing body, they had set up a democracy that presumed innocent until guilty. Charles had managed to talk his way out of his last encounter with the *Praetorium* and now he was creating problems again. "If they had, they wouldn't be coming to me to solve the problem." She and her fellow *venator*s who comprised the Order of Romulus, the internal affairs arm of the *Praetorium, had been* given the task of executing Charles. And she felt a moment's sadness because his blood ran through Lucas's veins as well as hers.

Lucas leaned a hip against the counter and sipped his coffee. "This is a really, really old story. Some of us sleep at night. Cut to the chase, Granny." He yawned, emphasizing his fatigue.

Lucas had always been impatient and demanding in a sweet way. He hadn't changed since he was a child. "A New Orleans police officer interfered, almost preventing me from sending Charles's newest converts to their final eternity, allowing Charles to escape—again."

Lucas raised an eyebrow. "How did a police officer interfere?"

Mignon crossed her arms over her waist. "He appeared to be on surveillance inside the morgue."

Lucas shrugged. "If you want to catch a rat, you have to use some cheese."

"Are you referring to me as a rodent?"

"Considering that you could snap me in half, no. No insult intended." An innocent smile played on his lips and his eyes sparkled with laughter. "Just using that old tried and true expression."

"Then what are you saying?"

"He's doing his job. The cops don't know you're one of the good guys. I would have done the same. Can't the *Praetorium* go to someone in authority and drop a hint about Charles?"

Mignon shook her head. "I can just see Elder Jubal walking up to the President of the United States and saying, 'By the way, Mr. President, did you know that vampires really do roam the earth? We aren't all the blood-sucking fiends of legend, but a race of superhumans. Some of us are the good guys trying to make certain that the vampire and mortal worlds can peacefully co-exist.' I can just imagine how that would be received." The present leader of the *Praetorium* would rather cut off his own head than deal with the mundane concerns of the mortal world. His words, not hers.

Lucas set the coffee mug down. "I understand the advantage of staying off the radar so your existence doesn't cause any panic, but that decision makes it damn hard to hunt Charles, doesn't it?

"More than difficult," Mignon conceded. "But we took an oath of loyalty to the *Praetorium*, agreeing to abide by their laws. And they demand silence."

Lucas shrugged. "I know. I know. But things would be so much easier if you didn't have to stay in the shadows."

She smiled. Lucas had his own way of seeing things and she had hers. "We tried to deal fairly with the world of humans, but in response we were hunted almost to extinction." Though that had been long before her time, the stories of the elders had been told and retold to her to impress upon her and the others who came after that humans and vampires could not live together in peace.

"I know, Granny." He leaned a hip against the counter, his face turning deadly serious. "Besides, if not for you and the rest of the vampire community, I'd have to find a real job. And I do so love to go down to the vaults every once in a while and roll naked in all your money."

Her mouth fell open for a second. "Lucas, that's so...so..." She couldn't think of the right word.

"Freaky?" He gave her an innocent grin.

Where he had obtained his outrageous sense of humor was beyond her. "Bizarre."

He shook his head as he picked up his cup and took a drink of coffee. "What are you going to do about the cop? And why didn't you just enchant him?"

He always kept her off guard with his remarks. "First off, he was immune to my enchantment, and my instincts tell me he's a good and honorable man." Her instincts were seldom wrong. "Nor is he stupid." She needed to talk to Max. Perhaps he'd dealt with this kind of problem before.

Lucas frowned. "There's always a first. What will you do if he gets too close?"

She'd already made the decision, one she would never tell her grandson. He had an honesty about him that she admired, but often their needs crossed and she didn't want him to know what she planned. He would object and even though he would eventually accept her decision, he would be troubled by the idea that any human blood would be shed. "He will be dealt with—on my own terms."

Lucas nodded. "Did you happen to get his name?"

"I didn't get it. Why do you want to know?"

"Because everyone has something in their past they want to hide. Maybe I can find something you could use against him. Something tawdry that would force him stay away from you and not interfere with your mission." The doubt on his face told her he was troubled by his own words.

"Maybe." Though the detective would make Mignon's job harder, she could get around him. After all, he was only mortal.

"We do have a contact in the N.O.P.D.. I can find all of the information I need," Lucas said.

She should have known Lucas would have someone in the department. He had the most interesting friends in low places. "Have Solomon and Max checked in yet?"

He shook his head. "As far as I know, they're still prowling the warehouse district."

She laughed. "You make it sound like they're looking for a night's companionship."

Lucas shuddered. "You make them sound desperate."

Mignon chuckled. "On that note, I think I'll take my leave."

"Have fun," Lucas said.

She intended to. She opened the door that led up the back steps to the second floor. "After I trade this axe for my sword." She ran up the stairs to the armament room and swapped weapons. The axe was not her weapon of choice, but in the confined space of the morgue was the better selection. Prowling in the open required a different sort of weapon.

The armament room was a large room with wood paneling and high plaster ceiling painted with a mural of some Greek gods. A variety of weapons hung from each wall, stretching back through a millennia of death. Most of them belonged to Max, who was the eldest and most skilled of the *venators*.

She hung the axe in its spot. It would be cleaned later. An enemy's blood was believed to make the steel more powerful. Mignon pulled down her broad sword. She smiled as she ran a hand down the wicked blade, satisfied at the sharpness. The steel felt comfortable in her hand. Tonight, she still had work to do.

The warehouse district was dark with only a few street lamps glowing. Though the streets were deserted, Mignon could hear the rustling of small animals in the black corners. The smell of rancid humanity on the pavement mixed with the dampness from the Mississippi. Hot, humid air weighed heavily on her as she strode down the middle of the street.

A few homeless people had rolled themselves into corners to sleep, strewing trash and debris about their beds to alert them should an unwary intruder approach. That they were still alive was testament to the fact that they were not Charles's sort of people. Charles lusted to overthrow the *Praetorium*, but he was still somewhat particular about who he changed into a vampire.

A pack of emaciated dogs slunk through the shadows, eyeing her with red, hungry eyes. Kamikaze moths fluttered about the lights, burning themselves on the hot glass globes. Tendrils of fog floated through the alleys.

The night was Mignon's domain. Even when she had been mortal, she had loved the night. Two hundred and fifty years later she could still feel the dampness of Martinique's humid air on her skin and hear the sighs of the wind in the palm trees that had shaded the house. Sometimes she missed Martinique and the indolence of island life.

She caught a whiff of something on the moist air. She stopped to sniff, trying to identify who of her kind was walking the night. She felt a deep sense of age, hunger, and viciousness, of someone who had been a vampire for centuries longer than she. She could smell the weight of the ancients, of those who could trace their heritage back to Egypt. Was this a follower of Charles? She stepped into a pool of light and waited.

Words, like the dry rustling of leaves on a winter meadow, reached across the air. "You are the one they call Mignon the Huntress, Mignon the Seductress."

Mignon turned toward the voice, reaching for the sword in a black leather sheath slung down her back. "And who are you, dead one?"

The dry voice chuckled. "Charles said you would come. I have been waiting. Charles said you would be hard to kill, but I don't believe so. He says that he made you. And that you belong to him."

The hissing voice poured over her like a cold shower. "Like you, Charles talks too much. I would like the name of the person I intend to kill." He was old, much older than Max who was the oldest vampire Mignon knew except for those in the *Praetorium*. "You are an ancient one."

"I am made of fire and destruction."

Mignon scoffed. "I've heard that one before. Many *many* times." Why did the old ones act like B-movie clichés?

The ancient one stepped into the halo of light cast by a street lamp. He held a scimitar in front of him with the ease of one who understood his weapon. He was thin and elegant looking with long, shiny brown hair curling about his shoulders like a cascade of new spun silk. He didn't look more than twenty-five in mortal years. And he was handsome—no he was pretty—with delicate, feminine features, a slender face and brooding dark eyes, almost too beautiful to kill. But the evil of his soul washed over Mignon and left a foul taste in her mouth.

"You are not impressed with me?" His voice held a tinge of wonder. "Even the pharaohs knew better than to show me such disdain."

Now she knew who he was. "You are the Egyptian." Mignon had heard of this ancient one. He was one of the first. His evil was legendary, and if the *Praetorium* could have caught him they would have executed him. But he had managed to stay out of their clutches, hidden deep in the nameless shadows of the underworld. "I heard you were in Cairo."

He smiled, revealing white, perfect teeth. "I have been many places. Now I'm here."

Taking his head would be quite a coup. "You should have stayed in Cairo where you would be safe." Excitement rippled inside her. Tonight she would kill a legend.

Again he grinned. "I was building pyramids while your ancestors were running naked through the jungle."

Mignon shook her head. Why did the ancient ones feel they had to offend others? "Now you have insulted my lineage. I will take your head last."

"What do you mean last?" His smile faltered slightly and his eyes flickered with the first sign of uncertainty.

Mignon felt pleased that she had shaken him. "First, I will take your arms. Then I will take your skinny legs." She leaped over his head, twisting her body so she would land on her feet facing his back. As her toes touched the ground, she sprang up before he could turn and kicked him in the back with both feet. He flew forward, than tumbled to the ground, losing his scimitar. "But first," she said with a predatory smile, "I will play with you." Leaping again, she sailed through the air and came down, burying her knee into his back. He flattened under her. Lifting herself off him, she picked him up and tossed him toward his sword. "I enjoyed our dance."

He picked up the scimitar. "I will cut you to pieces."

Mignon could see the rage and hate burning in his eyes. "You will try."

He screamed his outrage and ran toward her. He had no finesse. Mignon whirled and swooped so quickly he couldn't step back. Old vampires. They were so impressed with themselves, thinking they were invincible. Her sword cut through his thighs and his legs flew off. He fell back on his rear end, his pretty face stunned. His scimitar slid across the pavement.

"I'm sorry, my mistake. Had the order backwards." She walked around him and slid the tip of her sword into the pommel of the scimitar and flung it up. She caught the scimitar as the Egyptian glared at her. Nothing was more insulting than to be killed with your own sword. This evil creature deserved no respect from her.

He struggled to sit up.

As he braced his hands on the pavement, she chopped one off and kicked it away. He fell over sideways. "Where is Charles?"

He shook his head. "You will pay for this—"

"Tell me." She grabbed a handful of his hair. "Maybe I'll let you regenerate."

He smiled and shook his head. But she saw the fear in his eyes. He knew he was dead.

"Tell me something," she said as she yanked on his hair. "How can an old one like you be led by a baby vampire like Charles?"

He hesitated for a long moment. "Charles understands power. When the pharaohs ruled Egypt, Egypt was great. I would make her great again. I would rule with the gods of my ancestors."

She let go of his hair. "Ambition is a cruel mistress." Mignon swiped the sword and the ancient one's head fell off and rolled into the gutter. The body fell back, limp and boneless. "So is overconfidence."

Mignon studied the scimitar. Etched in the handle beneath a single red ruby was the symbol of Ra. The craftsmanship was excellent. Max would be green with envy. Not only because of the weapon, but because she had killed the Egyptian.

"What the hell are you doing, lady?" A voice came out of the mist.

Mignon whirled to confront a doughy-looking man wearing a police uniform. Down the street, the blue and red lights of his squad car flashed on the walls of the buildings, creating an eerie landscape of flashing color.

"Good evening, officer." Mignon sheathed her sword. She raised a hand and gently waved it in front of his face. His face went slack, his eyes blank. "I think you need a cup of coffee. And no sugar this time." She gently blew at him.

"Coffee?" He looked puzzled.

"Yes, coffee." She gently turned him around and steered him toward his car. "Black with no sugar. And stay away from the beignets while you're at it. Salad is good for you."

When the officer had driven away, Mignon turned back to the

ancient one's body and pulled a matchbook from her pocket. She lit a cigarette and took a puff, then threw the match at the old vampire's body parts.

Old vampires could be as dry as dust. The flame flickered in his clothing, caught, and suddenly erupted into a brilliant torch. In minutes, the body and all its parts had burned, leaving behind faint scorch marks on the pavement and a coppery smell in the air. Mignon finished her cigarette and when she was done, she flicked the butt at the feathery ash that littered the pavement.

Mignon returned her sword to its scabbard and walked down the street, the well-balanced scimitar in one hand. As she passed a stack of rotting crates, an old man with a grizzled beard gave her a toothless smile. "You're damn good with that pig sticker, little lady."

She smiled at him and with a wave of her hand, casually wiped his mind. She wanted to plant the idea of a job and respectability, but the older homeless drowning in liquor were too set in their ways, too far gone to change. She simply put him to sleep and gave him dreams more pleasant than the ones he usually had.

CHAPTER TWO

Charleston — 1748

Mignon stood outside the brothel watching it intently from beneath the branches of the fragrant magnolia tree. Night hadn't tempered the damp heat of the day. She felt the sheen of sweat on her skin. Usually, her body adapted to the climate, but Charleston was still recovering from a storm that had left the streets quagmires of mud. She lifted the damp curls of her hair from her shoulders. She longed for a breeze, something to cool the air.

The brothel was lit with lanterns hanging from tree branches and lining the intricate brick path to the front door. Carriages passed down the muddy street, splashing through the puddles. Men walked along laughing and drinking from flasks hidden in their coat pockets. Ladies of the night lifted the hems of their skirts to entice customers.

Mignon closed her eyes against the debauchery. Since she'd left Martinique, she had seen a world that still surprised her. How sheltered she'd been on the plantation. How naive of her to think she could so easily find her children.

She kept the memories of their sweet faces in her mind. She would find them. All she could hope for was that they wouldn't die before she found them. She didn't want to be alone in the world.

The weight of hunger pressed down on her. She wouldn't feed just yet. Not until she'd searched the brothel as she had searched a dozen similar brothels along the coastline. Three long years had been spent on the search as she kept herself one step ahead of Charles who seemed as reluctant to let her go as she was determined to remain free of him.

A man, dressed in velvet evening clothes with diamonds winking in the folds of his ruffles, approached the front door of the brothel and the door opened. A boy, maybe ten years old, opened the door and stood aside to allow the man inside. Mignon sniffed and the memory of Simon's scent returned to her. He had loved dogs and always smelled of puppies and molasses.

Simon. She almost cried at the sight of his youthful face. She had finally found her son. Even though she loathed what she had become, she luxuriated in some of the changes that had occurred. A more acute sense of sight and smell were only two of the changes.

Memories flooded back to her of Simon cradled in her arms as a newborn, of his first steps, his first words. She inhaled deeply of him as she studied him. He was taller now and his face had lines in it that hadn't been there before. His innocence was gone.

Simon was dressed as a footman—all fancy ruffles and black velvet. He bowed and took the man's hat, then started to close the door. He paused and stared out at the street where Mignon stood, his face quiet and closed. A tear started down Mignon's cheek. A tear of both joy and sadness.

She thrust her hands deep into the pockets of her shabby coat as she planned her next move. She'd been searching for so long. While part of her was overjoyed, another part was frightened.

Walking across the street, she dodged a man who seemed intent on a trollop who smiled enticingly at him. Another woman, shrouded in a dark cloak, glanced at her. Mignon knew exactly what the woman saw—a slender man of color dressed in worn clothing. In one pocket, wrapped in waterproof oilskin, Mignon carried her manumission papers indicating she was a free person of color. The papers had cost her dearly, even though they weren't a guarantee of safety.

At the front door she knocked. Inside she heard the shuffle of feet and then the door swung open and Simon stood in front of her. He glanced at her, his face blank for a moment. Then his eyes widened with recognition. She held a finger to her lips, grabbed his arm and pulled him out onto the veranda. He closed the door against the gaudy parlor and the half-dressed harlots who lounged on the sofas with men who pawed their breasts.

"Maman," he said in a husky, soon-to-be-man's voice.

Her heart almost burst with the joy that filled her soul. "You remember."

He hugged her tightly. "I told Angeline you would come."

"Angeline is here?" She silently thanked God for giving her this moment. Her search was ended. Both of her children would be returned to her.

Simon nodded, but his eyes grew haunted and his body went stiff. "She is upstairs."

Mignon needed no other explanation. She had been preparing herself for this, but faced with the knowledge that her daughter had been sold into prostitution brought a welling of grief so intense she almost fell down.

"We will take Angeline and leave this place."

Simon looked shocked. "But Maman, how will you do that? We are slaves. Someone will come for us."

"Let them come. I will take care of them." For a second her bravado almost left her. Then she remembered she was stronger and faster than any man. She could defend her children now. And no one could stand up to her.

Her son looked puzzled. "But you are only one person." He did not add, 'and a woman, besides,' though the words hung between them as visible as if spoken.

She kissed him on his forehead. "God has given me the strength of Samson. Now I want you to get your sister."

Simon laughed shakily. "But we cannot just walk out the front door."

"Then you will walk out the back door."

Simon nodded, but he looked frightened, not entirely convinced they would succeed.

"Trust me." Mignon stroked his cheek. "I can protect you now. Get your sister and meet me in the back garden."

Simon opened the door and stepped back inside. The door closed with a click and Mignon bolted down the path to the side of the house, elated at having found her children at last. She traversed an overgrown brick path, passing beneath a live oak and overgrown bougainvillea.

At the back of the house, a half-dozen windows lit the night, casting yellow pools into the darkness. Mignon could hear the faint laughter from inside the house. She could also smell the sadness and the fear.

She paced near a stone bench and prepared to wait for Simon and Angeline.

Charles had done her no favors in changing her, but some aspects of the change delighted her. She was physically strong in a way she'd never been before. She'd managed to defeat Charles and escape from Martinique. She'd eluded the slave hunters Charles had sent after her as though they were nothing. She would be no man's property ever again.

She could see as clearly at night as during the day. And her hearing was so acute, she could isolate and identify sounds and tell what direction they came from.

Closing her eyes, she listened intently, focusing every fiber of her being on the back of the house, separating the sounds. She listened to Simon's tread as he climbed the stairs, and the frantic laughter of the women inside, searching for a familiarity which would match to the memory of her daughter. But she could not remember her daughter's laughter. Angeline had always been a serious child, not given to much frivolity.

As Mignon waited, she thought about the future. Her plan had simply been to find her children and hide them, but now she realized that hiding might not be so easy. She would have to get them out of the city, probably out of this area. She thought about where they could go. Not back to Martinique. Maybe some place wild and uninhabited. The frontier? She had met a man who planned to trek west to the unknown territories. That idea held some appeal, though she felt a stronger pull to New Orleans.

Despite the disease and the cramped houses, she had fallen in love with the city the moment she stepped off the ship she had escaped on. New Orleans had its own colony of free people of color. There, she and her children could blend in, or fade away into the bayous beyond the reach of the slave hunters.

Simon's footsteps had stopped on the second floor. Mignon focused her attention on him. He started to pace back and forth and she found herself frowning. What was wrong? Why didn't he simply grab Angeline and run?

Panic rose in her, her body grew tense and she started to shake. Overwhelmed with worry, she jumped up and began to pace back and forth again. "Hurry, Simon," she whispered, "hurry." Suddenly the night seemed too short for what she needed to accomplish.

She pushed her fear aside and focused once more on Simon. She leaned against a tree and closed, her eyes listening for Simon's voice.

Suddenly Simon began talking quickly, his voice filled with fear. "I'm sorry, mistress. I'm sorry. I'm sorry."

"What are you doing up here?" a woman shrieked. "Get back to the front door. I had to answer it myself."

Mignon jumped into action. She flew up the steps to the back porch and flung open the back door. She raced past astonished servants and up the back stairs to the hallway.

Simon stood in the center of the hallway facing a heavily painted woman dressed in a heavy green dress with garish frills surrounding her florid face. Yellow curls bounced on her head and her eyes were circled with thick rings of kohl. Her cheeks were powdered and rouged, but Mignon could see beneath the powder to the pockmarks the woman tried to hide. The woman stood in front of Simon, her face contorted with fury, one hand raised as though she were ready to hit him.

A huge black man stood behind Simon holding his arms. Simon struggled for a second and then stood still as the woman smacked him across the face. Simon's head snapped back and his eyes rolled with the force of the blow.

Rage blazed in Mignon. She grabbed the woman's upraised hand before she could strike Simon a second time, and shoved her against the wall. The woman squeaked, her round blue eyes wide with surprise. Then her eyes narrowed as she took in Mignon's appearance, and she glanced at the man, an unspoken signal between them. The man tossed Simon aside as though he were nothing but a rag, and reached for Mignon.

Mignon dodged under the servant's grasping arms and came up between them, shoved him against the wall, and reached for his throat. For a second he looked surprised. Her hunger roared in her ears, lending her strength. She pushed against the man's windpipe until he gasped and his eyes closed. He slumped against the wall and slid down-ward. Mignon resisted the urge to kill him. He was a slave just doing what he had to do to protect himself.

But the woman wasn't a slave. Mignon turned with narrowed eyes. The madame shrieked and Mignon reached for her.

"Kill her!" the madame screamed. "Kill her!"

The servant pushed himself to his knees and started to mumble in a language Mignon did not understand. He crossed himself and backed away down the hall until he pressed tight against a wall.

"I've come for my children," Mignon said.

The madame's eyes flickered after her servant, but saw no help. "They belong to me." Her voice and look were superior and arrogant.

"Not anymore." Mignon's fangs slid out of their protective sheaths. She twisted the woman's neck to one side and buried her fangs deep in the jugular, drawing warm blood into her veins, feeling the strength of the woman's essence.

The woman slumped against the wall, her hands losing her grip on Mignon's arms. She went limp and her head rolled to the side. Mignon continued to feed. The rage she felt would not let her stop. She listened to the madame's heartbeat slow. Still she fed. When the woman's heart stopped, only then did Mignon step back and release the body. The woman slid down to the floor and lay limp, her life gone.

"Maman," Simon said, touching her hand. "What have you done?"

Mignon wiped a trickle of blood from her mouth. Her fangs retracted and she cradled Simon's face between her hands. "Forget, my son."

His eyes glazed over and closed. Mignon kissed him and at her touch, his eyes flew open.

"We have to hurry. Where is Angeline?"

He pointed at a door. "That is her room, but she isn't there."

Mignon opened the door. The room was empty except for a bed squeezed against the wall, a modest armoire and a rag rug on the floor. Mignon stalked out. She would find her daughter. She opened the nearest door, but it was empty. Methodically, she opened doors inter-rupting women, little more than girls themselves, with their clients who yelled at her.

Angeline was in the last room standing completely naked in the center while a naked man lolled on the bed with another young girl casually caressing him. The young girl on the bed was blonde and pretty in a faded sort of way. She looked barely ten.

"Dance," the man ordered.

Mignon stepped into the room and smiled at him.

His eyes flickered as they shifted to her. "You're a little old for my tastes, but still beautiful."

Angeline turned. Her eyes went wide and surprised. "Maman!"

Mignon picked up robes from the floor and flung them at the two girls. "Get dressed. Now."

The two girls simply stared at her. Mignon grabbed her daughter and dropped the robe over her thin shoulders. She grabbed the other girl and covered her, then pushed them through the doorway.

The man smiled lazily. He patted the bed next to him. Mignon growled. The hunger to kill pulsed through her. "So you like little girls?" Rage filled her and she clenched her hands and fought against the snarl that grew in the back of her throat.

His smile faded and he shrank back from the fury in her voice. "Are you going to hurt me?" He covered his genitals with his hands.

She advanced toward him. "How can I, I'm just a woman?"

He eased off the bed and picked up a poker from the fireplace and took a swing at her. She grabbed the poker and bent it until it broke. His mouth fell open at the demonstration of her strength and he started to sidle toward the door, his gaze darting back and forth as though looking for another weapon.

"I'm not going to hurt you." She dropped the broken poker on the floor. "I'm going to kill you."

Present Day — New Orleans

Ryan thought about just going home and getting some sleep, but he was too wired with adrenaline and the visions of the woman and her fancy moves. He had enough cases piling up on his desk without the added problem of trying to explain the axe-wielding babe and the carnage in the morgue. It was just easier to look incompetent than to look like a nut case.

He entered his office and paused a moment to pick up the pile of files in the center of his desk. The office was empty. Most of the night shift was still on rounds and the morning shift wouldn't arrive for several hours yet. He liked night duty, having never been much of a day person.

Somewhere in the building, a phone rang and was answered. A siren sounded in the distance. The hum of voices in the hall sounded weirdly normal after the oddness of his encounter with commando babe.

Ryan had reports to write and as he sat down at his cluttered desk, he realized he wasn't certain how to write them. No one would believe what he'd seen in the morgue. Hell, he still wasn't sure if he believed what he'd seen.

He'd seen his share of beautiful women from around the world, but tonight's honey had been beyond beautiful. She glowed. Sparkled almost. Everything from her sleek hair to her long, shapely legs had been nothing short of perfect. He'd bet her feet were just as fine. He could tell already she was going to be the star of his wet dreams until he died.

Mary Sanders entered the office with a stack of files in her arms. She sat across from Ryan. "Have fun at the morgue?" Her vibrant blue eyes danced with amusement as she spoke.

Mary was a small, trim woman with dark blonde hair pulled into a girlish pony tail. She still managed to retain her dirty-minded sense of humor no matter what dire things were going on in her life.

At least she had the decency not to mention that he had let the serial killer slip through his fingers. "I never have any fun playing with myself." Ryan pulled the bottom drawer out and propped his feet on it. What he really wanted was a stiff drink, which might, if he were lucky erase the vivid images of that incredible woman which still floated at the back of his brain.

"I am not going there." She jabbed a slender finger at him. "What happened? I don't see a suspect in cuffs waiting to be processed." And like a good partner, she pretended as though she hadn't already heard the gossip about what had happened at the morgue.

"No suspect, but five more heads rolling free." He rubbed his tired eyes. "This case is kicking my behind."

He trusted Mary with his life, but he didn't know if he could trust her with what had happened at the morgue. The whole bizarre quality of the experience was not the kind of thing a guy could tell his shrink, much less his partner, and expect to be believed. She'd be reaching for the phone to dial the hospital and have the men in white coats come get him.

"At least you had excitement." She leaned back in her creaky chair and sighed, "I filed papers. I hate riding a desk when I want to be out on the streets with you, kicking butt and nailing the bad guys."

"I know," Ryan reassured her, "that no one in this office has anything bad to say about you. Hang in there a couple more days. This whole situation will sort itself out." Or so he hoped. He wanted his partner back with him. Being on the street by himself, he felt as if he were cut in half.

"Yeah, right." She removed the band holding her hair back, shook her head, and her hair flowed across her shoulders, softening the harsh features of her face.

"Did you change your hair?" Ryan tilted his head to study her. A lot about her was different lately, but he couldn't quite put a finger on it.

She ran her hands through the blonde waves. "I have a new stylist."

"Stylist?" She'd spent money on a stylist. "You were the one who turned me on to the free haircuts at the beauty college."

She shrugged. "Sometimes a girl just wants to look pretty."

Ryan frowned, instantly jealous. His partner was having a life. "For who?"

She grinned, but he thought he saw a shadow cross her eyes. And he wondered who she was seeing.

"Maybe just for me." She pushed a couple of papers at him. "These need your signature before you take off." She changed the subject with a smoothness that was slicker than a water slide. "Is there anything I can do for you? Run down a lead, scare a suspect? Pretend to be a police officer while the powers that be are deciding my fate? Just give me a shout. You know I have your back."

He was tempted to ask her to run the license number of the woman at the morgue, but then decided against it. He could do that himself. Until he knew more about what was going on, he didn't want to involve Mary. She was in enough hot water as it was and didn't need to know about dead people coming back to life and his axe-wielding babe.

He signed the reports she'd typed for him. As he finished the last one, her phone rang. Ryan leaned back in his chair and watched her answer it. A slight flush touched her cheeks as she covered the mouthpiece with her hand. A private call. So she was seeing somebody. Again, that little bit of jealousy slid through him. Mary seldom kept secrets from him, but this one she wasn't sharing.

When she hung up, she frowned at him. "Is there anything else, Ryan?"

"Not at the moment. Want to get something to eat?"

"No. I'm going home." She ran her hands through her hair, suddenly looking tired. "And by the way, you had a visit from an FBI agent from Quantico. Guess you're going to get some help." She snickered at him as she stood, gathered her purse, and slung it over her arm.

"Not the Feds," Ryan groaned. "Where is he now?"

"Not a him. A her. I gave her directions to the executive bathroom and haven't seen her since."

"I guess," he said with a wry grin, "I better go check all the broom closets."

"See you later." She gathered up her purse and a light jacket and left the office without a backward glance. Just from the set of her shoulders, Ryan could see she was still feeling bitter about the investigation into her activities.

Ryan walked into the watch commander's office. "Tell me why I have the FBI horning in on my case." The FBI was the kind of agency that if the locals didn't play along, the Feds would confiscate everything and then run home to mama, taking all their toys. Ryan hated working with them.

Greg Fontaine was a large, muscular man with skin the color of newly tanned leather. If not for the squashed nose from his college years as a boxer, he would have been movie star handsome. He sat back in his chair and swivelled it back and forth slightly. "Because sometimes in a man's life, you have to realize that you have no control over who bounces heads off the mayor's lawn and causes the mayor's wife to lose her very expensive dinner. The mayor personally made a call to the attorney general. You know they went to Tulane together."

Ryan shook his head. "What do I do?"

Fontaine shrugged. "Consider yourself lucky the Feds only sent only one suit to mess up your life."

"Have you seen her?" Ryan asked.

Fontaine's eyebrows arced. "Hell no. I've been avoiding her. If you want to cooperate or not cooperate, I don't care. Just find me the killer."

Dismissed, Ryan headed back out into the hall. He glanced up and down the corridor, wondering if he should search the agent out, or just get the hell out and head home for some sleep. He turned, thinking if he could just make it to the parking lot, he'd be home free. Just as he pushed open the double doors, a tall, dark-skinned woman with an intense gaze stopped him. FBI oozed out of her, from her neatly-trimmed hair to her sensible, low-heeled shoes.

"Detective Lattimore." Her voice was hard-edged and irritated.

Ryan thought a long string of profanities. He'd almost made it out to his car. "I'm Lattimore."

The woman held out a hand. "I'm Special Agent Ursula Carlson."

Ryan looked her up and down. She was pretty in a fresh-faced way with her large dark eyes and full, generous lips. "Howdy do." He hadn't intended to sound so arrogant, but he was still pissed.

Carlson frowned ever so slightly as she withdrew her offered hand. Her lips thinned and her eyes narrowed. Ryan forced himself to keep from smiling at the quirky twist of Carlson's lips, the type of twitch that meant she was attempting to keep her smart remarks under wraps. Ryan had the urge to smack her on the back and say, 'Let it out, lady, you'll feel better.' But the FBI wasn't known for its humor.

"Sorry, we almost missed each other." Her voice held a clipped New Jersey accent.

Ryan wasn't sorry at all. "What can I do for you, Extra Special Agent Carlson?"

"First of all, Detective," She gave him a winsome smile that did not win him over, "I'm not trying to take over your case. My office received a call from the attorney general's office which received a call from your mayor. Someone had to come and check things out and that someone is me."

"You've checked things out. You can go home now and I can catch some sleep."

Carlson drew back stiffly and took a deep breath. "You know, I can pick up the phone right now and summon every agent on the eastern seaboard to give me a hand here. Either you deal with me, or you deal with the pack. I don't care."

Ryan's eyes narrowed. Damn she had big brass ones. He almost liked her. "I'm feeling threatened here."

"Have you ever dealt with a series of murders like this?"

Did she think he still had his cherry? The Big Easy was a rough town with all kinds of ugly to go around. "You mean with a serial killer? We've had one or two in our neck of the bayou before."

She sighed. "You aren't going to make this easy for me, are you?"

All Ryan could think of was that if Carlson had seen what he'd seen tonight, she'd head back to D.C. before the ink was dry on her plane ticket. Axe-wielding commando babes and headless bodies were just not the kinds of information one wanted to share. He wondered if the government ran mental hospitals for burned-out detectives who'd experienced the unexplained. Talk about a trip down the X-Files road. Hey maybe she knew Mulder.

Ryan shrugged. "I'm tired, I smell bad and I'm just not in the mood to deal with you."

Ryan opened the door and walked out into the early morning dampness to his car. As he drove out onto the street, he saw Mary get into a black limo with tinted windows so dark not even the interior ceiling lights showed through.

A black limo was not the standard dope dealer car. Usually dealers tried for more inconspicuous means of transportation. Though Ryan tried not to be suspicious of Mary, he wondered if she was being completely truthful with him or the Rat Squad over the incident. He tried to ignore the small seed of doubt that crept into his mind. When his case was over, maybe he needed to do a little digging into Mary's affairs, for his own peace of mind.

If she'd taken a turn down the wrong road, her actions could reflect on him. As much as he liked Mary, he liked being a cop more.

Ursula watched Detective Lattimore drive away, feeling annoyed. She'd known he would be reluctant to cooperate. After all, she was invading his territory and she understood how he felt. But he didn't understand what was really going on.

She took a deep breath and headed toward the street. As she headed for her car, a tan sedan was parked behind it. She recognized Colonel Hammett's driver, who nodded at her and gestured to the back. As she approached, the rear window rolled down and Colonel Hammett looked out.

Ursula straightened up and fought the urge to salute her superior officer. "Colonel Hammett, sir."

"At ease, Major." He smiled at her. "I see you've made contact with the good detective."

Ursula nodded. If she could call it contact, more like a sparring match. "Sir, tell me why I'm investigating Detective Lattimore when my prime objective is to recover Charles Rabelais?" Eight years ago Rabelais had brokered a deal with the Department of Defense for a lot of cash. At the time, the DOD hadn't a clue what he was, only that he was dealing in secrets and they'd wanted them. When the DOD discovered Charles was the culmination of all of humanity's worst nightmares, the government boys had wanted to find a way to put him to work. But when he'd disappeared, her unit was dispatched to bring him back into the fold.

The colonel shifted in his seat. "I don't have any proof, but dollars to donuts, my gut feeling tells me Rabelais is somehow connected to these murders. And if we're patient enough, Lattimore might just lead us to Rabelais. But in the meantime, we need to know what Lattimore knows about the vampire community."

"And then do what?"

Hammett didn't answer.

He didn't have to. She tensed. If the cop knew too much, he'd be eliminated. "I take it we're not going to get rid of him in a nice way, like a vacation to Antigua."

Hammett shrugged. "That depends. Is the detective going to cooperate?"

How the hell was she going to answer that? "He's feeling a little territorial at the moment." That was a nice, vague answer. She didn't want the colonel to think she couldn't handle the job. He'd gone to a lot of trouble to arrange this FBI cover story for her. "I wasn't expecting him to greet me with open arms." The military was just as possessive over their operations. Especially if they were top secret units like X-Ray company.

"True, Major. But this is too important to let the locals handle."

The existence of vampires was not going to go down so well with Mr. And Mrs. John Q. Public. She could see it all now. Pandemonium in the streets. People turning in their neighbors. And the chaos could ruin all the DOD's plans to draft the vampires into a crack anti-terrorist squad that would have no equal throughout the world. The DOD would finally have one up on Homeland Security. And that was gold. "I understand, sir. I have a tail on the detective. We've tapped his phones, tapped his home and office computer, and hidden a tracking device in his car. Eventually, we'll know what he knows." Which she hoped wasn't much. She'd liked Ryan. Everything she'd read about the guy told her he was as straight up as they came, and he was ex-military.

"Good."

"Personal question, sir," Ursula queried.

"Of course, Major, you're cleared for classified information."

Ursula nodded. "At the beginning of X-Ray Company, you tapped Detective Lattimore to be one of your operatives. What happened?"

She hoped he still had loyalty to the cause.

"Like you, his blood, DNA and hearing tests showed that he was immune to the...to the... what do you call it?"

"You mean the 'whammy?'"

The colonel laughed. "That sounds so ridiculous."

"Yes, sir, it does."

"Lattimore had a lot of potential, but when his aunt developed cancer, he resigned his commission, and returned to New Orleans to take care of her. We kept track of him. I consider it fate that he's the lead on this case."

"Why can't I just be honest with him?" He would understand about patriotism and the need to secure the boundaries from the terrorist threat.

"That's always a possibility, but the timing isn't right for openness."

"I understand," Ursula said. "Keep it neat, keep it tidy, keep it quiet." She wondered if Homeland Security had any idea what the DOD was doing. Ever since Homeland Security had been created, the DOD had been on the offensive, feeling as though it had been slapped in the face, as though the President didn't feel they were responsible enough to keep the country safe.

DOD had been trying to regain that lost confidence ever since and the idea of a vampire squad to combat terrorism was their way of assuring their one upmanship with Homeland Security. The program needed to stay on track. Recruiting Charles Rabelais had seemed the start of a great idea, until he flew the hen house.

"You're a squared-away soldier, Carlson. I'll be in touch." The window rolled up and the sedan slid away beneath the heavy New Orleans night.

Ursula opened her car door and sat down. Four years ago she'd been tapped by military intelligence to join the X-Ray unit, or as they affectionately called themselves, the vamp squad. At times, she wished they'd simply by-passed her and let her get on with her career. She had been the first in her family to get a college degree, to leave Newark for something else. She'd hated to give up her regular duties to chase after vamps. At times she wished she could go back to the days when she didn't know vamps existed.

She started the rental car and pulled out onto the street. The clock on the dashboard told her she'd been up all night. The detective was being tailed so she could afford a hot shower, some cool sheets, and some sleep.

CHAPTER THREE

After a couple hours of sleep and sluggish jog down St. Charles, Ryan had given up trying to not think about axe babe. He'd gone into the office and looked up the car license, which had brought him here to this French Quarter mansion. He fought a yawn as he parked in front of the three-story brick building.

Taking a sip of coffee, he studied the fancy wrought iron railings that twisted and turned up the front of the mansion. He recognized this place as having been a famed brothel in the mid-1800s. Duels had been fought in the courtyard and legend had it that a voodoo priestess had cast a curse on the house that was supposed to last for all eternity. No one knew what the curse was, but it apparently hadn't affected anything since the house was still standing and according to the historical building records, had been owned by the du Plessis family for over eighty years.

Ryan was impressed. Axe babe had cash to spare. The upkeep on the place must cost a pretty penny.

He glanced at his notebook. The Lexus SUV was registered in the name of Lucas du Plessis, age twenty-seven. The background check on Lucas du Plessis had netted Ryan little information other than the fact that he was a citizen of the Angeline Islands, the youngest son of the country's ambassador to the United Nations, and managed the local branch of the Angeline National Bank. He kept a low-profile, unlike his father whose politics often put him at odds with the other countries in the U.N. Ryan almost envied Lucas du Plessis. He seemed an upstanding, law-abiding person, except that he was somehow associated with the axe-wielding babe.

Ryan knew he shouldn't be here. After all, this house had diplomatic immunity, but he couldn't stop himself as he walked up the steps to the veranda and rang the doorbell. Inside, he heard the echo of footsteps on a wood floor and then the door swung open to reveal a young man who smiled at Ryan, a questioning look on his face. He was one of those high-yellow brothers, more white than black. And yet Ryan could see a faint resemblance around the eyes and mouth to the woman from last night.

The young man smiled. "Detective, we've been expecting you." He stepped aside and swung his hand toward the foyer entry. "Come in, please."

So the element of surprise was blown. He didn't like that. "Who are you?"

The man held out his hand. "I'm Lucas du Plessis."

The owner of the car. "And why were you expecting me?" Ryan entered the darkened house without shaking the other man's offered hand. At the moment, he didn't want to get too friendly. Despite the early morning sun, the windows were swathed with heavy draperies and lighted lamps cast yellow halos.

Du Plessis dropped his hand. "Miss Mignon regaled us with the tale of how she saved your bacon last night."

Miss Mignon! Ryan's honey now had a name. Or rather half a name. That woman hadn't looked old enough to have earned the designation of 'Miss,' an honorary title reserved for family matriarchs. She couldn't have been more than twenty-five, thirty on an ugly day—tops.

Lucas led the way up curving stairs. Ryan followed, aware of a tingling radiating up his spine. At the top, Lucas pointed down the shadowed hall. "Third door on the left. She's waiting for you."

Ryan's footsteps reverberated on the wood floor. The hairs on the back of his neck stood up. Miss Mignon was entirely too casual for someone who was about to be arrested.

He reached behind and checked on his Smith & Wesson. He'd retrieved it from the floor of the morgue after his encounter with the woman who now had a name. Not that his gun had helped him much last night, but he still felt more comfortable with it ready. He still didn't understand how she'd managed to slip past the other cops in the hall, and then out again without any of them seeing or hearing her. Or why the bodies had come back to life again, or why he hadn't been able to do his job. Those were only a few of the questions he needed answered as soon as he saw her.

As he traversed the hall, he heard the sound of voices. He reached the door Lucas had directed him to, opened it and stepped into a small room to find the axe-woman spread out on a table while a masseur gently massaged her arms.

Miss Mignon was naked except for a towel covering her firm, well-rounded butt. He could worship that butt. He felt a tightening in his groin that had nothing to do with his being a cop.

She glanced up at him. "You're late. I expected you much earlier than this." Her imperious tone was filled with the music of the bayous, lilting and soft with a whiskey undertone that reminded him of late nights, naughty girls and clandestine sex in the backseat of old cars.

Who the hell did she think she was? The queen of New Orleans? "Then why aren't you dressed and ready for me to take you into custody?"

She gave him a silken chuckle that sent shivers radiating outward from the center of his body. She rolled over, tossing the towel away, and sat up, displaying herself without seeming to realize she wore no clothes. Or maybe she was teasing him. Frankly he didn't care. He just wanted to enjoy the view.

"Antoine," she said, "leave us."

The masseur obediently turned away and left through a door that was so carefully disguised in the far wall, that Ryan didn't notice it until the man opened it and stepped out of sight. The door closed with barely a sound.

Ryan couldn't look away from her. His body took on a life of its own as he gazed at her lush, up-tilted breasts, narrow waist, and rounded hips with the dark triangle of hair between her legs. Ryan felt a slow heat build in him. She was a damn fine looking woman.

He caught the hint of a amusement in her dark, almond-shaped eyes, and knew he didn't care. He was a guy, after all. He liked his women naked and his sex raw. He wasn't ashamed. Obviously, she wasn't either. So why not indulge himself in a look-see?

"Miss..." Ryan couldn't look away. She was absolute perfection from the gentle rise of her breasts to the long supple toes of her feet. He should have known she'd even have sexy feet.

Women didn't get much better than this. She had a lap dancer's body and a commando's skills, his fantasy come to life. He could fall in love with a woman like her. His brain suddenly shook him awake. She was a killer, and he was mooning after her body like an eighteen-year-old after a long drought.

"Du Plessis," she replied. "But please call me Mignon." She slid a dark red silk oriental robe up her arms, drew the lapels over her breasts, and tied a belt about her waist. Her actions were slow and teasing. To achieve what? To distract him? He wasn't sure, nor did he give a flying flip. He was just going to enjoy the show.

The robe was worse than seeing her naked. The silk slithered down her body in a wave of undulating sensuality. Every curve was more visible, from the gentle flare of her hips to the pertness of her nipples. And when she moved gracefully toward a sideboard to lift a bottle of red wine from an ice bucket, Ryan could barely repress a sigh. She poured herself a glass and lifted it to her lips. Ryan wondered what type of red wine was served chilled.

"May I offer you a glass of wine?" She reached for a second wine glass.

"I'm on duty."

"Are you absolutely certain I can't tempt you?" The corner of her mouth lifted with just a hint of flirtatiousness.

Wine wasn't the temptation he wanted to give in to. Ryan held up his hand. "I'm good."

"Pity." Her full mouth formed a flirting pout. "I have the most exquisite merlot."

Danger, Will Robinson, danger. The mantra from the old *Lost In Space* TV show repeated itself. Long-legged, full breasted, slinky danger—the kind a man can only hope to find before he's too old to do anything about it.

The invitation was so blatant, so open, Ryan's knees almost buckled. He grabbed the back of a chair and hung on for dear life, determined not to disgrace the department. If the seductive act was her ploy to keep him off her trail, he'd be happy to let her lead him on a merry chase. Up to a certain point.

She opened the lid of a green marble box and with long, sinuous fingers delicately extracted a cigarette. Ryan leaned toward the musky scent of the tobacco, thinking that this woman wasn't his killer. He didn't know where the thought came from; it simply slipped into his mind.

Her head tilted to one side and she seemed disappointed. "If I can't tempt you with drink, perhaps I can offer you a cigarette?" she asked in a voice that seemed to caress him.

"No. I quit."

She sniffed the air. "When?" A slight smile danced at the edges of her lips.

"At eight this morning."

Her eyebrows rose as she glanced at the diamond encrusted watch encircling her delicate wrist. "It's only one o'clock now."

"Have to start sometime." Ryan had quit smoking every morning for the last five years. Actually, he was almost proud of himself. Some days he could make an entire shift without a smoke. But he could tell right now he was going to have to stop and pick up a carton after this.

"I see." She lit the cigarette and inhaled. She exhaled a long stream of smoke and it curled outward from her mouth. "So tell me. Are you going to be the good cop today, or are you going to play the bad cop?"

"You make me want to be bad." He couldn't stop the leer in his eyes. He was almost ashamed of himself. Here he was on cop business and he was ogling the merchandise like a dumbstruck rookie.

She didn't smoke domestic brands. The fragrant smoke came from a French brand that Ryan had once tried and lusted after but couldn't afford on the modest salary the city paid him to keep the citizens safe.

"Charming." Taking a puff of the cigarette, she laughed. "You're here to arrest me?" She held her wrists out in front of her.

He wanted, more than anything else, to get her in a pair of irons and play suspect interrogation with her. His instincts were to let her hang herself. Years of doing interviews told him that she wouldn't respond to a hard hitting Q&A. They were going to dance. And if he wanted answers, he was going to have to let her lead. He could do that, because he was leaning toward the theory that she wasn't the killer. But she was deep in his investigation somehow, and he wanted to know how much. "For the first time in my career, I'm not sure."

She took another drag off her cigarette. "Why is that, Detective?"

"Last night, I saw five murder victims who the coroner had already confirmed as very, very dead. One of them tried to take a bite of me after I pumped two .45 caliber slugs into his chest from three feet away. I don't know what to think." He'd spent most of the last twelve hours reliving the episode in the morgue and he was no closer to an answer than he'd been last night. He suspected she had the answers, but getting her to part with them was going to take some adroit handling and manipulation.

She tilted her head in a flirtatious manner. "Would it be too much to ask you to just trust me?"

Not for all the silk panties in New Orleans, lady. "Five dead guys got up and walked. I saw you cut off their heads. You dragged me outside like I weighed four pounds—and I'm ex-Special Forces—without anyone doing jack squat to stop you, much less notice. I know if I say one thing about what happened in that room last night, I'll be laughed out of New Orleans P.D. on a psych discharge. I don't know what to think. Until I get some decent answers, trusting you is probably not going to happen."

She smiled at him as she exhaled another puff of fragrant smoke. "Detective, will it suffice to say that there are things in this universe that are unexplainable? Mystical?" Her voice took on an ethereal quality that lulled him. The room seemed to shift out of focus for a moment, just as it had last night.

He snapped back, pushing away the calming sense of well-being that surrounded him. "I don't like to think about things unexplainable or mystical. That crap makes my job harder, and I hate that. I like answers, the kind of answers everybody will understand."

"One would think that being a detective you would enjoy a good mystery."

She was giving him a headache with her hoodoo voodoo talk. "It's pretty mysterious that someone can assemble a ship inside a whiskey bottle, but when dead bodies just pop on up and walk again, that's too hard for me to understand."

She walked to a high-backed wing chair and sat. Slowly she crossed her legs. Silk rippled as the robe slipped open to reveal a shapely knee, long slender calf and narrow foot. "Would it be enough of an explanation to say they weren't exactly dead to begin with?"

A few more inches and he'd see the promised land. Was he bad in wanting the robe to ride up a bit more? Ryan knew he heard her words, but they just weren't computing in his brain. He needed some sleep. "They were sliced and diced, lady. All their insides were in jars on the shelf. They were dead. Give me a good reason why I shouldn't arrest you." Maybe he should just get drunk and forget the whole damn thing. The world had gone way beyond plausible during his encounter in the morgue with the "walking dead."

She took another drag off the cigarette, then stubbed it out in a marble ashtray. "I'm not the murderer you seek."

Where had he heard that story before? From the mouth of every criminal in New Orleans. I'm not your guy. Wasn't me. I didn't do it. I was playing cards in a back alley, couldn't have done it. Yet he believed her. "Are you telling me that you are a murderer, just not the one I'm looking for right now? 'Cause if you want to confess about anything, I'm happy to listen."

She gave him a sultry smile that rocked him to the core. "Which would you like me to be?"

Let me get you a list. "Okay. Then what were you doing in the morgue last night decapitating already dead bodies?" But they weren't dead. "Well, sort of dead bodies." Ryan frowned getting confused. "Non-dead dead bodies."

Miss Mignon was taking him for one long-assed dance. Which was okay. As long as he got what he wanted, Ryan would boogie to her tune until she was ready to call it quits. Rule number one of detective work: An interview was never about the detective but a suspect's moment in the spotlight. If he kept her talking long enough, maybe she'd unwittingly drop something to convict herself, or better yet, let something loose that he could use to catch his killer. Because he had the strangest feeling that she knew the killer, the person he was looking for.

She chuckled. "Preserving truth, justice and the American way."

Rubbing his forehead, he wondered how long he was going to let her spill her story—-as nutty as it sounded. "I need more than that. How about we pretend I'm an unbeliever." Not that he'd be stretching his acting abilities. She knew that. But would she really tell him the truth?

As she ran a hand through her curly hair, her breasts pushed against the lapels of her robe. "I don't think that would tax my talents."

She had skills all right, she could wield an axe, mess with his head, and give him a hard-on all at the same time. Talent like that took years to hone. The last time he'd been outclassed was when he'd had a hot drop in Somalia and ended up in the middle of a street fighting with kids who looked as if they should have been playing Little League. He'd got through Somalia with his ass intact; he'd make it through this.

She sipped her wine. "Those bodies were in the process of changing."

"Yeah? Into what?" He really didn't want to know but damned if he could stop himself from asking

"A metamorphic change."

He eyed her. What the hell was she talking about? "Do you mean like a butterfly?" He didn't know human beings could morph into something else.

A flash of annoyance crossed her face. "They were in the process of becoming vampires, and you were about to be their first meal."

His mouth dropped open, his witty reply stopped in its tracks. "Come again?"

"They were becoming vampires."

He stared her. She'd said *vampires* like regular people talk about getting a haircut. Vampires! The woman was nuts. Vampires didn't exist except in the murky depths of fiction. Now he'd heard it all. "Did you hit your head in the morgue? I didn't see you take a dive, but you must have to be talking crazy like this."

Her lips pressed together tightly for a moment. "I'm not crazy."

"Vampires are a myth, a legend to scare little kids into eating their lima beans." Did she think he was so gullible he'd believe her fairy tale? This wasn't an *X-Files* episode.

She burst out laughing. "Vampires have been used for a lot of dirty work over the centuries, but encouraging lima bean consumption is not one of them."

"That's it! I've had enough. I haven't slept or taken a shower in four days. You're under arrest." He reached behind him and pulled out his cuffs. He had no particular reason to arrest her, but she didn't know that. And hopefully the lawyer wouldn't be around to stop him. At the moment he didn't care either.

She tilted her head up at him, an amused expression on her lips and in her eyes. "On what charge?"

"For getting on my last nerve. And when I'm done with you, I'm taking you to the psych ward. You can commune with some Prozac."

She threw back her head and burst into a hearty laugh that filled the room and surrounded him like a velvet cloud.

Ryan noticed she had a nice neck. Long and supple, it reminded of him of a swan. Funny, he'd never noticed that part of a woman's anatomy before. He was a confirmed T and A man.

"Put your toys away, Detective," she said in her husky, 'do me' voice. "I don't have to go anywhere with you and you know it."

Damn, she'd called his bluff and he had to admit, it was kind of sexy. He'd never been outwitted by a girl before, except his grandmother, and she didn't count. "Okay, lady. Give me one extra-good reason not to take you in."

She waved her hand at a chair, gesturing for him to sit. "This is going to take awhile. Are you sure I can't get you a drink?"

This was going to be entertaining. Too bad he didn't have any Milk Duds, popcorn and a soda. "I have time." He settled down in a dark red chair that seemed to curve to accommodate him. "I don't want to hear anything about blood-sucking vampires or any demon shit you might come up with. I want the truth, the whole truth and nothing but the truth."

"Then shut up and listen." She took another sip of her wine.

"Ouch." Damn, he was getting smart-assed in his old age.

She set her glass on a table. "Vampires aren't demons. Vampirism is a...medical condition."

He rubbed his forehead. "I told you I don't want to hear about no vampire shit." He didn't even like reading about them.

She gazed at him, her brown eyes filled with something he thought was sadness. "Vampires exist whether you want to believe or not."

Her words sent a chill through him that made him shiver with dread. He knew when a suspect was lying. He could almost smell it on them. She wasn't lying. She really believed this crap. That made him sad. So beautiful and yet so loony. There was no justice in the world if a woman this fine wasn't firing on all cylinders. "So you're saying that being a vampire is a disorder, like schizophrenia or paranoia?" She had the most delectable, kissable lips. Every time the pouty curve of her lips touched the edge of the glass, he couldn't help wishing she were kissing him, touching him, using her lips to rouse him to insatiable passion. Her voice, her whole body, indicated a carnal knowledge that would knock his socks off.

"Not a mental condition, but a physical change." Her chest rose and fell with contained emotion. Her voice was tight, and her lips pressed together with annoyance.

Yeah! Yeah! Yeah! He'd pissed her off good. And that bothered him. When had that happened before in his career? The next thing he knew he'd have to wrap her head in tinfoil so she'd stop getting signals from the mother ship. The least he could do was play along, even if he did-n't believe one word coming from her so delectable lips. "So you're telling me that those corpses weren't really dead despite the lack of blood in their very empty veins, along with no pulse and no working heart, lungs or brain. And they were waking up and wanting to suck my blood. Do they turn into bats, too?"

She closed her eyes for a moment, then opened them. She glared at him. "Only shape-shifters can do such a thing."

He hit his forehead with the palm of his hand. "I should have known!" He pondered her words for a moment. "Are you saying that shape-shifters exist, too?"

"What I'm saying is that you need to pay attention and believe me because if you don't, humanity will cease to exist in the manner to which you are accustomed."

"Right. And if humans die off in some sort of cataclysmic action, what would vampires do for food then?" He was pretty proud of his statement. Damn, was he smart. He'd watched his share of horror movies and was amazed no one had ever asked that question.

She drew back her shoulders, the silk rustling about her breasts and then settling down against her skin. "Human blood is not the only food source available to them. Just the tastiest one."

He was afraid to ask what the alternative food source was. He found his eyes staring at the V between her breasts where the fabric crossed over itself. The roundness of her breasts pushed against the red silk and he felt his blood roaring in his ears. He'd never in his life had such a strong reaction to a woman. Especially a woman he was questioning.

"Okay," he said in a soothing tone, willing to play along. Anything to get her to tell him the real truth, not her version of it. He could only take so many lies in the course of a day, and he'd reached his limit an hour ago. "What kind of medical condition?"

She paused as though considering her options. "Vampirism is like a viral infection that affects the brain's function."

"Obviously deadly." Excuse the pun, he told himself, but every once in a while his sense of the macabre wouldn't stay bottled up.

She didn't smile. "It's not deadly, but it transforms the human brain and the body."

Like he was an idiot and willing to listen to her drivel. She was sumptuous and heady, but he couldn't believe she was telling him fairy tales, or rather, vampire tales. Did she have any concept as to how wacky all this sounded? "Yeah. Right. Sure."

She leaned forward and the robe gapped, revealing the smooth side-crescents of each breast. "I'm breaking a lot of rules here telling you this. The least you can do is shut up and listen to what I have to say."

Okay, he could play along to get what he wanted. "I'll bite. Why the blood sucking?" Even he winced at his pun.

She frowned at him. "Vampires have to replenish their blood every few days."

"That explains the bloodless bodies lying around lately." Way too many of them. Even though all the victims had been on the wrong side of the law, he still needed to stop the killer. No one went vigilante in his city and took the law into their own hands. "Why do they only attack at night?"

She eyed him with the look a parent gives a misbehaving child. "They are sensitive to light."

"Sensitive how?"

"Sunlight causes a chemical reaction and their bodies burn. From the inside out." She shuddered.

Only yesterday morning one of the beat cops discovered one of the victims just as the sun was coming up, and claimed the body started smoking and turning black. Like everyone else in the squad room, Ryan had thought the man was tripping. "Like a Lean Cuisine in a microwave oven?" He couldn't resist that one.

Her grip on the wineglass tightened. "Don't be crude, Detective."

Ryan shrugged, hoping he looked ashamed of himself. He was getting to her. He could tell. Good. Pushing all the right buttons was his favorite interview tactic. "I'm a guy. What do you want? We live for crude."

She eyed him. Her dark pupils were like pools of blackness against the whiteness. "Ryan Maurice Lattimore, you're thirty-six years old. You graduated magna cum laude from Tulane University. Afterward, you joined the army, became a member of the Special Forces and served with honor and distinction in the Persian Gulf and Somalia. You joined the New Orleans P.D. and rose through the ranks with a jacket full of commendations. You made it to detective in record time. You have a seventy-five percent clearance rate. No, Detective, you're not just a guy."

Hearing his history sent a chill through his body, but he wasn't going to let her know how much she had just rattled him. "Do you know I also like Captain Crunch Peanut Butter cereal for breakfast and prefer cotton boxers?"

She took a deep breath. "No, but I'll add that to my dossier on you."

"You have a dossier on me? I'm impressed." Actually, he was worried, but he wasn't going to let her know it. "Why?" How had she found out so much about him? His records were so classified he didn't even have them. Maybe ten people on the planet knew what he had done in the military.

She tapped a thick manilla folder on a side table with a long slender finger. "Information is power. Or didn't your stint in military intelligence teach you that. I'm rather disappointed."

How the hell had she known that? "Now you're delving into the classified. Where did you get that information?"

She smiled. "The old fashioned way. But the fact is, I was able to find out all I needed to know about you in precious little time, which is why I expected you earlier. After all, you had the license plate number of Lucas's car."

Now he was at a disadvantage. He didn't know anything about her except her name and her silly theories about vampires. "So who are you?"

"I told you before my name is Mignon du Plessis."

Not enough, he thought. "What are you?"

She sighed. "If you must give me a label, I'm a Venator."

Searching his memory, he knew that word. "That's Latin for hunter, right?"

Miss Mignon graced him with a dazzling smile. "Very good."

"Jesuits, they learn a boy right."

"I'm impressed."

Score one for Lattimore, he'd impressed the babe. "So what do you hunt?" he asked innocently.

"Vampires."

They were back to vampires again. Just when he was beginning to like her. She might have had a body designed by the hand of God, but her brain had a short circuit regarding vampires.

His instincts told him she wasn't lying, at least not in her mind. "Okay, Buffy, is that your story? Are you sticking to it?"

She frowned and leaned toward him. "Never call me that. That's a television show and they don't know anything about what a real vampire is like. In fact, they wouldn't know a real vampire if they fell over one." Her body stiffened. "Where they got the idea vampires transform into such hideous creatures is beyond me."

Chalk one up for TV expediency. "Don't tell me, let me guess. Vampires are really beautiful and misunderstood."

"Some are. But I can tell you this. They don't overpower their victims for a meal. They simply enchant them."

All right. Vampires can use enchantment, whatever the hell that is. All this information was so very interesting. "You're saying vampires are boring creatures and their existence goes back to the viral infection thing?"

A sad look passed over her face. "I realize the myth is so much more exciting. Vampires are average people who have been enhanced."

This was the spookiest conversation Ryan had ever had. And he'd had some humdingers in his day. "Enhanced how?" He almost hated asking.

"They become superhuman."

"Then why are you killing them? Which I might remind you is a felony."

"Then let me remind you, since you haven't taken me into custody or Mirandized me, this is nothing more than a simple conversation."

"You are good." Admiration rose in him. He liked a smart suspect. That made his job so much more enjoyable when he was able to get a conviction.

"Nor," she continued, "can you arrest me for killing someone already pronounced dead by your esteemed coroner in his or her limited experience."

"I see you found a technicality. But we do have laws about desecrating the dead." Let her chew on that.

She smiled as she spread her hands out in front of her and stared at her blood-red fingernails. "I'm very smart."

A hot, flossy babe with a brain. Did it get any better than that? "You're all that."

"Detective, we can sit here and banter, telling jokes all morning long. But there is a plague hitting New Orleans, one that will overrun the city, then the state and the whole country. I am the only person standing between you and the apocalypse."

CHAPTER FOUR

Mignon closed her eyes. Maybe if she kept them closed long enough, this vexing man would just fade away. She couldn't seem to make him understand without telling him the entire truth. Ryan Lattimore had no idea just how much danger he and all the citizens of New Orleans were in.

"So," he said, "is this an apocalypse of biblical proportions or just get-out-the-riot-gear kind? 'Cause I think I should start preparing now."

She opened her eyes and glared at him. How could such a handsome, intelligent man be so infuriating? "Detective Lattimore, you're mocking me." She couldn't keep the exasperation out of her voice. Why did it matter if he believed her or not. she just needed him to stay out of her way for the next few days until she found Charles. But unless she gave him something to satisfy his curiosity, he'd be nipping at her heels. For a second that prospect didn't seem so unappealing.

She knew he was interested in her in more than just a work-related way. The scent of desire rose hotly off his skin. He wanted her. Was that why he'd said nothing to his superiors about her actions at the morgue? No. How would he have explained what had happened and even if he had been able to, who in their right mind would believe him?

"I'm going to explain this one time," she said quietly and firmly. "Vampires transmit the virus through the sharing of their blood, so vampires can feed without turning a victim into a vampire. There are only three ways to kill a vampire—decapitation, fire, and exposure to sunlight. Stakes, crosses and garlic do not work. At this moment a vampire named Charles Rabelais is amassing an army. I have to stop him. So you can help me fight him or you can go home. I don't care which."

He held up a hand. "How come you know so much about these vampires?"

Mignon stared at his large hand, noticing that he didn't wear a wedding band. This pleased her for some strange reason. "The best way to snare your prey is to know them, to think like them. I have studied them for a lifetime."

He leaned forward, his elbows on his knees. "Why is Rabelais on the warpath?" His tone was almost conversational, as if they were talking about the weather.

Mignon suppressed a smile. Make the suspect your friend. He was wooing her, trying to make her talk. She liked his technique. It had been a long time since a man had tried to dally with her. "Some vampires believe they should rule humanity. I am, to use a police expression, the thin, blue line between good and evil, between us and them."

A condescending expression crossed his face, as though he were preparing to disbelieve her but would let her talk anyway. "What do you know about that?"

Sensing that she was losing him, she wondered if she should let him think she was insane. "You're uncomfortable, because you've grown up with the knowledge that humans are the apex predators on this planet."

"I like it on top."

This man was so infuriating, yet at the same time she was thoroughly enjoying the banter. If the circumstances weren't so dire, she would enjoy Ryan Lattimore's company. Quick-witted and cynical, he was self-confident without being arrogant, everything she enjoyed in a man, except the fact that he was mortal. "I'm sure you do, but sometimes you just have to lie on your back and take what you get."

He grinned at her. "I'll bet you do pretty good on top yourself."

She bit her lip to stop herself from laughing. The man had the most wicked smile she'd seen in years. His full lips revealed straight white teeth against mahogany brown skin. The only word she could use to describe him was lethal. "When all else fails, resort to sexual innuendo." Men, she thought. Vampire or mortal, they never change. She hadn't had such a stimulating conversation with a man in a long, long time. "Are you a betting man?"

"Maybe," he admitted, "but I gotta tell you, I'm still on the fence about your vampire tale."

"If I can prove to you that vampires really exist, will you stand back and let me do my job? I promise I will stop your killer."

A half smile curved his lips. "You prove to me vampires exist, and I'll *let* you help me stop the killer."

Putting her hand on her hip, she studied the smug expression on his face. His brown eyes glittered with humor. "How very kind of you."

He shrugged. "I do my best."

She pursed her lips, knowing that he had won this battle. "Is that the best offer I'm going to get from you?"

He smiled again. "I have plenty of offers for you, lady, but none of them involve solving these homicides." His gaze raked her up and down, his eyes lingering at the base of her throat.

Fire curled in the pit of her stomach. Her throat went dry. If she were human, she could see herself being with this man. But she wasn't human any more and she'd seen a lot of history—too much to overcome. "Check your libido, Detective. Tonight, you and I are going to hunt."

He jiggled his eyebrows. "Should I slip into something slinky and black like you?"

Amusement bubbled inside her chest. "I believe I might enjoy that." She could see him clothed in black leather, tight across his thighs, molding his firm behind, and a black mesh t-shirt showing his dark, muscled body to sinful perfection. A wave of yearning washed over her. An ache to live a normal life with a normal man who would give her children. But that dream was long gone and she felt a moment's sadness that she would never reclaim the innocence she'd been born with.

"What time is the party?" he asked.

"We're hunting vampires. After sunset. Say seven."

"That'll work for me." He stood. "Where should I meet you?"

"Here." Mignon rose to her feet. The red silk rustled about her skin.

She watched him leave the room. He had the grace of a leopard and the haughtiness of a lion. Having him around could be fun. She hadn't had much recreation for a long time. When a woman spent two hundred fifty years as a vampire, playfulness was hard to come by. She'd become jaded.

After Lattimore had closed the door, leaving her alone once more, she picked up an old daguerreotype from the sideboard. Her youthful face stared back at her. She clearly remembered the day the photographer had done the sitting. She'd worn her best silk gown with jet beads on the sleeves and collar. Her hair had been swept up under a tiny black hat with a black feather. She had been seated on a bench with her great-grandson, Jean Pierre, and her great-great-grandson, Victor. Jean Pierre's face had already been lined with age and his hair had gone completely gray while she remained youthful and exuberant with tendrils of black hair curling about her temples.

If she could live her life over again, would she choose to live? Not that she'd known the results of her decision at the time. She had watched her children die, her grandchildren, her great-grandchildren. She'd seen many things. Great wars, inventions that were supposed to save the world, and she'd met men and women who'd been the best humanity had to offer and the worst. And she had watched the life drain from some of them, while others had changed to stay at her side.

A knock sounded at the door and it opened. Maximus Severus walked in. He was tall and muscular with tanned skin, brown eyes and lean face. He'd been the son of a whore during the reign of Tiberius Caesar and had been sold into slavery to fight in the gladiator arenas where he'd become a champion.

"Where do you stand with your detective, *Piccola*?" His voice was deep and sensual. His muscles rippled as he poured himself a glass of pig blood.

After all these years he still called her 'little one.' He made her feel protected and cared for. "He's going to be a problem."

Max took a sip. "How will he be a problem?"

She had to tell him the truth. "Have you ever failed to enchant someone?"

He turned, one eyebrow lifting. "Once. Many centuries ago." For a second, a wistfulness passed over his face. "She was a courtesan in Venice."

"Tell me." Max had the most interesting past. After all the years of knowing him, he still had the ability to surprise her.

"Madeline made me feel young again, like you did when first we met."

Max was a terrible flirt. He could not help himself. Women adored him, and even though her affair with him had ended over seventy years ago, Mignon would always love him and over the years their friendship had only deepened. "And what did you do, Max?"

He sighed, "Those were the days when no rules existed forbidding intimate contact with mortals, so I let her seduce me. She was very skilled in the art of pleasure, and I was," he sighed, "grateful."

Mignon burst into laughter. "And gratitude is one of your finer qualities."

"Yes," he acknowledged with no lack of pride. "But back to the question at hand. Being unable to enchant a human has been known to happen, but it's rare. Are you saying you could not enchant the detective?"

"Yes."

His blond brows drew together. "That does pose a problem. What does he know of us?"

"I told him I'm a vampire hunter, but he doesn't believe me, nor does he believe in vampires. Everything he thinks he knows, he learned from television and movies."

"So he's an avid television viewer." Max shook his head knowingly. "Why didn't you just kill him and save yourself the trouble? You could have broken him in two. You didn't have to share any information with him."

Like most vampires, Max was at odds with the modern world. Not that she was steeped in it; she just understood mortals much better. "He's not one of the faceless masses. I couldn't enchant him. He saw me and saw the bodies rise. One nearly killed him. He's a New Orleans police officer and his turning up dead or missing would galvanize the whole department. Charles chose his prey from the dregs. Thank God for that, but police look after their own, the same way we look after our own."

"Why didn't you let the newly risen vampire kill him? That would have solved our problems."

Mignon was still connected to the mortal world through her descendants. She was a baby in vampire time. "Letting him die would have been wrong."

"Your conscience is your cross to bear."

They'd had this conversation many times before. The stakes were too high for her to ignore. "Then why are you helping me hunt Charles?"

"Because Charles created you and he still has power over you."

She curled her hand into a fist, trying to control her rage. Even after all these years, the anger refused to go away. "Charles has no hold on me." She didn't believe her words and she knew Max didn't either. Her sire's blood ran through the veins of her descendants. She and Charles would always be connected in a way other vampires did not understand. Too many of them had distanced themselves from humanity, but Mignon could not abandon those she protected.

Max glanced at her. "What is between you and Charles will never be over."

"When I take his head, it will be."

He kissed her lightly on the forehead. "Your hate is a powerful thing, Mignon. Don't let it consume you."

"Charles sold *my* children to a brothel. My hate is why I am here. Otherwise I would have been content to remain on Angeline Island with my descendants. The job I do there is important to the brethren." And for their future survival.

"I recognize that maintaining the bank is what keeps us safe, but you are more than a banker. Your compassion for mortals is something the rest of us have forced ourselves to forget. Your descendants keep you human. Your hatred keeps you focused."

"You aren't telling me something I don't already know."

"I was a slave once, too. To the emperors, gladiators were only livestock to be used for their own blood lust." He touched her cheek. "I never did understand, why after what Charles did to you, you consented to the change."

"Because I thought if I pleased him he'd bring my children back. Nor did I truly understand the consequences. I did what I had to do. I will do the same now." She waved him away. "I am weary of this conversation. I need to rest for this evening."

He ran a finger down the side of her breast and circled her nipple.

Mignon grabbed his hand to stop him and backed away just out of reach.

"I intended only to offer you comfort," he said, his tone sad.

"We do not have time. While we've managed to find most of the fledglings, Charles still eludes us and the time grows short." She held his gaze. "Charles is growing strong. We must stop him—soon."

"We will."

His confidence washed over her and for a moment she thought of Ryan. He'd had the same confidence that right would always triumph over wrong. She wasn't so sure. Charles had grown stronger than any other vampire she had faced in the past. Even stronger than the Egyptian who'd had four thousand years to grow his power. She closed her eyes. "Why do you put up with me?"

"Because you are the type of woman who marks a man's soul forever." He gently pushed a tendril of hair away from her forehead.

"And you," she responded, "are the type of man who can almost make me forget my failures."

He kissed her cheek. "I will never stop caring for you."

"I know." But he could never quiet the guilt that filled her with bitterness. For all his flaws, Max had a streak of nobility that ran through him, keeping him from becoming like Charles. And as long as she had mortal descendants, she could never truly give herself over to the life of a vampire.

"Rest well, *Piccola*." He left her to her loneliness.

For a long time, she sat in her chair staring at the door and remembering. After she had escaped Charles and found her children, she'd hidden with them in New Orleans, only coming out when the need for money or blood drove her.

New Orleans — 1751

Mignon moved through the room dressed in a heavy brocade skirt and matching bodice she'd stolen from another fancy woman. The smokey, crowded room teemed with activity. Men sat around tables playing cards. Music played in the background.

Crystal chandeliers hung from the ceiling, the candles casting soft light across the many card players. She hated what she was about to do, but had no choice. Her children, not only her own blood children but the ones she had liberated from the brothel and taken in, needed food.

Mignon smiled and slid into a chair next to a fat man, who looked as if he would never miss a few drops of blood or any one of the rings on his fingers. His florid face was thick and round with rolls of fat beneath his chin. He would feed her well tonight.

A strange prickle crawled up her skin and she looked around. Something was not right this night, but she couldn't decide what the problem was.

She gently ran her fingers down the man's thigh. "Come with me. I cannot wait another moment for you." She tried not to stare at his bejeweled fingers.

A man brushed against the back of her neck. A tingle started where he touched her and she again felt the strangeness resonate through her. She glanced up at the man. He smiled at her.

He was handsome and lean with eyes that seemed to see directly into her soul. He smiled lazily and slipped a coin into her cleavage. Then he bent over and nuzzled her neck. She stood and faced him. "Good evening."

"For a night with you, I'd give a king's ransom." He slid a finger down her cheek.

"I am willing." She didn't care who she preyed on, though this stranger would be more pleasurable than her first choice.

The fat man reached out a thick-fingered hand to stop her. "You're mine."

"Not any more," she replied with a throaty purr and jerked her hand away. He'd had his chance. In exchange for blood and money, she always left her 'dinner' companions with the most seductive of memories of her. This man would miss his treat.

She let the new man lead her to the rooms above. She'd been working this brothel for only a few months and even though she knew her way around, she was still awed by the luxurious beauty of the hall with its elaborate paintings of nude women on the walls and the thick red carpet.

They reached the man's room. He opened the door and stood to one side, politely allowing her to enter first. For a second Mignon didn't know quite what to do. No man had ever treated her with the respect usually reserved for a noble-born lady. She hesitated. Then he urged her into the room.

The understated elegance of the room reminded her of Charles's plantation on Martinique.

"It's a pity, you are so beautiful," he said as he closed the door.

Mignon turned to look at him and frowned. "I don't understand."

He gave a slight, almost sinister smile. "One hates to destroy such beauty, no matter how evil it is." He set a finger under her chin and lifted it.

Mignon felt a moment of superiority. As though he could kill her. "Do you think you could harm me?" She stepped away from him. His touch seared her flesh and he made her uncomfortable. A flash of fear went through her as she realized this man was like no other. She hadn't felt this kind of fear since Charles had been her master.

"I have been hunting you for three years."

"Hunting me?" He was a slave hunter. "I am a free woman. I have my manumission papers." She held up the little bag she carried.

For a second he frowned. "I have no interest in your slave past. I am hunting you because in Charleston, three years ago, you killed twenty-seven people."

A chill raced up her spine. How did he know what she had done? All the children had come with her and she had erased their memories of that one night of rage. She'd left the slaves alive and put false memories in their heads. Had she failed to bewitch one? "It was a brothel and they had my children. They had other people's children." Her voice took on a pleading tone, begging him to understand. She had to survive; her children would die without her.

He walked casually across the room and reached inside the armoire. He withdrew a sword, so huge that it seemed to stretch from his hand to the floor.

Her body turned to ice. "What are you going to do?" She forced herself to stand still and face him, even though every instinct shouted for her to flee. She would have to kill again. She hated the killing and tried her best to avoid taking anyone's life.

The man smiled, revealing even white teeth. "I will take your lovely head."

"My children," she moaned. She couldn't die. Who would look after Simon and the others?

He raised the sword over his head. "Vampires are unable to breed."

"Vampires!" She stared at him. "Is that what I am called?" She repeated the name in her mind even as she tensed, ready to stop him.

He hesitated, looking puzzled. "You did not know?"

She shook her head, her fear adding to her confusion. Her stomach twisted and she felt bile rising in her throat. Simon. Angeline. To never see their faces again, or touch the sweet softness of their skin. To miss out on her granddaughter's first words. A terror so great rose in her that she thought she would choke. She couldn't let this man kill her.

He lowered his sword. "Who is your sire?"

She prepared to fight. "I do not know who my father was."

"Who made you into a vampire?" He took a step closer to her.

"My master."

He nodded. "His name?"

Would he kill Charles, too? If so she could go to her grave knowing his evil had been ended. Her past would be eradicated. "Charles Rabelais."

"Ah, Charles. He is another I would execute if I could find him. He's a slippery bastard."

Keep him talking, she thought, then grab the sword and use it against him.

"Rabelais must have told you what you are? What we are."

He was like her. There were more like her? She'd thought she and Charles were the only ones. "He told me nothing before I ran away from him. I had to find my children."

His grip on the sword relaxed and he stepped back, the tension in his face gone. "Tell me about your children."

Mignon began to relax. Perhaps she could talk her way out of this after all. "Charles sold my children, then made me sick. I went to a healer, but she cursed me. She said I was evil. Even the priest refused to help me." The meeting with the priest had been the worst. He had crossed himself over and over again and held his crucifix out in front of him as though he'd expected it to save him. Mignon had come close to killing the priest, but had run away instead. She had thought to find help and had instead found damnation.

"Why did you kill those people in Charleston if not to feed?" He tossed the sword on the bed.

"I was so angry. They forced my son, my daughter and the other children to sell their bodies. My daughter was pregnant and she was still a child herself. I had to save them. I have refused to kill since then. I learned how to take enough blood to live. I only take money to feed everyone, to survive." She thought of her son and daughter, the rest of the children hidden deep in the swamps. They were all Mignon had left in the world and she wouldn't let anything happen to them. She would guard them with her life.

He sheathed the sword and put it away in the armoire. "You have no idea what you are, do you?" He sounded frustrated.

"The sun burns me. But I am stronger. I hear and see things better. I can smell better. I can even make people forget that they saw me or allowed me to feed on them." Bewitching people was a pleasing benefit of her illness. But according to this man, she wasn't ill.

He sighed. "That is what happens when we are changed."

Surprise filled her. "I didn't know."

He ran a hand through his dark hair and then gestured for her to sit down. "You have a lot to learn, and I will have a lot to explain to the *Praetorium*."

"You promise not to kill me?"

"Not at this moment."

Her knees grew wobbly and she sat down harder than she'd intended. "Dawn will be coming soon and I have to return to the children."

He opened a drawer in the desk and took out a bag of coins. "First you must feed."

He opened the door and stood aside to allow her to precede him. For a second she hesitated, thinking about her children. She sensed that this man would change her, that he would show her a whole new world, and she didn't know if she wanted that world. She was happy with things the way they were.

She took a step forward, knowing that she had no choice. She had to know what she was and he would show her.

CHAPTER FIVE

Present day — New Orleans

Max had shown her that vampirism could be a blessing, not a curse. He'd taught her more than she could ever have imagined. He had become her teacher, her mentor, and years later, her lover. He had remade the frightened ex-slave into the self-confident person she was today. She was a *venator* of the Order of Romulus, an executioner, the person who guarded the secrets of the vampire.

Max had always been filled with suppressed energy, constantly filling his time with activities. He seldom stayed in one place too long, while Mignon yearned to be home with the serenity and peace she had built for herself.

Now on to her newest problem. Detective Ryan Lattimore. He intrigued her as much as he irritated her. She couldn't say why she'd saved him at the morgue. His death would have made her task easier. But something had stopped her. When the newly risen vampire had attacked the detective, Mignon had gone into action.

Having met him, she found she enjoyed his company, his banter and his lack of pretense. She had told him the most outrageous story, leaving a few parts out, and even though she knew he didn't quite believed her, he wanted to trust her because he didn't want her to be guilty.

She could use that knowledge.

At the wall, she opened the panel that led to her bedroom. She needed to rest.

Mignon crouched, her Chinese broadsword tight in her hand as she faced Max with a pair of butterfly short swords. Solomon stood at one end of the large room watching, his arms crossed over his chest and his dark face impassive.

Max swung his swords and Mignon slid to one side, avoiding him. "You're sluggish today, *Piccola*."

"I'm fine." Her footsteps were loud on the wood floor as she whirled.

He executed a drop spin kick. "Perhaps you are spending too much time in the company of mortals."

Mignon felt a flash of annoyance as she back flipped to avoid his kick. Righting herself, she raised her sword and swung. He ducked as the blade nicked the side of his throat.

"It's not my head you want." The blood trickled back into the small wound and Max's skin immediately healed.

"Then don't annoy me." Again, irritation flared in her.

He came at her, both of his blades slicing through the air. "You're very angry today."

Mignon took a deep breath and blocked each of his blows. The sound of clashing steel rang in the air. "I'm here for practice, not analysis."

Max lunged at her. "One bad dinner party with Siggy and you've never forgiven the man."

With her sword she blocked his blow and hit him in the solar plexus with her free hand. He staggered back a few steps. She would have loved to have had Sigmund Freud *for* dinner. He had been the most misogynystic, petty, boorish mortal she'd ever had the displeasure to meet. How dare he tell her that all she wanted in life was a penis.

That was why women had the power, because men were too concerned about finding a place to bed their penis. Wasn't that what courtship was all about? In another place and time, she wouldn't mind being courted by that handsome detective. She'd bet he had a penis to die for.

Max danced around her, swinging his swords. He nicked her cheek and she felt the sharp painful prick of the tip of his sword and the hot blood trickle down.

Shrugging off the pain, she knew the cut would heal in a moment. He had her on the defensive with his blitz attack. She needed to focus, to put thoughts of Lattimore and Charles out of her mind.

She wasn't at her best today, but she would never admit such a thing to Max. He was a master at playing on people's weaknesses, whether they were physical or emotional.

Max launched another barrage, forcing her back, parrying her own attack as though she were nothing but an annoying insect. She backed against the wall and jumped straight up and gripped the ceiling. She hung there, laughing. Being a vampire had some advantages. She loved the ability to defy gravity, her added quickness and the way her mind worked.

"No fair, Mignon," Max chided her as he stood with one hand on his hip.

"Don't pout, Maximus, it's so unmanly." She dropped back down, intending to land on him, but as her feet touched his chest, he changed, shrinking down until he'd shape-shifted into a fly. He buzzed around her face and she swatted at him but missed each time. She could just barely hear him laughing. She swung a hand at him. He turned back to human form just as her hand impacted with his cheek.

He staggered back, sitting down hard on his butt. He had one hand on his cheek. "Mignon, remind me to never speak of Freud when we spar again."

Solomon stepped forward, his hands up as though to keep them apart. "Children," he chided them, "cease your petty squabbling. I believe we have company." He took a sniff of the air. "A B negative."

Ryan presented himself at the front door promptly at seven o'clock. When Mignon opened the door, Ryan had to stop and stare for moment. She wore tight black spandex pants and a sleeveless tank tube top. *What this woman did for the color black should be considered illegal.*

"Good evening, Ryan." Her voice was an aged whiskey purr that married the gentle cadence of the Caribbean with the indolent accent of the bayous. Shivers vibrated up and down his spine.

"I thought I'd let you know there were no bloodless bodies today. I don't need to camp out at the morgue tonight."

"None that were found." She turned and started up the stairs to the next floor.

Ryan could barely breathe as he followed her. He could hardly take his eyes from the sensual sway of her hips that matched the exotic sway of her ponytail. She opened a set of double doors and beyond them Ryan could see a huge room which had probably once been a ballroom.

In the ballroom he found two crouched men facing each other holding swords. They thrust and parried, dancing on the balls of their feet, moving with grace. Both were seriously muscled, making Ryan think he should be putting in more hours at the gym. He hadn't been this muscled up when he'd been playing army commando.

The ballroom was huge with a wood floor and paneled walls that held several racks of antique swords interspersed with huge double-headed axes that looked as lethal as the one Mignon had used the night before. In opposite corners, two suits of ornately decorated medieval armor held court.

For a second, Ryan thought he'd stepped into a medieval castle. Doors opened to a deck that overlooked the heavily shaded courtyard, and the gentle scent of magnolias and bougainvillea drifted in on the evening breeze.

At his entrance, the men stopped their practice and faced him. They weren't breathing hard. They weren't even sweating. The tall black man nodded at Ryan.

"Are these your peeps?" Ryan asked as Mignon entered the room.

"My what?" An expression of confusion spread over her beautiful face.

Did the woman own a TV? "You know, your people, your posse, your crew."

She frowned. Sometimes with mortals one needed a translator. Why did the language have to change with the times? By the time she figured out the slang of one generation, the next generation's jargon had replaced it. "Max and Solomon are my associates. They are also hunters."

"You tussle with them? They look like some bad ass dudes. Don't you get your behind kicked?"

She rolled her eyes. "Hardly ever. This is not a job for the weak. Don't let my girlish figure fool you. I can break you like a twig."

He kinda suspected that, but he had to keep his macho on. "Are you casting aspersions on my masculinity?"

She grinned. "Aspersions? That's a big word for a man like you."

"I studied the dictionary this morning. Makes me feel eddicated."

Her mouth worked at trying not to smile, and then she shook her head.

He slapped her on the back. "You want to laugh. Go ahead. I'm a funny guy."

"I haven't met anyone like you in...forever." She walked up to the two men and motioned Ryan to follow her. "Let me introduce you."

Up close, the two men were even bigger than Ryan thought. The black man stood well over six feet and he carried himself as if he owned the room.

"This is Solomon ben Zafir." Mignon gestured at the black man. "And this is Maximus Severus." She tilted her head toward the blond man with the hair almost down to his waist.

Ryan measured both men. He wondered which one would be his competition for Mignon. The second the thought popped into his head he pushed it away. He wasn't here for a little nookie, no matter how tasty the lady was. She was bad news. "Ben Zafir, sounds Arabic."

"I'm from Ethiopia." Solomon's voice was a deep, almost menacing rumble.

Ryan didn't want to come up against Solomon ben Zafir in a dark alley without some serious backup. This man was intimidating. Hell, they were both menacing. Ryan was six foot one but he felt like a dwarf. Now that he'd thought about it, he realized Mignon was tall, too. The top of her head was just even with his eyes, making her around five ten.

The blonde man shook hands with Ryan. "Detective."

Ryan studied the man. If this man was Italian, Ryan decided he ought to be investing in Miss Clairol. He turned to Mignon, "I thought you and I would be solo. Are we going to have a party?"

"You're going to learn to hunt. These two are the great masters."

"Cut off the head or they regenerate. What else do I need to have three teachers for?" He knew he sounded flip despite the fact that the specter of the previous night's activity still haunted him.

Mignon gestured at the display of swords over the fireplace mantle. "Pick a sword," she ordered.

"Any one?"

She nodded. "The one that speaks to you."

How did one find a sword that spoke to a person? He sauntered around the ballroom looking at each display carefully, expecting some sword to start singing in Disneyesque style. After a few minutes, he found a katana nestled in an silver scabbard sitting on a red wooden cradle.

The katana had a wicked curve to it and the second Ryan saw it, he knew he had to have it. The sword seemed to call to him. The ache to hold it, to touch it, echoed in his mind. Was that what she meant by, the sword speaking to him? He reached for it and heard Mignon sigh behind him.

He drew the sword from the scabbard and held it. A snarling dragon, etched into the blade, curled up the curving metal. For a second he had the odd feeling that the dragon had winked at him. He almost sheathed the sword and put it back. Carved dragons did not wink.

"An elegant weapon," Mignon said, "Masamune made this in the thirteenth century. He was one of the finest blade makers in Japan." She touched the hilt and glanced at Max. "He made this especially for a hunter."

Several Japanese symbols were carved into the hilt. "What does this mean?" Ryan traced the symbols with his fingers. The metal warmed with his touch and seemed to rearrange itself to fit his grip.

"It's an old Roman term translated into Japanese. 'Strength and honor.'"

He found himself staring at her, fascinated by her ease with the world of a warrior. "You're really different from other women. I've never known a girl into swords and butt-kicking. That's kind of sexy."

"I like pretty things, too."

He remembered the silk robe flowing over her skin and the way the neckline plunged to reveal the half-globes of her breasts.

Someone cleared his throat and Mignon whirled to stare at Max.

"Excuse me, you two." Max's voice held a mocking tone. "I think it's time we begin." He walked away from them.

Ryan leaned toward Mignon. "Do you and the white boy have something going on?"

She slanted a glance at him. "Are you afraid of a little competition?"

Ryan gave Max the once-over. He cracked his neck, letting the bones slip into place. "No."

"I'm assuming you remember your Special Forces training. You should be able to pick up the basic elements of sword fighting quickly. All you have to remember is to duck and slice."

"Don't the baby vampires have swords, too?" He liked the feel of the blade, as though it belonged to him and him alone. When he closed his eyes he thought for a second the blade sang to him. Then he shook himself and ordered his imagination to stop being so fanciful.

Mignon shook her head. "Baby vamps have appetites, and while they are searching for food they aren't thinking about defense. That is the moment in which we must kill them."

"Cool." He hadn't felt this alive since his Special Forces days. He was gonna like this job.

"And," Maximus added, "never forget that vampires are as cunning and as strong as when they are hungry. Don't let them get too close."

Ryan shook his head. "Or I'll end up a few quarts low. Got it."

Mignon stood aside and watched Ryan as he swung his blade, practicing with Solomon. He was a natural swordsman. His balance was incredible. His eyes never strayed from his intended target. His sleek moves and supple grace reminded her of a leopard. Properly trained he would be an exceptional opponent.

What a fine *venator* he would make, if he were a vampire. He quickly grasped the intricacies and complexities, almost as though he'd used a sword in a previous life. Maybe he had. Mignon didn't believe in rein-carnation, but a few strange things had happened over the years that made her suspect it could happen. Though not to her.

If she survived the hunts, she would be thousands of years old before her death arrived. Unlike the TV vampires who were immortal and didn't age, real vampires aged. Slowly. Max was almost two thou-sand years old and he looked about thirty-five. In another two thousand years, he'd appear fifty. And if life were kind, he'd live another two thou-sand after that before dying of vampire old age.

"What do you think?" she asked Max, nodding at Ryan and Solomon.

"He still thinks this is a joke."

"That will change when he tastes his first battle. It was the same with me." Mignon admired the way Ryan's body moved. He was pow-erful, commanding and in tune with himself. He used his body to advantage. Mignon sensed he would be a magnificent lover. Strong and passionate. A tingle built in her body.

"Mignon?"

She stopped fantasizing, realizing Max had asked her a question. "What?"

Max's menacing scowl said it all. "What do you plan to do with him once this is over and Charles is dead?"

Mignon took a deep breath. She didn't want to think that far into the future. "I don't know."

"The *Praetorium* doesn't like loose ends. He's human and he knows about us."

"He knows nothing about us. He knows only about vampires, though he still doesn't believe. But he will eventually."

"How long until he finds out that we are the same as the ones he hunts?"

Mignon was not going to think about that, and didn't answer Max. She knew she was skating on thin ice and that Ryan was not stupid. If they didn't find Charles and kill him, Ryan would eventually find out that she was a vampire. Like most mortals he'd painted all vampires with the same brush. When he did find out, he would come after her and there would be no other option. She would have to kill him. After a few seconds of silence Max walked across the room.

Ryan and Solomon put up their swords. Ryan was sweating and breathing hard. "Had enough, man? Ready to throw in the towel? Are you tired? I was just playing with you before. I have my game face on now. I'm ready. Let's get busy."

Solomon laughed, a deep rumbling laugh that seemed to originate in the pit of his stomach. Mignon hadn't heard Solomon laugh so heartily since 1924.

Solomon draped an arm around Ryan's shoulders and punched him playfully on the cheek. "I like you."

Ryan blanched. "Thanks, I think."

Solomon laughed again. "I'll hunt with you any day."

Ryan glanced at Mignon. "So tell me, brother man, how do you get this kind of gig? Slicing and dicing vampires. Do you have dental insurance? Is the pay good? What's your retirement like?"

Solomon shook his head. "He's good. He makes me laugh."

"Just call me good-time Charlie." Ryan replaced the sword in the scabbard.

The men had bonded. Good. Solomon would be a powerful ally. If things became hard, he would protect Ryan. Mignon stared at Solomon. This was the most lively conversation she'd heard out of him in years.

Ryan turned to Mignon. "How about you and me doing a little sparring?"

"You're not ready for me, yet." Mignon stepped back. "I don't want to hurt you."

"Not ready!" Ryan squared his shoulders. "Did you see me? I was Samurai Man. I could take you on."

"I doubt that." Mignon arched an eyebrow.

"Any time. Any day, baby." Ryan beat his chest with his palm. "I'm the man."

Max shoved Mignon toward Ryan. "Why not? Teach this puppy a lesson."

"No." She didn't think she could spar against Ryan and not be distracted by him. He was too much in her thoughts. She would falter and if he injured her and witnessed her heal, he would know her secret.

Max raised an eyebrow. "Yes."

Mignon knew she wasn't getting out of this. She glanced at Ryan's face. He wore a challenging grin. Perhaps the detective needed a lesson. "Fine." Later, she promised herself, she would deal with Max.

Max eyed Ryan. "A word of warning, Detective. The lady is also a master."

"I can do her."

Mignon nearly dropped her broadsword. The heat of embarrassment tingled over her skin.

Max grinned. "I think you'd like to."

Ryan jiggled his eyebrows. A cocky half-smile slid across his mouth. He knew he had gotten to her with that last remark.

Mignon was so hot, she wondered if she'd incinerate at any moment. What was it about him that set her body aflame? While he intrigued her and fascinated her, he was a mortal. Fifty years ago he would have been nothing more than a snack for her. She would have seduced him for the blood flowing in his veins, not because she found him exciting. She mentally shook herself. *Focus on how he irritates you*, she ordered herself. *Then you'll be able to concentrate on beating him.*

Mignon removed her sword from its scabbard, enjoying the hiss of steel on steel. The polished metal blade of the medieval broadsword gleamed in the light. She flexed her calf muscles and bounced on the balls of her feet. Quickly she sliced the air, testing the weight of her favorite blade.

Ryan lunged at her.

She parried his thrust and spun out of his way.

Ryan wiped a trickle of sweat off the side of his face. "The lady has style. I'm impressed."

"Be careful, detective, she's just toying with you," Max said from a distant corner of the room.

Mignon could see Ryan was tired, having pushed himself to exhaustion in keeping up with Solomon. He was running solely on his pride. That alone might keep him alive when he faced the vampires.

Their swords met, and the clang of metal echoed in the room. Mignon pushed against him and Ryan fell back. He stepped aside and she slipped past him. Their swords met again. Ryan was almost too tired to be aware of what she was doing. As she manipulated him backward toward the wall, she found herself grinning. For all his exhaustion, he was fighting well. He'd make a splendid vampire. He would be a great hunter. If only the *Praetorium* had not put a two century moratorium on changing over humans, Mignon would have seriously considered bringing him across.

He thrust at her and she parried his blow. He was breathing hard and sweat dripped into his eyes. Suddenly, he swept out a leg and caught her calves. She tumbled backward and sat down with a thud. Her rear end smarted almost as much as her pride. Where had he learned that move?

"Dammit!"

"Are you okay?" He loomed over her.

"Perfectly."

"Hurt anything vital?" He pointed the sword at her. "I was taking it easy because you're a girl."

She rolled away and got to her feet. "You will pay for that."

Ryan followed her. "I've got you on the run."

"Not yet." She lifted the sword to defend herself. For all his exhaustion he was still fighting hard. Mignon swung her blade with all her might and knocked his sword out of his hand. The sword went flying across the floor. She kicked him to the ground and straddled him, standing over him with her sword at his throat. "Not so blasé now."

He smiled weakly. "Just enjoying the view."

"Do you yield?"

"I'm down, but I'm not out. You can't have your way with me yet."

"Are you so sure?"

He gave her a sexy smile that just about melted her insides. She almost groaned. She flicked her sword against his shirt and a button flew across the room. Then one by one, she relieved his shirt of its buttons until she reached his belt buckle.

The edges of his shirt fell apart to reveal his bare chest. He was the color of strong, dark coffee. His flesh glistened. The veins in his throat throbbed and she found herself staring at the veins, each pulsing sweet blood. He smelled of hot, sultry nights in the bayou, primal and dark. Her fangs slipped out and sank into her bottom lip. She felt the pain. Blood slid across her lips.

"You win," he said.

She calmed herself and her fangs retreated. She sat down on his chest and smiled at him. She leaned over and grabbed his shirt. Yanking him, up, she brought him up until their lips nearly met. Their eyes were level. She licked her lips, then kissed him hard. Lightning exploded inside her. Panicking, she knew she had to stop. Ryan began to kiss her back and she yanked her head away. "It's good that you know your betters." Mignon let go of his shirt and he fell back against the wood floor with a small thunk.

She stepped over him and replaced her sword in its scabbard. Turning away from Ryan, she tossed the scabbard to Max, who deftly caught it. "Find him a shirt. Tonight he will see what we are all up against." She left the room and ran to her bedroom. Her heart raced as she entered the cool room. Slamming the door closed, she leaned against the cool wood, eyes shut, searching her mind for the meditation that would calm her raging emotions.

A few seconds later, a knock sounded.

"Miss Mignon," came a voice. "Are you all right?"

Mignon stepped aside and opened the door. Lucas's wife stood in the doorway. "Come in, Sarah."

Sarah had a smile on her sweet, round face. As she walked into the bedroom, a riot of dark curls bounced around her mocha-colored head and neck. "I watched the practice session on the security camera. The police detective learns fast."

"I noticed." Mignon's voice was flat.

"I have some information for you." She handed Mignon a piece of paper. "I played a hunch and hacked into the building department's computer files and found a list of abandoned warehouses along the river front. Several of them look promising." Sarah pointed at the top of the list.

"Your talent for snooping never ceases to amaze me. I can't imagine how you mortals lived so long without your technological wonders." Sarah had been searching through the city data bases looking for areas where Charles might hide. One by one, Mignon had searched through each district in the city. They had narrowed the search to the warehouse district and several unused port facilities along the river.

Sarah laughed. "Don't get on your high horse just because the TV remote baffles you. You're going to be around a long time, Miss Mignon. You need to get with the times."

This tired argument again. "I have mastered the cell phone."

"Just barely. I could not even contemplate existing without such conveniences."

Mignon glanced down the list. Sarah had been thorough. "You and Lucas should get yourself out of the city. Charles knows I'm here and he might decide to come after you." Charles had a history of strikes against others in ways that hurt the most. Mignon did not want to think about the children she had almost lost to Charles. Charles, who did not care that he killed his own blood, simply wanted to hurt her, to strike at her because he thought her abandonment of him was a sign of disloyalty.

Sarah shook her head, smiling. "Who will look after all of you? You need me to switch on the computer."

"I will look after myself. Go home to the island. I will see you after this is done." She patted Sarah's round stomach, feeling the strong sensation of life growing inside the woman's body, a son. She could tell by the beat of the heart. But she didn't tell Sarah, because she and Lucas wanted it to be a surprise. "Take care of the newest member of my family."

Sarah put her hand over Mignon's. "But you might need more information."

Mignon laughed. She touched Sarah's face. Her skin was warm and vibrant. She always smelled of caramel and peaches. "I think you have liberated enough information for me."

"You're going out tonight? Are you taking the detective with you?"

"Yes." Mignon felt a small thrill of excitement skirt along her spine. A tiny corner of her mind wanted to impress Ryan Lattimore. "I intend to show my detective that what haunts the shadows is much more frightening than anything he could ever imagine."

Sarah kissed Mignon on the cheek. "Kick ass tonight, Granny."

"With pleasure."

CHAPTER SIX

Ryan surveyed the dark buildings around him. The smell of mold and decay mingled with the smell of the Mississippi. Mist floated around the street lights, casting a ghostly halo on the buildings. A barge floated like a shadow on the dark river. Overhead the moon lit the night sky with a spectral light.

For the first time in Ryan's experience, the city felt eerie and otherworldly: like Congo Square at midnight when the haunting sounds of drums seem to permeate the air, or the old mansions of the Quarter that lined the narrow streets, or the cemeteries—the cities of the dead—that New Orleans was famous for.

"Do I get to kill some vampires?" Ryan asked as he watched a lone car turn a corner and disappear down the street. Like New York, the Big Easy kept night hours. Usually the port was alive twenty-four hours a day with the flow of cargo barges and cruise ships docking at the Julia Street terminal. But with a double digit maniac on the loose, no one wanted to be out at night.

"Tonight you're just an observer." Mignon handed him night vision goggles.

Their fingers brushed and the chill he'd been feeling evaporated at the touch of her skin on his. God, he wanted her. He couldn't stop thinking about her. Everything about her fascinated him. He almost felt embarrassed that a woman had gotten to him that quickly.

Ryan cleared his head as he adjusted the goggles to his face and found himself looking at the wharves in an entirely new light. Green to be exact. The green quality added a spookiness to the already seedy area. Overhead the bridge connecting the city to the west bank rose like a guardian, the huge stanchions glowing. Cars moved across the bridge.

"How long do we have to wait for some action?" Ryan asked, feeling like a goon in the stupid goggles. How was a man supposed to look sexy in hardware like this?

Solomon laid a hand on Ryan's shoulder. "The hunter has to be patient, Detective."

"They'll be here." Mignon flexed her fingers.

"We have irresistible bait," Max said as he rotated his neck.

"What is that?" Ryan adjusted the tension strap. The goggles were a little too tight.

Mignon leaned over close to his ear. "Human blood," she whispered.

He just loved being on the menu. Casting a sidelong look at her he smiled. "They're gonna go after you first."

She chuckled. "Because I'm a girl?"

"You smell tastier."

She flexed the muscles of her neck. "I'll remember that." She moved away from him.

Minutes passed as they waited.

Ryan watched Mignon prowl the street looking like a big sexy cat in her black leather pants and vest. She pulled a pair of sunglasses out of her pocket and slipped them over her eyes. Max and Solomon did the same with their own pair of wrap-around dark glasses.

He wanted the cool stuff, not the geek glasses. "How come you get the designer sunglasses and I get goggles?"

Mignon shrugged. "Because we're special."

I'm special, too, he thought. "How much more special are you than me?"

Max sighed. "You're not going to win this kind of debate with a woman. Retreat would be a wise course, detective. Save your pride."

Ryan scanned the area for any signs of movement. "Maybe, but I still want those shades. Tell me how you rate a pair."

"Our organization does a lot of research and development, and I pay my union dues," Mignon said.

Ha, ha, funny, funny. "Just because I'm not a member of the bad-ass club, I have to look like a nerd?"

She nodded, smiling. "Yes."

"Do the Feds fund you?" He couldn't imagine the federal government believing in vampires, but hey, a person never knew who was in his business.

"No." Mignon swiped the air with her broadsword. "We're a centuries old privately-funded organization."

Ryan would have to check up on this organization. "Do you have a name?"

She stopped swinging her sword and tossed a saucy grin over her shoulder. "The League of Bad-Asses. Or as we like to call ourselves, the LBA."

Ryan didn't like cryptic. "The LBA, my left pinkie toe," he mumbled. Somebody paid for their nifty toys and he was going to find out who. That was another thing to add to his to-do list. Staring at her lean body moving through the night air, he could add a few other things to his to-do list, things involving the lovely Mignon. But that was for another time.

As always, the waiting was wearing on his nerves. He had to do something and do it soon.

"Let's go." Max headed into the dark.

They spread out and moved down the deserted street, Ryan in the rear. The hair on the back of his neck stood straight up. The tension was a palpable drumming against the blackness. A few street lamps lit small halos at their bases.

Mignon stiffened. Max disappeared into the darkness, and Solomon went on his guard. Mignon stopped and hefted her sword, assuming a combat stance.

Ryan held his own sword ready. He might be an observer, but he wasn't going to sit back and let everyone else handle the action.

"Do you feel that, Detective?" Solomon asked in a hushed tone.

He searched the darkness, trying to feel what Solomon had felt. "Feel what?"

"The eyes of the night are here."

Ryan turned just in time to see Solomon blend into the shadows.

Mignon sighed. "Solomon is enjoying himself far too much at your expense, Detective. Boys never change."

Jokes, at a time like this, Ryan thought as he gripped his sword more tightly. Mignon stayed at his right, so close he could feel her subtle jasmine perfume on his skin. Focus, boy, focus, or you'll end up as some vampire's midnight snack.

The shadow of the bridge was a distorted shape against the night. An occasional truck roared down a nearby street. Though the areas closest to the river were usually alive with activity, the more distant warehouses were dark and silent.

He heard a rustle, the clang of a sword and a head flew up and over Ryan, spattering him with blood. Two days ago, a disembodied head would have been a shock. Now all he wondered was whether he could get out of this alive.

A dark figure approached and Mignon whirled, her sword a slashing arc. Another head flew by him. The surreal quality left him unnerved. Flying heads. He remembered the flying monkeys in the *Wizard of Oz* and how their numbers had obscured the sky with the Wicked Witch of the West cackling in the background. He didn't want to think about vampire heads doing the same thing.

The sounds of labored grunts and swords clashing surrounded him. Mignon moved into a puddle of light and he saw she was surrounded by three men and a woman who wore dirty, tattered clothes.

Ryan started for her, intending to help, but something seemed to stop him. Hard, dense air pressed against him and kept him immobile. He pushed against the invisible barrier.

He glanced down and saw feet, then calves appear, then a body and a head. Ryan blinked. The man who materialized in front of him was dressed in an elegant three piece suit as though he were on his way to a corporate business meeting. He smiled in a friendly manner at Ryan and then whipped out a thin sword from the end of a walking stick.

The heavy air suddenly released him and Ryan raised his sword to strike, but man the danced out of the way, disappeared and reappeared in another spot. The softness of laughter enveloped him.

"Hello, Detective," the man said. "I understand you've been looking for me."

Ryan remained fixed, not sure what to do. This was one big 'oh shit' moment. The man's fangs seemed to slide over the edges of his mouth. Ryan felt a movement at his side and Mignon appeared and tackled the man in mid-section. The man grunted and he stumbled back.

Mignon shoved Charles away from Ryan. Charles snarled at her, but she was already in motion. She righted herself. "I have been waiting for this moment." Poised on the balls of her feet, she lifted her sword and Charles lifted his slender fencing sword, preparing to defend himself against her attack. She laughed. "Are you going to kill me with that little thing?"

"Heavens no." Charles grinned. "Another time." He whirled and ran for a bridge support and scrambled up the suspension cable.

Mignon hesitated only a second and then she was after him. She yelled at Max as she passed him, "Keep Ryan safe." She raced after Charles and leaped up the pillar after him.

Charles's laughter filled the night. He leaped from truss to truss and onto the bridge roadway. A car dodged around him, brakes squealing. Mignon clung to a cable. Stay cool, she ordered herself. She thrust at him, but he jumped up onto a cable and raced along it toward the suspension tower.

Mignon swung herself onto the cable, balanced on the roundness beneath her feet, and followed behind him. This would end today, she vowed to herself. Charles was not escaping.

She followed his movements as he backed up, his sword held out as she thrust and parried.

A bank of clouds slid across the moon, obscuring it, and then drifted away. Moonlight reflected on the river below, showing a slow moving barge heading toward a port.

Charles grinned. "I like what you've done with your hair. It's very free."

Mignon gritted her teeth. He was trying to appease her by using his charm. Here she was trying her best to kill him, and he was wooing her. As if he had a hope in hell of winning her affections.

Charles slipped, but righted himself quickly.

Mignon jabbed at him, but she missed him by an inch. Her concentration was off; she needed to calm herself. She'd made dozens of kills. Not since she was a new *venator* had she been this sloppy.

Charles continued backward up the cable, talking as he deflected her blows. "I've never approved of women in britches, but I must say they certainly suit you. After all this time, you still take my breath away. You are magnificent, *ma petite*."

Her grip tightened on the handle of her sword. She could see a glint of humor in his eyes. Charles didn't take her seriously. He thought he could talk his way out of her killing him. Or he didn't think she had the fortitude to punish him. He was wrong. She would take his head and end his existence tonight. "I'm so glad you approve of my attire. I will extend your compliments to my personal shopper."

"Please do."

"Always so civilized and so polite."

"Good breeding, my dear, always shows." He deflected a blow and their swords crossed. "Speaking of breeding, how are our descendants, Mignon?" Charles backed up the suspension cable on sure feet. He wasn't even breathing hard.

Mignon pushed him backward, concentrating on her desire to kill him. She jabbed her sword through him and said through gritted teeth, "Fine." She backed up and Charles simply smiled as he sat back against the cable.

Suddenly, the sound of helicopter blades filled the air above her. The wind from the blades whipped at Mignon's hair as the helicopter swooped toward them, distracting her. She glanced back at Charles just as he jumped to the road below.

Mignon felt a sting on her arm. She grabbed at her arm and her fingers curled around a long, cylindrical object. She pulled the dart out. As she tried to make sense of what had just happened, numbness spread down her arm and up across her shoulder. She slipped on the cable, losing her balance. Without thinking, she leaped from the side toward the dark water below.

London — 1813

Mignon stood out on the balcony watching the dancers inside the ballroom whirl around. The ballroom was festive with candles in a dozen chandeliers, casting a golden glow on the dancers and brightly colored ribbons that fluttered from the windows. A table at one end of the ball-room was laden with food and servants patiently waited on the dancers.

Mignon wanted to join the dancers. Music was in her blood and in the back of her mind she heard the drumbeat of her native Martinique and the wild dances held on the beach. But London was a society that was different from what she knew. She had no entree here because of her skin color. But yet, she was sworn to protect these humans who considered her inferior.

Max passed, flashing a smile at her as he whirled a pretty young girl dressed in clingy white muslin that gave her an ethereal look. Mignon was jealous. She wanted to be the one in Max's arms, feeling his hands on her.

She felt envious that Max fit so easily into a society where she could never be accepted because of her skin color. Yet here she was, protecting those same humans from a menace they would never understand.

A blood-curdling cry sounded behind her. In an instant, Max disengaged himself from his lovely dancing partner, was out the door and at Mignon's side.

Solomon dropped lightly on the ground from the tree he'd been in.

"Tell me," Max demanded. He reached for his sword. Mignon had kept it safely in her grasp for the time when he would need it. Their fingers brushed and she felt a tingle that made her smile.

"I saw the old one." Solomon pointed. "By the maze."

Max sprinted across the gravel of the garden path, darted around a gurgling fountain and into the shadows of the garden paths. Mignon and Solomon split up, taking different paths. As she moved through the garden, she felt the weight of the night and the pull of the old vampire.

The old vampire had been terrorizing London for almost a year. The *Praetorium* had sent Max to stop the murders. And as his apprentice, she had joined him. He was teaching her the skills of the *venator*, the same way he had taught her to read and write.

A man and woman, arm in arm, wandered down the path, their feet crunching on the gravel, heads bent toward each other in a seductive manner. Mignon circled around.

The old vampire stood in the center of the gravel path waiting for his prey. Mignon turned as the man and woman entered the area. She drew their gaze and casually planted the thought that they should return to the ball. They obediently turned around and hurried back the way they had come.

Mignon whirled to face the old vampire, wondering where Max and Solomon were. She pulled out the two Roman short swords Max had trained her with.

The old vampire was thin and elegant with a tilt of his head that told Mignon he had once been of the nobility. "You are Mignon, Max's new pet." His voice was a whisper of leaves on the air.

"Careful old one, my bite is deadly." At least she hoped so. This was her first mission and she felt a subtle nervousness as she tried to keep Max's training in her mind.

He dismissed her casually. "You are nothing but a suckling. And an inexperienced one."

Annoyed by his words, Mignon said, "First I'm going to take your head, and then I'm going to take your sword." Stay calm, she ordered herself. Max would be here in a moment to aid her even though this was to be his kill.

The old one pulled out his sword. It was large and bulky, but deadly. Polished jewels winked on the hilt. "My sword has been to the Holy Land and killed many of my enemies before I was reborn. I have wielded it for a thousand years as did my father before me and his father before him."

"Enough," Mignon said, anxious to get on with the kill. "Stop before I die of boredom."

He gave her a quirk of a smile, his lips lifting in his slender face. "Where is your keeper?"

"Here," Max replied, and stepped out of the shadows.

"Three against one," the old one said, "is hardly fair odds."

Max shook his head in agreement. "But we are not here to do what is fair, John Forrest."

John Forrest said, "Please don't tell me you're here for justice." He gave a dry, papery laugh edged with contempt.

Mignon hefted her swords. "You know the rules. We do not prey on innocents. How old was that child? Thirteen, fourteen, fifteen?"

"Do you consider yourself the twit's champion?" Forrest taunted her.

"How refreshing to have someone on the side of justice." He sidestepped as though to slip away down a side path, but Solomon stood there, arms crossed over his massive chest, his face stoic and his scimitar ready.

"The greatest gift of the strong," Mignon said, "is the honor of protecting those who are weak."

For a second Forrest stared at her. Then he broke out into hearty laughter. "Humans are food or pets."

"No, they are what we used to be." She had been weak and no one had protected her from Charles's lust, and no one had protected her children. This bastard was evil and evil had to be destroyed.

"We are the same kind," Forrest said. "We understand each other. You and I should be able to come to some agreement. What if I promised to behave from now on? I'll dine on the scraps from the table." Again, his soft laughter sounded.

Mignon grinned. "Let me sheath my swords and be on my merry way."

Forrest looked startled. "Mignon, you wound me. You don't believe me."

"And here I thought I was a much better actress."

"Then shall we proceed? I have virgins to slaughter." He raised his broadsword and swung it around.

Mignon stared at his descending sword. Before she could react, he cut off her hand and it flopped to the ground. One of her swords clanged as it landed on the gravel. Pain flooded her and she dropped the other sword and clutched her wrist to her chest.

Forrest smiled. "Now if you will excuse me, I am outnumbered, but not outmatched. I believe I will take my leave."

Forrest turned and ran from her. She reached down and hefted one of her swords. As the old vampire glanced back at her over his shoulder, triumph on his face, she flung the Roman sword. The steel flashed as it arched through the air and slid neatly between his shoulder blades and impaled him on a tree.

Forrest dropped his sword with a fierce, agonized cry. Mignon grabbed her other sword and ran to him with Max on her heels. The old vampire pushed against the tree, but the sword was deeply imbedded. Mignon smiled. She raised her sword and waited for permission from

Max to kill the old one.

"You trained her well," Forrest whispered to Max.

"Unlike you, she will never betray us."

Forrest pushed against the tree once more.

"I told you," Mignon said as she advanced toward the old vampire, "I would take your head and then I would take your sword. You should have listened to me." She swung with all her strength and his head fell back and rolled on the gravel. She stared at it for a moment.

She glanced at the sky. "The sun will be up in a hour. We can leave him to burn." She lowered the sword. She thought she would feel something for the vampire, but she felt only a void and a distant satisfaction in the kill.

Max removed all the jewelry. For someone as old as he was, he still possessed a vanity that required diamonds and sapphires. Max ripped open Forrest's shirt and drew it down the limp arms. "Mark your kill," he ordered Mignon.

She pulled a small knife out of her pocket and wrote in Latin across the old one's back, '*Strength and Honor.*' When she finished, she wiped the blood from her knife on the old one's shirt. When she turned, she found the small area crowded by the vampires who had been at the party. She stared at them, seeing the sadness and horror on their faces.

"Behave, children," Max chided them. "The *venator* numbers grow." He eyed the other vampires, and one by one they slid away to disappear into the darkness.

Solomon stood to the side. As the other vampires slipped away, he stepped forward. "I have a souvenir of your first kill," he said to Mignon with a wry grin on his dark face.

"Presents." She would have clapped her hands if she'd had two. Hopefully, it wasn't a ring.

She held out the stump which had already healed over. The small bumps of fingers showed where regeneration had begun. "Your generosity knows no bounds."

Solomon held out her hand. "In case you need a hand."

CHAPTER SEVEN

Ursula Carlson swore a blue streak as she watched the female vampire dive into the dark water of the Mississippi River. She'd missed Charles and hit the unknown female instead. Her second dart had gone wide as wind buffeted the helicopter and it had swerved.

"Dammit," she said into her headphones. "Head back to base." She radioed the recovery team on the ground. "An unknown target has fallen into the water. Female, black, definitely a vamp. Track and recover." The recovery team leader acknowledged and signed off.

Operation Night Eyes was off to a rocky start, but she did have an unknown vamp almost within her grasp.

The helicopter took her back to Clover Island, just off the coast of Alabama. Colonel Hammett waited for her in the operations hut, observing the video feed. He looked up when Ursula entered, removed headphones and handed them to a technician. He didn't looked pleased. "For once your timing was bad, Carlson." He drew her out of the hut into the night. He pulled a cigar out of his pocket and lit it as he studied her silently.

She waited, mentally preparing herself for the ass chewing she so richly deserved. "I'm sorry to disappoint you, sir." She couldn't excuse herself by blaming the wind or the unknown female. She had been trained to consider all options. And failure was not an option.

His steely eyes bored into her. "If you'd been ten seconds earlier Charles Rabelais would be back in our control. Who was the woman?"

"Unknown, sir. The recovery team should be picking her up soon and bringing her back here. My surveillance team tracked Lattimore to a house where a female vamp fitting her general description appears to be living."

He took a puff of his cigar. "Do you have a name?"

"We're searching the records now. The only thing we know now is that the house is owned by Lucas du Plessis, the son of the U.N. Ambassador from the Angeline Islands. It's one of several houses the ambassador owns in the United States."

Hammett nodded. "Interesting, I may be able to help you with that search."

"How so?"

"The bank." He smiled as though he knew something she didn't.

She couldn't help noticing how satisfied he appeared with himself. Ursula respected her boss, but she wasn't blind to his over-active ego. "The bank? I don't follow."

"Since September 11, the U.S. has been rigorously investigating offshore banks, looking for ties to terrorist money, and the Banque D'Angeline was one they investigated. Unfortunately, it was clean as a whistle."

"Until this afternoon, I'd never even heard of the Angeline Islands, much less its bank."

He puffed on his cigar for a moment, then said, "The bank has been in operation since 1801 when the islands were purchased from France by the du Plessis family. The islands are twenty-seven miles out from the coast of Louisiana."

She still didn't know where he was going with his comments. "What's the word on these people and why the super low profile?"

"The government is headed by a regent who keeps a very discreet profile. The regent has declined diplomatic relations with all nations except the U.S. And even then, our relations with them are best described as hands off. The regent does little more than he has to in order to maintain a minimal level of diplomacy. He keeps a house in Georgetown and another in New York City."

This was getting way too complicated. There would be no breaking down the doors and dragging these people off into the night. "They probably have ties to drug smugglers."

Hammett shook his head. "Not even close. Do you remember Miguel Juarez Gomez?"

"The big Mexican heroin guy? He was busted three years ago in New Orleans."

"Yes. He sought refuge in the Angeline Islands and one night he was escorted to the New Orleans Police Department in chains and turned over to them."

"That's kinda strange. Drug money is about as good as it gets for offshore banks."

"The Angeline government is very odd. There isn't a standing army or a police force. Their only industry is agricultural research. The bank is one of the wealthiest ones in the world. The regency has been kept in the du Plessis family for over two hundred years."

This was getting murkier by the second. "Have we ever done any in-depth research into these people?"

"We've tried on several occasions and found nothing out of the ordinary." Again he flashed that mean grin. "Which makes them all the more suspect."

She wanted to roll her eyes. This guy was a little too interested in making mountains out of nothing. But she knew how to play the game with him and said nothing. "I have a team watching this house and there appear to be three vamps living there and a couple of humans. So this tells me the vampires are somehow linked to the Angeline Islands. From the way the female was fighting with Charles, I think she was very upset with him. Do you think we should approach her?" The female had been more than aggressive. Her body language had indicated complete and total fury. Ursula wondered what could make a woman, or anyone for that matter, so angry.

He shook his head. "Major, do you think we can afford to trust another vampire? Look what happened to our trust in Charles. He sucked us dry and gave us nothing."

"Sir, the old saying goes, the enemy of my enemy is my friend."

"Or, the enemy of my enemy is still my enemy."

He had her there. "Understood, sir."

"For the moment, I want this woman put in the wait and see category."

"Yes, sir. Maybe with a little luck, this female vamp will do our dirty work for us." Not that Ursula was too hopeful. Charles Rabelais was a slippery bastard. And if he could outfox Colonel Hammett, he could outfox the female vamp.

"One can only hope."

"Why not just knock on the door and see what happens."

Hammett shook his head. "That house is considered sovereign territory, giving its occupants diplomatic immunity. You can't knock on the door."

Ursula ground her teeth in frustration. "There has to be a way around that."

"Until someone from that house commits a major felony, no, there is not." Colonel Hammett glanced at his watch. "I have a meeting in an hour. I want you to get all the information you can about the vamps in that house."

"What about Rabelais?" He had been her first objective. Things were changing so fast, she didn't know what would happen next.

"He's slipped through our fingers again. When the recovery team finds the female, she might have the information we need that will lead us back to Rabelais. Concentrate your efforts on capturing her."

"Forget Lattimore?"

"Forget nothing. You can multi-task, Major." He stalked off in a plume of fragrant cigar smoke.

"Yeah, no problem," she mumbled. Ursula closed her eyes. She reentered the operations hut and sat down in a corner, preparing to wait for the recovery team.

When she had first joined the army, she'd had dreams of making a difference. But of late, she'd been rethinking her objective. In some ways, she felt trapped. She couldn't leave the vamp squad; she knew too much about things otherworldly. Yet at the same time, she wished she'd never accepted the invitation to join.

Ryan stuffed his hands in his pockets and paced the living room of Mignon's house. Where the hell was she? They'd been back for nearly two hours and she hadn't shown up. For the first time in a long while he prayed. She couldn't be dead. He glanced at Max who sat on the floor sharpening his sword, looking as though not one moment of his mind was concerned with Mignon's late return. What kind of friend was he? "Am I the only one who is worried about Mignon?"

Max stopped scraping the pumice stone across the blade. "Mignon can take care of herself."

Ryan had the distinct impression he was being indulged like a little kid. He didn't like it one bit. "Shouldn't we have waited for her?"

"Detective, our job was done. We killed all the vampires and disposed of the bodies. Mignon will return. She always does." Max lowered his sword.

Ryan rubbed his neck. "Now that we're back in the house and all the door and windows are locked, can someone explain to me how that vampire dude was able to appear out of nowhere?" Ryan flopped down on the sofa and took out a cigarette and flipped open his lighter. His lighter wouldn't catch. He stared at the cigarette with longing and then stuffed it into his pocket.

Max sat in a chair and sipped a glass of wine. "Solomon, would you like to answer that question?"

Solomon prowled the large room. "How much did Mignon explain to you about the vampire brain?" He sat down and crossed his legs.

Ryan tapped his fingers on his knee, trying to rid himself of his excess energy. "That they're super brainiac people who can use their whole brain and can do special stuff."

Somewhere in the house a phone rang. Max stood up. "I'll get the phone. Solomon, you explain vampire physiology."

Solomon seemed to ponder something and then he began to speak. "Once a vampire reaches two or three centuries of age, they come into what is called their *dos,* or gift, if you will."

"A talent of sorts." Ryan didn't like the sound of this.

"Exactly. Some vampires are able to walk in the daytime, shift into animal form, fade into nothing, or defy gravity."

What had he gotten himself into? "So this guy was able to disappear?"

"In a way, yes."

Damn, damn, damn. This shit was just getting deeper every freaking second. "So that means he's an old vampire."

"Not as old as some," Solomon replied. "But old enough."

Ryan had the sense that Solomon was hiding something. What? "This is so not right."

"I once thought that many years ago."

Ryan felt a shiver start at the base of his spine and skitter upward. Undead, all-powerful creatures of legend were going to give him nightmares. "How long have you been fighting vampires?"

"Too long."

Although Solomon had given him a nice non-committal answer, Ryan could feel that he was holding a lot back. Getting info from this guy was like pulling teeth. "Why do it?"

Solomon shrugged his massive shoulders. "One tends to think of it as a calling."

"Aren't you afraid of getting bitten and turned into one of them?" Ryan asked.

"You were a soldier and put yourself into harm's way for little more than a pittance. Were you afraid?"

"Sometimes." Who was he kidding. Hell, he'd been scared shitless every time he went out on a mission. Fear had kept him alive.

"Yet you went anyway because you believed in what you were doing."

The fear had never been as great as the love of job. He still missed the rush. "Yeah!"

"And now you're a police officer, putting yourself in harm's way for little monetary gain, because you believe in justice. In a way, being a *venator* is like being a police officer. Though I think we're better paid than you."

Ryan chuckled. "Everybody's better paid than me."

Max entered, still rubbing his neck. He looked tired.

Solomon looked at him expectantly. "Who was on the phone."

"Later," Max replied. "Detective, can I offer you some coffee?"

"I have to go the office and check in." Something was up. And he knew they weren't going to share anything else in front of him. Ryan wanted time away from these intense men to figure out what he'd just seen. Vampires! Who would have thought that a nightmare could come true so easily?

The door flew open and Mignon entered and slammed the door behind her. Her hair hung about her face in long, tangled ropes. Water still dripped from her wet clothes, and the leather of her outfit molded even tighter to her slender curves. Ryan thought he was going to start salivating.

"My dear," Max said, "what have you done with your hair?"

She tossed a strange word at Max. Solomon chuckled.

Ryan didn't recognize the language, but he was certain it wasn't nice. "Did you take a tumble into the river?"

She glared at Ryan. "No. I thought I needed a bath."

Ryan grinned. "You're upset, aren't you?"

"Detective, I am many things. At the moment, upset is only one of them. Another one is that I'm not in the mood for your pithy conversation. Go home. Get a good night's, or rather, day's sleep. Because tomorrow you're back in the training room. The sooner I ready you to fight the vampires, the sooner we're done and I can go back home."

Damn, but he liked a take-charge babe. "I believe I was just dismissed." He headed for the door and stopped next to her. "Nice smell." As he left the house, Ryan wasn't sure but he thought he heard her growl. Getting under her skin was the most fun he'd had in a long time.

The first rays of dawn were lighting the sky. He glanced up and down the street. Across the way, heavy humidity had left rivulets of sweat on the banquettes. Trash bags lined the gutter, waiting for the early morning trash pickup. Parked halfway down the street, he noticed an unmarked car that stuck out in the line of other parked cars, and wondered who was watching the house. As he watched, the car suddenly pulled away and a nondescript van parked in its place.

Lucas came out of the kitchen holding a cup of coffee. "Granny, you look nappy."

Mignon hissed at him, and her fangs came out.

"Ooo! Look at the big scary monster." Lucas covered his eyes and in a mocking tone said, "I'm shaking." Then he laughed and kissed her on the cheek. "I didn't think vampires could smell bad, but you stink."

"Remind me why I love you."

He gave her a winsome grin. "I'm your favorite."

Her fangs retreated and she smiled at him. Like Ryan, Lucas had this playful way about him that always amused her.

The door opened and Ryan marched back inside.

Mignon felt a small spurt of annoyance mingled with the excitement of seeing him again, but she'd burn in hell before she'd let anyone know how he twisted her emotions into knots. "Detective Lattimore, why are you back here?"

Ryan put a finger over his mouth. Everyone stared at him.

"What is the matter?" Mignon said, a small shiver of apprehension spiraling up her spine.

"I forgot to give you this." He reached in his pocket for a notebook and a pen and put his finger over his mouth again. He wrote quickly on the paper.

He handed the note to Mignon. *House under surveillance. They have listening devices.* After reading it she handed the page to Solomon. Solomon read the note, handed it to Max, and walked to the window fronting the street and pushed aside the drapes to look outside.

Lucas took the note from Max. "Not to worry, Detective. This house is secure."

Ryan stuffed his notebook back in his jacket pocket. "How?"

Lucas tore the note into small bits and stuffed them in his pocket. "I'm the son of a U.N. Ambassador and therefore this house not only has diplomatic immunity, but it's completely safe. If I've learned one thing over the years, it's that information is power. If people have information on me, or what goes on in this house, they can cause untold trouble. This house is already set up to keep unauthorized ears from listening. Trust me, my jamming equipment is the best to be found."

"In other words," Ryan said, "you don't trust anybody."

Mignon smiled. Lucas had been taught well to protect his surrogate family.

"Trust is a luxury," Lucas replied, "one of the few I can't afford."

"Thank you, Detective," Mignon said, "for your vigilance." She felt pleased that Ryan had been so concerned for their safety. Perhaps she could trust him with other secrets of her kind.

Ryan jiggled his eyebrows. "This is the best gig I've ever had. You guys are so much fun. When can we go hunting again?"

Mignon loved the playful expression on his face. He could be so open. "Detective, you make it sound like we're going on a date."

"We're not?" Ryan's eyebrows arched in surprise. "You mean, all of this sword swinging and vampire killing isn't a dating activity? And here I was trying to impress the hell out of you."

Mignon fought the urge to kiss him. "We'll see you tonight." She hustled him back out the door.

"Same time, same station?" he asked as he opened the front door.

She again pushed down the urge to kiss him. She hadn't felt such a thing in centuries. "Tonight," she said and closed the door firmly in his face.

When she returned to the living room, Lucas stood near the door still sipping his coffee, a frown on his face. Max and Solomon had poured themselves some blood cocktails. Her own stomach growled.

"I think you like him," Lucas teased.

Mignon glared at him. "I don't trust him completely. Not yet."

Solomon continued to stare out of the window. "He did tell us about the surveillance. That must count for something."

Her thoughts of Ryan confused her. One moment she wanted him desperately and the next she couldn't wait to be away from him. She hated this feeling of not being control of her emotions. She felt weak and unfocused. If she were not careful with her heart, she'd lose her head. "Maybe. But I do know that we have more of a problem than whether we trust the detective or not."

"Are you going to tell us what happened?" Max said. "Did you kill Charles?"

She pushed a hand into the tight leather pocket of her pants and pulled out the dart. "No. But I seemed to be the target for this dart." She held it out to Max, who took it and examined it.

"Do you think Charles is responsible for this?" Max transferred the dart to Solomon, who smelled it.

"Honestly, I don't know. But that doesn't seem like Charles's style.

We were on the bridge when a Blackhawk helicopter flew overhead and shot this at me. I don't know what was inside, but whatever it was, it was strong enough to at least stun me enough that I lost my balance and fell into the river."

Max gripped the dart. "I've never heard of a chemical that could stun a vampire."

The possibility of chemical warfare against the vampires frightened her as well. "And then I had to play hide and seek with commandos. Human commandos who seemed to know exactly what I would do. I don't like this."

Silence hung over them. Finally, Solomon said, "We may have a new enemy."

"Besides Charles?" Mignon replied, unwilling to accept the possibility. No way would Charles align himself with mortals. To lower himself by mingling with what he considered his inferiors would be unheard of. She'd smelled Solomon's anxiety.

Lucas frowned. "Who would have access to Blackhawk helicopters?"

"The military," Max replied.

Mignon glanced at Lucas. "Call your cousin David at the Pentagon and see what he can find out."

"What if David can't find anything?" Lucas asked as he rubbed his eyes. He looked so tired.

"Then," she replied, "we will find out who our new enemies are the old-fashioned way."

"They've come this far," Solomon said, "let them make the first move."

Mignon snorted. "I'm still feeling the effects of their first move. I say we strike back."

Solomon shook his head. "What happened on the bridge was unexpected. Do you think Charles could have been the target and you were in the way?"

Mignon hadn't considered that. She had considered a lot of different scenarios during her long underwater trek fending off curious fish and slogging through the mud. "Charles is an evil bastard who can make an enemy out of a saint. I would not be the least bit surprised if he has made more enemies than just the *Praetorium*. But until something more concrete happens, I'm taking a shower." She carefully handed the dart to Lucas. What was an irritation to her could be deadly for a mortal. "See what you can find out about what's inside this thing."

Lucas accepted the dart with alacrity. He studied it, frowning. "I'll send it back to the Islands and see what the lab can come up with."

Mignon nodded. "Send Sarah. Better yet, both of you should go. I don't think the two of you are safe here anymore. If someone is setting up a surveillance, than obviously your diplomatic immunity is not an issue for them."

"I think someone knows what we are," Max said. He'd been standing at the window, the drapes parted slightly, watching the van down the street.

"Then we must be doubly vigilant." She smiled at Lucas. "When you get the report, just call me. Don't come back."

"But I have business here. I can't just stay away. Sarah can take the bank's private jet, and she'll make sure the dart gets to the lab. I'm not leaving, Granny."

Lucas had always been her staunchest defender. "Don't call me that. You make feel old."

Lucas coughed. "You are old."

She batted him on the arm. "All right then. Just do everything you can to make sure Sarah is safe. We can't have the next generation in danger." Every child born to her family was doubly precious to Mignon.

Lucas ran up the stairs, calling for his wife. When he was safely gone, Mignon turned to Max. "You've been making faces at me since I returned. What is wrong?"

"We're expecting company. Very old company," Max said. "Elder Turi will arrive tonight. He says he has something important to talk to you about."

"Did he give you a clue?" Mignon hated when the Elders stepped in to interfere with her job. Once they gave her an assignment, she expected to be allowed to complete it her own way. Why couldn't Elder Turi just stay on the islands?

"Not a one," Max replied.

Mignon ground her teeth. "Well, until he arrives, I'll be resting, after I've had a shower." She thought about her own house on the beach and how the night breezes cooled it. She wished she could simply forget Charles and go home. What had started out as a simple plan to get rid of Charles was turning into a complicated situation. Mignon didn't like complicated.

"You need one," Max said with a grin.

"Careful, Max. I'm not in a good mood right now." She had a new unknown enemy and Elder Turi would be arriving to make her life even more complicated.

Mignon stalked up the stairs. Her best leather pants had been ruined and she wasn't in a mood to be anything but angry.

CHAPTER EIGHT

Ryan sat at his desk typing a report and stifling his yawns. After leaving Mignon's he could have gone home for a cat nap, but had been unable to sleep and decided to complete some paperwork at the office.

Mary sashayed into the squad room and leaned a hip against his desk. "Where did you disappear to last night? Anything you care to share?" She tilted her head as though to soften the hint of desperation in her question.

Ryan shrugged. Since he'd seen her get into the limo, he'd been ambivalent about her departmental issues. He wondered if maybe something more was going on that she wasn't telling him. "Just running down a couple of leads. Nothing earth-shattering, just busy work." And nothing he wanted to share with her. For some reason, he felt wary in her presence and he didn't understand why. He wanted to share what was going on, but his gut told him not to. Something about Mary had changed. Something he couldn't quite figure out.

"Was I being nosy?" She stood and crossed her arms under her breasts.

Ryan wondered how to handle this volatile situation. Mary had never taken offense before. He knew she was feeling left out of the case, and his life. "Nice watch." He noticed a gold Rolex on her wrist. Where the hell had that come from?

She tilted her head at him, her hair hiding half her face. "It was a gift."

"So tell me about the new man in your life." Please don't let it be a drug dealer. Mary had always been steady as a rock, had always known exactly who she was. The thought that maybe Internal Affairs wasn't wrong ate at him.

She caressed the gold watch band. "He's very generous." She smiled. "You know how us girls like that in a man."

A shy smile crossed her lips, the kind of smile that told Ryan she was already in deep with the unknown lover who could afford a limo. Generous wasn't the word he would have used. Overpowering was a better fit. He knew exactly how she felt. Mignon made him crazy.

"So you're not going to share a name?" Ryan wanted info so he could do a little snooping around and make sure everything was on the up and up and that Mary wasn't compromising her future.

Mary bit her lip. "We'll talk about it later. I have some busy work I can do."

He grabbed her wrist to stop her from leaving. "Let's have a bite to eat."

"Can't." She jerked her arm out of his grip. "I'm busy. Talk to you later." She headed back out of the room. Ryan had the impression that if he'd asked the right questions, she would have told him what was worrying her.

He went back to his typing. The door to the squad room opened and Agent Ursula Carlson walked in. "Detective Lattimore, I need to speak to you."

Ryan smiled. "Extra Special Agent Carlson. What a surprise."

"I brought you a peace offering." She set a Starbucks container down on his desk. She looked as if she'd been up all night, too. "Let's be buddies."

"Thank you." Coffee. He took an experimental sip. Not that he was expecting anything in it, but with the FBI, a good cop couldn't be too careful. "What's on your mind, Special Agent Carlson?" He leaned back in his chair, propping his feet on his desk.

Carlson plopped down in Mary's chair. "How's the case going? I missed you last night."

Why was everyone suddenly interested in what he'd done last night? First Mary and now Carlson. "Just doing routine police work." He could still feel the heaviness of the sword in his hand and a thrill of using it against one of the vampires. Last night had made a believer out of him.

She grinned at him. "If you and I were partners, it wouldn't be so dull."

"Are you interviewing for the job?" Crossing his arms over his chest, he leaned back in the chair and studied her wondering what her angle was.

She leaned forward with a sweet smile. "Just hoping to get a piece of the most sensational murder case in the last five years."

"What can I say, Special Agent Carlson? I'm a solo kind of guy."

She took his statement in a good-natured kind of way. "I'm not the enemy."

He wasn't so sure about that. "Maybe, maybe not. But you are the competition."

"Nothing wrong with a bit of good-natured competition." She flashed that winning grin again. "It's healthy."

He couldn't help grinning. She reminded him of a scrappy little terrier. "You're not ready to be on my team." She didn't want to know about his team. No one in the world was going to believe how bizarre his new teammates were.

"What are your plans for tonight?" she asked. "Maybe we could have dinner."

Was she coming on to him? With Mignon in his life, he had about all the women he could handle. He pointed at the stack of paperwork on a corner of his desk. "I'm taking these reports to a nice quiet spot and working on them. Then I'm going to revisit some crime scenes." And somewhere in between, find a few hours' sleep. And then maybe, if I live through all this excitement, I'll take myself a shower and a nap." And hopefully, someday, he'd get back to a normal life again.

She leaned in closer. "Ryan, what do I have to do to get you to trust me?"

Wow! He'd had two trust issues in the space of an hour, one with Mary and now with Carlson. His life had definitely taken a turn toward the more exciting. "Maybe you should stop trying so hard. Talk to you later." He determinedly picked up the next report in his stack and opened the folder, blocking her out.

Carlson stood for a moment in front of his desk, and finally he heard her shoes tapping as she walked across the empty squad room to the door. When the door swished shut, Ryan closed the report, rubbed his eyes and sat back in his chair, trying to figure out why so many people were so interested in him all of a sudden.

Lieutenant Barton entered the squad room. "You've been avoiding me, Lattimore," he said. "My office. Now. I want an update on everything you've come up with in the last twenty-four hours. My ass is on the line. And I don't want any of your nonsense. The mayor is pretty annoyed over that situation at the morgue the other night. I want some answers."

Ryan pushed himself out of his desk chair and followed Barton out of the room. He had lots to say, but who would believe him? He rolled out his usual spiel and prepared to snowball Barton with comments that he was working down some leads and that Barton would know things when he knew them.

Mignon spent the day resting and preparing herself for Elder Turi's visit. By the time darkness arrived, she was ready, even though she didn't know how or if she would tell him about Ryan. And when Solomon and Max escorted Elder Turi into her office, she felt composed and ready for whatever he would say.

"Elder Turi, a pleasure to see you again." She took his hand in both of hers.

Elder Turi was one of the oldest members of the *Praetorium*. He was a small man with almost dainty hands and feet. He wore his four thousand years well. White hair framed his narrow, hawk-nosed face. The three-piece suit he wore was a suitably conservative black.

Elder Turi had been one of the first changed. His age had recently started to show in the faint crinkling around his eyes. For all his smallness, he was a dangerous man who could best any of the *venators* with little effort. Mignon adored him no end.

He tapped Mignon on the arm. "Always such pretty words for me. As if you miss me."

"Old one," Mignon said respectfully, "can I get you a blanket to take the chill off your ancient bones?"

"Insolent puppy," Elder Turi said with wry amusement. "Your

humor brightens my night." Though his voice was light and teasing, it held an undertone of seriousness.

Mignon kissed him on the forehead. His skin was as dry as aging parchment. She adored him beyond reason. "I live to serve your needs."

He tapped her shoulder. "If I were a thousand years younger, you'd have to work a lot harder to satisfy my needs."

Mignon laughed. She escorted him to a comfortable chair and sat across from him. Max and Solomon arranged themselves on chairs close to the fire. Though the night was humid, a chill hung in the air. A storm brewed in the Gulf.

Solomon crossed his legs. "Did Max and I come here to watch the two of you exchange sexual innuendo?"

"Do not try my patience, Solomon," Elder Turi said with another fond chuckle. Elder Turi and Solomon were old friends.

Solomon grinned, his teeth white and straight against the darkness of his skin.

"What brings you to us?" Mignon asked politely. Ordinarily Elder Turi would have summoned Mignon to him. Having him come to her was highly unusual. When he wasn't on the island, he preferred to live in Rome. She forced a sense of unease from her mind.

Elder Turi folded his dainty hands across his lap. "We might be facing a bigger problem than Charles."

Max leaned forward. "You mean Charles isn't enough. He's wreaking havoc on New Orleans and is in danger of alerting the whole world to our presence. What could be worse than that?"

"I don't think Charles cares. Some new information has been uncovered indicating that the United States government is interested in vampires."

"The whole government?" Mignon's voice rose with surprise. "I can't believe they would keep our secret. They can't keep their own secrets." Talk about a leaking sieve. The government couldn't manage its own affairs without compromising themselves.

Elder Turi shook his head. "It's a small contingency inside the Department of Defense."

Max frowned. "The Blackhawk helicopters."

Elder Turi glanced curiously at Mignon. "Explain."

Mignon told him about her fight on the bridge with Charles, the helicopter and the dart. "What does this small group want with us?"

He sighed. "I could think of several reason why they would want to control vampires, but I honestly don't know."

"Share your thoughts with us," Mignon said.

Elder Turi looked grave. "The first thing that comes to mind is an army of vampires. Unlike some of our brethren, I am up on current affairs and I know what has been happening in the world and how this country is under siege from terrorists. Imagine a soldier who is bullet-proof, chemical warfare-proof and possibly even radiation-proof."

Mignon chewed at her lower lip. "We have purposely taken ourselves out of the world arena so that we can never be pawns of any government. Are you telling me that Charles has been sharing our secrets?"

"You better than anyone should know that Charles gives nothing away for free. I don't know what he's told the government, but I suspect he's betrayed them as he has betrayed us and they want him back."

Charles must have been the targeted victim and they'd missed, hitting her instead. That also explained the group of commandos diligently searching the river for her. She felt a sudden chill. "How do we counteract this new threat?"

Elder Turi shook his head. "I have no idea. I'm just the bearer of the news. But the *Praetorium* believes that we are about to be compromised on the island. Someone from the Department of Defense has taken a new interest in the workings of our bank."

"And if they find a way to infiltrate the bank," Mignon said, "they will know about us." The Banque d'Angeline was not only the repository of vampire money, but of their whole history, including the names and locations of every vampire in the world.

Mignon stood up and went to the intercom. "Lucas, you need to come here." She sat down again and a few seconds later, Lucas entered. He glanced at the Elder, nodded respectfully, and then sat down.

"What's up?" Lucas asked.

Mignon explained what was happening.

Lucas frowned. "Leave it to the United States to make things difficult for us." He sat back, his eyes half closed as though he were thinking. "Temporarily, we can route money to our accounts in the

Caymans, the Antilles and Switzerland. We can diversify our assets so that if the threat from the U.S. government is real, they don't catch us uncovered."

"But it's more than just the money," Mignon said. "It's the information about us." About the whole vampire community. They were all at risk.

Lucas nodded. "Not to worry. None of the information regarding any vampire is on computer."

Max said, "You've never told us that."

Lucas grinned. "Any computer can be hacked into by someone determined enough to get through the fire walls. The decision to keep all vampire records off a computer was for your safety."

"Thank you," Max replied, looking surprised.

"You're welcome." Lucas looked pleased with himself. "Genevieve has spent the last century planning for every contingency. We've learned from the past. We're never going to be caught again with our pants down as we were during the war of 1812. Lafitte would have given his left kidney for the Angeline Islands."

Hell, Mignon thought, in the last two hundred years, her descendants had fought off pirates, smugglers, the Mafia, and even the U.S. military, who thought the Angelines were perfect for their strategic position off the coast. Forty years ago when the government had been preparing for battle with Latin America, the Angelines would have been a perfect spot for a base. Instead, they'd used Guantanamo, which hadn't been as convenient or as friendly.

"It seems you have the situation well in hand," Elder Turi said. "Is there anything else on your mind?"

"This house is under surveillance." Mignon hated telling him. Elder Turi had enough to worry about.

"Charles?" he asked.

Mignon shook her head. "We think it's the U.S. government."

Max stood and walked to the window. He parted the drapes and glanced out at the street. "The van is still there."

Elder Turi frowned. "This is not good. Our greatest advantage is secrecy."

As though Mignon didn't know that. Her whole life had been lived in secrecy. Maybe now was not a good time to talk about Ryan.

Elder Turi said, "We will deal with the humans the same way we always do." He nodded at Solomon. "Investigate them. Enchant them and see what they have waiting for us."

Solomon walked out and a few moments later the front door opened and closed.

"Is there something else, Mignon?" Elder Turi asked gently.

He knew her too well. Should she just come clean about Ryan and keep her secret? "We've found an unexpected ally."

Elder Turi's eyebrows rose. "A vampire we don't know about?"

He was playing with her. "No, not a vampire. A detective with the New Orleans Police Department. Charles has been more than sloppy."

Elder Turi looked thoughtful. "This detective, what does he know of us?"

"That we are vampire hunters, not vampires."

Turi let out a long sigh. "Why didn't you enchant him?"

"I couldn't. He is immune."

"Then why is this detective still alive?"

Because she wanted him. Because Ryan Lattimore had made her feel like a woman and not just a *venator* or the matriarch of a family. When she was around him, everything wonderful about being human rushed back to her. And she had missed those feelings after keeping them in check for so long. "Killing him would have been murder. I'm an assassin, not a murderer."

"There is a difference?"

She didn't have to think about her answer. "Yes. My prey knows the game and the rules. The detective is an innocent."

Turi tapped his long fingers on the chair's arm. "You are playing a dangerous game. If he suspects for one moment that you are what he hunts, you will have to put your principles aside and eliminate him." Turi leaned back in his chair. "Will you be able to do that?"

She paused for a second. "Yes." But the word came out reluctantly.

"I hope so. There are those among the *venators* who will not hesitate to hunt you down, but for the moment I will forget this conversation ever happened."

She smiled. "Thank you, old one."

"Now tell me about Charles."

"As I said, he's gotten sloppy. He leaves his victims to be found. He allows them to hunt before they have learned to control themselves. The humans will know about us soon, if Charles is not stopped." And panic would follow. She thought of all the ways the humans would react if they knew their ancient fears were more than myth. Max had told her of the vampire hunting during the Middle Ages and how the determined humans had almost brought the vampires to extinction. She did not want such a thing to happen again.

Elder Turi tapped his temple thoughtfully. "Charles has never done anything without a reason. That is what has always made him so dangerous. He's playing with you the way a cat plays a mouse. What better way to bait a *venator*?"

The *Praetorium* should have executed Charles when they'd had the chance. Because of Charles, the vampire way of life was being jeopardized. "I am not his prey."

"Yes, you are," Elder Turi said with a sadness in his eyes. "Do not fool yourself, Mignon. Charles has never given you up. He wants you back. You are the one who got away."

"Charles is a fool," Mignon spat, fear in her soul. Though her years as Charles' slave were long over, the memories would never go away. "I have not been his slave for a long time."

"Little one, look at me. What do you see? A man? No. You see me as though I am your grandfather. Do not be fooled. I am a man with a man's passion, hatreds. Our lives will stretch out for thousands of years, and because of the length of our life spans, we don't drop things and move on. Vampires have a long, long time to let things fester. How long has your hatred for him lasted? Why do you not think that his lust for you would last just as long?"

Mignon knew her hate fueled her. That was what had kept her alive for a long time. "I've moved on with my life."

"Have you? I have seen you cleaning the burial crypts of your descendants. You never miss lighting candles to your family on All Saint's Day. You named your home and the islands after your daughter. Your house is a shrine to your children who have passed. You are a complicated woman, Mignon. I don't remember the names, not even the faces of my parents, my sisters. You can recite the histories of all your descendants. You know all their names, you pay homage to their lives. The *Praetorium* was formed to protect our brethren from the humans. You became a *venator* to protect the humans from us. No matter how long we are together, no matter how you feel about your brethren, we will always be your second family. We will never be first in your heart."

"Old man, you run on and on like a babbling brook."

Elder Turi grinned. "The privileges of age, puppy. The true death may claim me tomorrow, so today I will speak my mind."

Mignon stood and bent over him to kiss him on the cheek. "Never forget, I adore you. I always have and I always will. You are the father of my heart."

"Such pretty words, Mignon." He stroked her cheek. "I can never stay mad at you."

"I know. But now I have to get ready to hunt." She headed for the door.

"Mignon?"

She stopped and turned. "Yes, decrepit one."

He drew his finger across his neck. "Bring me Charles's head."

"With pleasure." Before she was able to leave, Solomon yanked the door open and stepped into the room, a puzzled look on his face.

"What's happened?" Mignon asked, alarmed. She'd never seen Solomon look so unnerved before.

Solomon pointed at the window. "I was unable to enchant the people in the van."

"More who cannot be enchanted?" Mignon felt fear radiate outward from her stomach.

"Not even a glimmer." He flexed his fingers. "This makes us extremely vulnerable."

More than vulnerable. Killable. The front doorbell rang. Mignon went to open it. Ryan stood on the veranda. She caught her breath. She could smell a subtle scent of fresh citrus on his skin. He reminded her of sunny mornings on the island, after a summer rain. "Detective, here for more lessons?"

"I like being teacher's pet." He entered without being asked, but stopped just inside the foyer. He scanned the assembled group. "Looks like I interrupted a family pow-wow."

Mignon pointed to Elder Turi, wondering exactly how she would explain his sudden appearance. "This is our boss, Turi. Elder Turi, this is Detective Ryan Lattimore."

"Good evening, sir," Ryan said respectfully.

"So courteous for one so young." Elder Turi tossed a teasing glance at Mignon. "Some here could do with better manners."

Mignon smirked. "I wonder to whom you are referring?"

Elder Turi seemed delighted to meet Ryan.

Ryan seemed puzzled. "Did I come in on something I wasn't supposed to? I could go right outside and listen from the other side of the door." Ryan gestured at the window. "You still have your company outside, I could join them."

Mignon smiled at his teasing. Relaxing, she let the tension ease from her shoulders. "There is no need for you to eavesdrop from the veranda. You are welcome here, Detective."

"I got a look at one of those guys sitting on the house and he looks like a straight-up commando type to me." He leveled a glance at Mignon. "Who did you insult?"

Mignon glared at him. Her mood always seemed to be in flux around him. "Don't be insolent."

He took off his jacket and slung it over his arm. "That's my stock in trade."

"Mignon," Elder Turi said, delight in his voice, "I like this puppy of yours."

"Puppy?" Ryan queried with one eyebrow raised. "I'm gonna let that slide because you have that old big, bad dog vibe hanging around you."

Mignon patted Elder Turi's hand. "This one is a very old dog."

Elder Turi pinched Mignon's cheek. "Dog. Now I'm a dog?"

"No, old one," Mignon said, her voice light and teasing despite the worry and fear that hovered inside her. "You're the alpha wolf."

Ryan looked amused. He leaned toward Mignon. "Kiss ass."

Mignon told Elder Turi, "Ignore him. He is jealous of your great and imperial status."

Elder Turi took Ryan's hand and turned it palm up, and traced the lines. Then he glanced into Ryan's eyes. "I see you are an honorable man. You have sacrificed a great deal for those you love. Very noble. And unlike some in this room, you have no secrets."

Ryan pulled his hand back, frowning. "Thanks."

Mignon said, "Please forgive him, he is stuck in his ways." Elder Turi was a soul catcher—an *animus capio*. One of the rarest of the skills given to vampires. Mignon had known only one other.

Ryan's tone was harsh and filled with pain as though Elder Turi had brought back long held memories. "Am I here to practice or to get analyzed?"

Mignon slipped her arm through Ryan's. "Why don't you go up to the ballroom and I'll be along in a minute."

Max and Solomon accompanied Ryan up the stairs. Mignon listened to them as they ascended to the second floor and entered the ballroom. She turned back to Elder Turi. "He is my complication."

"For a mortal, your complication intrigues me."

What exactly did he mean by that statement? "He's just a man."

He took her hand. "But he is a man who attracts you as well."

Mignon pulled away. She didn't need to be psychoanalyzed by Elder Turi. "Are you staying or are you heading back to the islands tonight?"

"I think I'll have a little fun with the surveillance team." He grinned. "I feel like hunting. I haven't felt that way since the Spanish Inquisition. I'm rather excited by the prospect."

"Don't get too excited. You might get careless. You are an old man."

"Insolent puppy." He tapped her on the cheek. "I have forgotten more about survival than those mortals will ever learn."

"I think those people in the van are very dangerous. I don't want to think about a future without you."

"I will be around another thousand years, Mignon. You are not to worry."

When he was gone, Mignon turned to Lucas. "You have work to do. See what you can find out about our guests across the street."

He held up a small instrument. Mignon wasn't up on tech, but she did recognize his hand-held computer. "While you old guys were swapping stories about the old times, I've been taking care of things." He grinned at her, rose and kissed her on the cheek. "Not to worry, Granny, I'm on it." He walked out.

Mignon went to the bar and poured herself a blood cocktail. She was going to need all her strength tonight.

South Carolina-1862

Mignon stood outside on the veranda of the old plantation house watching the activity going on inside. A group of Confederate officers stood around a table looking at maps while a black servant served them food and wine. The servant was Mignon's great-great-grandson and she was trying to contain her annoyance with him. After all the time she'd spent working to keep her family safe, Louis had to put himself right in the midst of danger to play spy for the North.

He should be up in Boston where he would be safe. But he had insisted on putting his law career on hold to work for the North. A pox on men with principles.

She shifted, her sword heavy in its sheath across her back, and wondered when he would notice she was here. After all, he'd summoned her. She wiped dust from her boots and trousers and pushed her hair back out of her face. The night air was hot and damp. She fanned herself with her floppy-brimmed hat. From the dovecote came the gentle sound of cooing. A rooster crowed sleepily.

Mignon was sometimes amazed at how much went on during the darkness. Until she had been changed, she'd had no idea that so much happened. While some of her people longed to walk in daylight and feel the sun on their skin, she was quite content with her life in the darkness. She loved the peace and quiet, the moments between sunset and dawn when a different world appeared.

She had already done her bit for the war by helping runaway slaves and spying for the North by using her ability to ferret out information.

But headstrong, willful, idealistic Louis had taken it into his fool head that he had to do his part for the war effort. His mother had indulged him way too much and when Mignon returned to her island home off the coast of Louisiana, she'd have something to say about that. She was proud of Louis, more than proud, but she would never tell him. He had the audacity to defy her.

Finally, the meeting broke up and Mignon hid in the shadows as the assembled officers stepped out through the windows to the veranda for a last minute smoke of their smelly cigars. As Louis cleaned the room and put it back to order, she watched him. She'd like to throttle him for putting himself in such danger.

As he put out the last lamp the veranda emptied, he stepped out and stood on the edge of the veranda staring out over the gardens. "Grandmama," he said, "I know you're here. I can feel you."

"You sent for me." She stepped close to him, inhaling his humanity. "Did you want to gloat about your success as a spy?"

He chuckled. "Grandmama, I am as safe here as I ever would be in Boston." He leaned over and kissed her cheek. "It's nice to see you, too."

"Forgive me, Louis, but no member of our family has been a slave since I took Simon and Angeline from the brothel. To see you acting the part of a slave unsettles me."

"I'm just pretending, Grandmama. Besides, the war isn't going to last much longer and then all of our people will be free."

"If victory is within our grasp, then what is so urgent to bring me here?"

He picked up a discarded cigar, lit it and puffed a moment. "General Jonah Wentworth has been turned to the blood and is in the process of turning his officers. He has this grandiose scheme to unleash a vampire army on the North and win the war."

Mignon went cold with fear. The war was being won by the North because they had more money, more men and an almost inexhaustible supply of resources. But with a vampire army, the South would be victorious in a matter of weeks. No human army could withstand such overwhelming odds. "Where is this general?" She would have to destroy him. Immediately. She wouldn't even have time to send for

Solomon or Max. For a moment, she hesitated. She'd never killed another vampire without Solomon or Max at her side.

"A two-day ride down that road." He pointed at the dusty lane spiraling around the edge of the garden and disappearing into a grove of live oaks covered in Spanish moss.

Mignon kissed her grandson on the cheek and said, "Don't forget your duties."

He grinned. "Yassah, massa."

She punched him on the arm. "Keep yourself safe, Louis." She jumped down from the veranda and ran across the garden toward the road.

The general's camp was set back from the road, partially hidden by tall live oaks. Rows of men asleep inside tattered blankets, or just lying on the ground, lined the meadow. Pickets on guard at the perimeter caught quick naps or visited with each other.

General Wentworth had set up his headquarters in a small house off to the side of the peaceful meadow, away from the rows of tents that probably housed his officers. As Mignon approached, she saw several officers standing at the foot of the steps leading into the house. After a few minutes the officers dispersed back to their tents. Two passed near Mignon.

One grumbled between yawns. "Heard about the general? Giving orders and having staff meetings on the porch at night, all of sudden. Don't he know we need our sleep? Hell, he don't even let us sit down. We're fightin' a war."

"He's a general, who cares?" the second man said.

The two officers walked on to their tents.

Lamplight lit the inside of the house. The windows were dirty, and the whole house had a sense of desolation and abandonment about it. She slipped onto the porch, sensing the general and three others inside. From their scents, she could tell all of them had been turned.

Inside, someone laughed. The general seemed to be enjoying his new life. She eased around a corner of the house and found a window not as dirty as the others. She glanced inside. A dead Union soldier lay in a corner on the floor, a trickle of blood drying on his neck, obviously the evening meal. Newly turned vampires were so sloppy about their dining habits. The body should have been removed and destroyed. She wondered how many other bodies he'd left lying around for the superstitious to find. That was the problem with baby vampires, they thought of nothing but their own amusements. Whoever had turned the general had been a fool.

Mignon opened the front door and entered. "Good evening, gentlemen." She stepped into the parlor, a large room that held nothing but a table set off to one side and four folding camp chairs.

General Wentworth was a thin man with intense blue eyes that seemed to shine with a fanatical fervor. The three staff officers stared at her uncertainly.

The youngest officer with the soft down of youth still on his cheeks smiled at her. "Are you the entertainment or the dessert?" He laughed.

Mignon smiled. "I'm definitely the entertainment for the evening."

"Who are you?" Wentworth snapped. He was a man used to command.

"A *venator*."

"And that is?" he demanded impatiently.

She sighed. "Your judge. Your jury." She unsheathed her sword and swung it. One officer's head fell off and rolled toward the dead soldier. "Your executioner."

Another officer pulled out his pistol and shot her. The bullet passed through her with a stinging pain. Before she said her next words, the wound had closed. "Have you learned nothing about what you have become?" She tried not to let the lingering pain show. She hated when people shot at her.

"What do you know?" The general's interest was piqued.

"Since I'm over a hundred years old, much more than you."

"You're nothing but a woman," he scoffed, and she could see in his eyes that what he really meant was 'black woman.'

Mignon studied him. "I will save you for last."

"Wait!" One officer held up his hands. "If we are like you, why did you kill Major Dunne?"

"You have sinned against the brethren." She whirled her sword and his head slid down his arm. "I have no time to explain anything. Let's just get to the killing."

Wentworth reached for his pistol. Mignon simply smiled at him. Then she whirled and killed the third officer.

"You don't understand." Wentworth backed away from her. "I'm raising an army to preserve the South."

"You don't understand." She took a step closer to him, backing him further in the corner. "I'm defeating your army to free the South."

"You're a fool," Wentworth snarled.

"Do you think your good intentions will stop there? I was once a slave and I know the evil you and others like you have preached. I'm not an animal, nor am I stupid. I am not a savage." All the rage of the past built in her, consuming her. "What you want to preserve is your stranglehold on power."

He shook his head and shrugged. "You're wrong." He put his pistol down on the table and drew his sword. "You have no idea what you're trying to destroy."

"Who sired you?" She sidestepped around him, preparing to do battle. She had caught his officers by surprise, but he wasn't of the same fabric. He knew how to fight with a sword.

"He said to never tell anyone."

"Too bad you won't survive to tell your sire what a poor job he did in preparing you for what you have become."

They circled each other. "He did what I asked him to do. He gave me the tools I needed to survive."

"You have endangered us all with your petty ambitions."

"You're one of us."

"And you are dead." She swung, but he stepped back and her sword fell short.

Solomon and Max had prepared her for this moment. She had to stop Wentworth; she had to put the balance back. He swung and she danced away from him. As he closed on her, she searched for his weaknesses and when the opportunity came, she severed his head from his body. As he crumpled to the ground, she turned and for a moment she felt an exhilaration that had nothing to do with Wentworth.

After a hundred years, she finally felt free. She was no longer a slave, but a woman in control of her life, understanding who and what she was. No one owned her body, her mind, or her soul. She was finally free of the shackles she had lived with since her birth.

She turned and looked at the table with the maps and realized that she was looking at plans for a major offensive against the North. She gathered up the maps and all the paperwork she could find and stuffed it into a valise she found under the table. Louis would know where to send all this.

Next she bent over the Union soldier, saddened that he had died for an unjust reason. She searched his pockets and found a letter tucked inside an envelope with his name and battalion. Inside the letter was a daguerreotype. The picture was of a soft, pretty woman with a little girl and a toddler boy leaning against her knees. She eased his wedding ring off his fingers and carefully opened the letter. The woman's name was Sylvia and the letter told Mignon how proud Sylvia was of her husband's decision to fight for what he believed in. She wrote of their children and their son's first steps. She couldn't wait for her husband to get home.

Tears gathered in Mignon's eyes. She gently touched the soldier's forehead. "Go in peace, Lieutenant Bower. I will see that your wife knows only that you died with honor." She tucked the letter and the ring into the valise. She didn't know how she would contact the woman, but she intended to return the young man's personal possessions to her.

She blew out all the lamps but one and took the globes off. As she poured kerosene around the room, the smell made her gag for a moment. When she was satisfied that each corner of the room and each body was thoroughly soaked, she threw the lit lamp at the center puddle. With the general's sword in hand, Mignon slipped out into the night as the fire flashed and the dry timber of the house was completely engulfed.

CHAPTER NINE

With his feet apart, Ryan held his sword in both hands and faced both Max and Solomon. Max held two swords, short and lethal. Solomon's scimitar gleamed. He kept his gaze on the two men facing him, and he felt rather than saw Mignon enter the room.

He hadn't expected to have the two men gang up on him, but assumed this was another lesson for his practice. When Mignon joined them, he realized he was in for a hard workout. Mignon held a thick stick with a blade at the end. She was really an unusual woman. In all his life, he'd never been so attracted to a woman the way he was attracted to her.

"What the hell is that thing?" he asked her.

"It's a halberd." She balanced it in her hands.

"What's it for?"

"To eliminate your enemy."

"I want one."

She swung the halberd over her head and then in a graceful arc behind her back. "Let me give you a little history on this fine killing tool."

Damn, but she looked hot carrying that thing. He didn't care about who, what, why, or where. He just want to see her wield that thing naked.

Max and Solomon relaxed and stepped back, giving her room.

"Foot soldiers," Mignon said, "carried halberds during the fifteenth century and used them to thrust upward into the belly of horses. But a well-balanced halberd can do a lot more." She demonstrated as she talked. She held the halberd balanced in both hands and swung it, then held it up.

"You just have the best toys," Ryan said. "I'm consumed with jealousy."

She twirled it over her head. "What is that saying? The one with the most toys at the end of game wins."

"Do you mean that literally?"

She hooked the halberd under the hilt of his sword and flipped it up. The katana flew through the air and fell on a mat with a muted clang.

"I don't get it." Ryan walked over to the sword with as much dignity as he could muster. As he picked up the katana, he didn't take his eyes off her just in case this was another one of her painful lessons. "You use swords to kill the vamps. But what prevents them from using guns on you? If they can kill you first, then they don't die."

Mignon lowered the halberd. "What is the answer to that, Solomon?"

Solomon said, "Would you believe using guns to kill humans is considered the ultimate in rude. Besides, it's not sporting."

Better to be rude and win than dead and polite. "Rude?" Ryan asked. "If I was a vamp and you were my next happy meal, do you think I'd care if it were rude?"

"Me either." Solomon grinned. "One of our greatest advantages against the vampires is their enormous egos. Killing humans with a gun is saying that humans are as powerful as vampires."

Ryan shook his head. "You're still pulling my leg." Why did he get the sense they weren't telling him everything he needed to know?

Mignon jabbed the halberd at him. "Unless you can shoot well enough to sever the spinal cord, guns are useless against a vampire anyway. They barely even slow them down."

Now that was interesting. "Even if you shoot them in the head?"

"As long as the primitive brain in the back of the head continues to function, a vampire can regenerate any part of their body."

Just how the hell were they supposed to win a war against an enemy that didn't die like they were supposed to? "That is so not right. Don't you think you guys should bring in the government? How do you handle this all by yourself?"

Mignon shrugged. "We just do. Shall we get back to practicing? I want to check out a bar at the waterfront tonight. But I don't want you going in half-prepared. We will practice for another two hours." She nodded at Solomon and Max, who took a flanking position on either side of her. Ryan had just enough time to bring up his sword before she attacked.

"That's not fair," Ryan said, "three against one."

Solomon grinned. "Neither is life." He thrust at Ryan and when Ryan parried, the clang of metal rang in his ears.

Mignon swirled and stabbed at him and he danced out of the way. Her agility still surprised him. She punched him in the stomach with the pole end of the halberd. He grunted, his wandering thoughts brought back to the task at hand. Damn, if he wasn't careful the training would kill him.

Ryan opened the door to Robby's Bar and Grill. Loud blues music from an old-fashioned jukebox blasted at his ears as he held the door open. Mignon walked in ahead of him.

He'd worked plenty of undercover and black ops operations, yet he didn't seem to be able to find the groove on this one. "Why do I always end up at the dives?" He eyed the huge man behind the bar who sported thick, muscled arms that looked like they could break him in pieces.

"You're nervous?" Mignon sounded amused.

"I can see the case report now." Ryan tried to picture himself hacking off heads and then writing it up in his daily report. Barton would laugh himself into a heart attack. "This *is not* the kind of undercover operation that goes over really well with the department brass."

The smokey air of the dark bar enveloped them as they walked across the hardwood floor. A couple of men near the door eyed Ryan incuriously. Their gazes settled on Mignon and the light of interest showed in them. Ryan didn't like that at all, but Mignon could take care of herself.

Discarded peanut shells crunched underfoot. Ryan thought they should have a sign on the door that stated, **'Low-lifes welcome here.'**

A cocktail waitress wearing a skimpy black skirt and a blouse that barely covered her assets sashayed up to Ryan and Mignon and pointed out an empty booth at the back of the bar.

Mignon led Ryan toward the booth. She had changed into tight black leather pants, a white low-neck, sleeveless knit that clung to her luscious breasts. Again with the black leather. Ryan licked dry lips. That woman was made to wear leather. He couldn't imagine any steer that wouldn't roll over and give its life to be a pair of her pants.

He looked to the heavens. *God, if I die tonight, let me be reincarnated as the steer that was chosen to cover her ass. I promise to be a good boy for the rest of my days.*

She slid onto one of the wooden benches. Ryan sat opposite her.

"Beer," Ryan ordered from the waitress.

The young woman looked expectantly at Mignon and she ordered a bourbon, neat, no ice. When the waitress was gone, Mignon glanced at him. "I didn't think you drank on duty. I'm rather disappointed."

"It's my undercover drink. If I sat here and didn't drink anything, I'd be noticed. Blending in with the unwashed masses is an old undercover trick."

She simply nodded.

The waitress brought their drinks and Ryan paid her. After she left them, he poured his beer into a mug. "Why are we here? Why this particular bar?"

This bar was reputed to be one of the roughest in the city. Ryan had already recognized several men who'd made the N.O.P.D.'s top ten most wanted list. Hunching down in the seat, he hoped no one recognized his face from his days as a beat cop.

When Mignon took out a cigarette and lit it, the flame from the lighter illuminated her finely-boned face. "Besides being dead, what stands out about the victims to you?"

So she'd noticed that tidbit too. "That they were all hoodlum scum." Not one victim had been an upstanding member of society.

She lifted her drink to her lips but didn't take a sip. "Do you know why?"

"Karma?"

She put the drink on the table. "Amusing as ever, Detective."

"I try my best." Ryan saluted her with his glass. "I'm assuming they just couldn't run fast enough."

This time she narrowed her eyes at him. "Detective, with the smart mouth you have, it's a wonder you've made it this far in life. Let me tell you a little something about vampires."

"I'm all teeth."

Her nostrils flared. "Funny."

"You're not laughing."

"I'm laughing inside."

He glanced at her breasts to see if they moved.

She leaned forward. "Are you enjoying the show?"

He wriggled his eyebrows. "Just checking to see if you really are laughing inside."

She grinned at him. "Getting back to the subject. The reality of vampires is that there are good vampires and bad ones. Bad people make bad vampires. Bad vampires do evil things. Evil vampires must be destroyed."

"I'm for that." He lifted his beer and pretended to take a sip. "Since you're being chatty, tell me what you tried to do to me at the morgue."

She gave him an innocent grin. "Besides saving your sorry life?"

"Yeah. That and the 'forget' thing." Like he could ever forget her with her black hair dancing along the edge of her shoulders and her dark face intent with her mission.

"It's called enchanting, something we learned from the vampires."

His hand went to the hilt of the sword. "Is that how we walked right in here with our swords and no one noticed?"

She nodded.

"How did you pick up that little skill?"

"What's that old saying? If you want to hunt a duck, you have to think like a duck."

"That's a skill that could come in handy. How does it work exactly?"

"Low frequency sound."

"Draw me a picture. I was a political science major."

Mignon touched the base of her throat. "You can train your vocal cords to emit a sound so low that it affects a chemical in the brain that puts the person you're aiming the sound at in neutral, preventing them from processing the sensory information in the normal way."

"You mean like a parlor trick. Like reading a Ouija board?"

Mignon grimaced. "Ouija boards are not to be trifled with. And I resent you comparing the ability to enchant with parlor tricks. It's not a parlor trick. Your mind isn't very open, is it, Detective?"

Ryan fiddled with his beer bottle. "I've seen babies blown to bits, cities leveled, and the ugliness that is humanity. I keep my mind closed because that preserves my sanity. I'm following you on this little jaunt because logic does not apply here and I need to know why."

Mignon dipped a finger into her bourbon and then licked it off her skin. "I use whatever tools I have at my disposal to win. I refuse to allow wickedness to overrun this world. And maybe it doesn't make any sense to you, but to me, the reality is that there's a very fine line between the mortal world and the supernatural. I keep that line intact so that the mortal world is not overrun. Up until now, we hunters have done very well in keeping the ugliness of vampires hidden."

He admired her dedication. She would have made one hell of a cop. He was glad she was on his side. Sort of. "You have nothing but respect from me."

"I'm glad you approve." Her tone was laced with bitter sarcasm.

A weaving man approached. He leaned over, his palms against the table, and whiskey fumes swirled through the air. Ryan sucked in his breath. This was going to get ugly. He could just smell it.

"Honey pants, let's dance." He grabbed her arm and tried to wrestle her out of the booth.

"Take your hands off me." Mignon didn't budge.

"Or what?" He leaned over. "Shut up, bitch. I wanna dance."

Ryan just knew what was going to happen. This loser had just rattled the wrong cage and things were gonna get ugly fast. And Ryan intended to enjoy the show.

A warning smile crossed her full mouth. "Since you put it that way, how can I refuse." She stood and moved away from the table.

He slapped her on the butt. "I knew you liked me." He put an arm around her waist. "Show me your nasty stuff, honey pants."

"Let me show you what I learned in charm school."

Ryan leaned back in his chair almost feeling sorry for the bozo about to get his ass handed back to him. He didn't have long to wait. Mignon whirled around, kicked the guy in his stomach and when he bent over, elbowed him in the middle of the back. The man collapsed with a grunt and lay unmoving on the floor. Mignon leaned over him for a long moment, her face taut with concentration. Then she stood, sauntered over to Ryan and sat down, her face as composed though nothing unusual had happened.

The drunk sat up after a few more moments and without even a glance at Mignon, he made his way to the door and out into the dark night.

"You enchanted him."

"Yes." She pushed the bowl on the table toward him. "Nuts?"

"Don't mind if I do." Ryan picked up several and tossed them in his mouth. He chewed and swallowed. "So tell me something."

"Anything."

Yeah, right, he thought. He placed his elbows on the table top and trained his best detective stare on her. "Why do all you superhero types know kung-fu?"

She pushed a strand of hair out of her face. "Because it's in the superhero rule book."

Ryan burst out laughing. "Mignon, you told a joke. I didn't know you had it in you."

Leaning closer, he picked up the seductive scent of jasmine on her skin. Just the way she smelled made him crazy.

She tilted her head and stared at him. "I have abilities you don't know exist."

He could think of few things he'd like to have in her. But he was smart enough not to say them out loud. "Really?" He scooted closer to her. "I love women's secrets. What kind of abilities?"

She leaned closer to him and smiled. "Things that would curl your hair."

His gaze held hers. He could see the heat of desire burning bright. When this was all over they were going to have some one-on-one personal time together. He just knew it. "But I would love to find out."

Suddenly, Mignon's back stiffened. She turned and stared intently at the door.

"What's up?"

Mignon inclined her head. "Look at the door. The man in the green jacket. Does he look familiar to you?"

Ryan, without seeming too obvious, checked out the man at the door. Faces clicked through his memory. He recognized the man. "Yeah. Billy Joe Willis. Small time arsonist and leg breaker. Someone filed a missing persons report on him about a week ago. Is he one of them?"

"Yes."

As Ryan watched Willis, four more men entered the bar. He recognized them all, three petty criminals and one paroled murderer—all listed as missing.

The bar seemed to change. One second it was filled with high-pitched conversation with blaring music, and the next a chill silence spread over the patrons as the juke box coughed and went still.

The five men glanced around the room, their eyes stopping at Mignon. A seeping coldness filled the bar, or maybe that was Ryan's overactive imagination playing tricks on him.

Mignon stood and approached the men. Ryan followed.

Billy Joe Willis studied her. "We've been warned about you. Get out of the way." He was about five inches taller than Mignon and had a good hundred pounds on her.

She sized him up. "No."

Ryan clinched his teeth. That was it. Heads were gonna fly. Ryan remembered what fear smelled like from his days in the military. He didn't smell that particular acrid aroma now. Nope, but he could almost taste Mignon's excitement. Blood would be spilled tonight.

"I'll tear you apart, *venator*," Billy Joe snarled.

Mignon reached to her side and took out her sword. "Then let's take it outside."

"We're ready for you and your pet." He flicked a contemptuous glance at Ryan.

"Good. Shall we proceed?" Mignon pointed her sword at the door.

The vampires turned and led the way out the door. Ryan exchanged glances with Mignon. Five guys with no swords. Ryan waited by the door while Mignon spent a few extra minutes enchanting the patrons. Then they both stepped out into the street.

Street lights cast an eerie glow over the pavement. Fingers of mist curled around the edges of the buildings. On the river, a barge sounded its fog horn.

Ryan's eyes adjusted and he found himself facing five strange vampires with swords in their hands. They stood in a line along the curb. Ryan stared at them. The baby vampires from the bar had disappeared. "Who are these guys?"

Mignon was poised on the balls of her feet. "They are *patronus*."

Here we go, more with the Latin.

"Protectors of the young."

Ryan leaned close to her. "Maybe I'm being a little paranoid, but I think we've been set up." The old bait and switch tactic again. Criminals were so predictable.

"I'm inclined to agree with you."

Damn, she sounded calm. The kind of calm that made him nervous.

The five vampires hefted their huge swords and started forward. One of them twirled his sword in the air, showing off.

Ryan drew his sword from the scabbard. "Buffy, I think it's time to break open that can of whoop-ass."

The vampire twirling his sword grinned, revealing the tips of his fangs. He was joined by a big biker vampire with a sword straight out of the movie *Braveheart*.

Things were going downhill fast. Ryan grimaced. "Better make that a six-pack." He gripped his own sword. "Five to two is good odds." He doubted he would be much good with his sword. A few hours of practice wasn't enough for facing the vamp version of the A-Team. These guys held their swords with confidence, the expressions on their face clearly stated you-are-my-next-cheeseburger, but he couldn't let Mignon face the five protectors by herself. Hell, he'd always wanted to buy the farm with his boots on.

She pointed her sword at the group. "Which one do you want?"

"I think I'll take that little guy over there." The little guy didn't look so dangerous with his tiny Asian face all crinkled up and his curved sword at a right angle to his body.

Mignon chuckled. "I think I'd better take him. Hiramoto is a

BLOOD LUST

Samurai master and over six hundred years old."

A shiver of anticipation ran down his arms. "Damn, he looks good for his age."

Mignon started laughing.

Ryan glanced at her. "Your timing sucks. This is not the time to be giggling at one of my jokes."

"Ryan, you're a treasure."

"Yuck it up later, we have work to do." Out of the corner of his eye, Ryan saw Max step out of the shadows. Ryan was glad to see him. "Max, my man."

Max held an axe and a short, broad sword. "Children, did you think that we would let you play by yourselves?"

Relief flood through Ryan. Five to three. The odds were evening up. "What happened to the baby vamps?" Maybe he'd make it tonight.

Max aimed the big axe at the dark alley. "Solomon is having fun with them."

On cue, a head rolled out of the alley and one the bad guys side-stepped it as it rolled to the curb.

A woman stepped out of the shadows. She was tall, lithe and her face a mask of fury.

"Keenan," Mignon said to the woman, "you've arrived. Welcome to the party."

The red-haired woman smiled. "I wouldn't miss it."

Ryan revised his odds. Okay, six to three. The odds kept changing. Ryan wondered who else was in reserve.

The vampire named Keenan stepped forward and engaged Max. Mignon faced the Samurai warrior. Ryan found himself facing a short, plump man. He wanted to think the kill would be easy, but his sword was as unwieldy in his hands as an unbalanced club.

The plump man attacked, yelling, "I want you, mortal."

Ryan lifted his sword. "Let's get it on, fat boy." Ryan had barely finished his words when the man swung his sword. Ryan blocked the thrust with one of his own. The swords met with a ringing clang and Ryan forgot about Mignon and Max. He fought as though he were a seasoned warrior, the sword singing in his hands. After a few seconds he felt as though he had fought for years, so easy was the weighted sword

128

against his palms. Not that this guy was in any way a slouch. He was strong, fast and handled his own sword with more skill that Ryan would ever know.

Ryan danced outside the range of the other blade. The man swung and Ryan blocked. He pulled his knee up and slammed it into the man's groin. The vampire looked surprised and bent over. Ryan sliced his head off. It hit the ground with a heavy thud. Ryan felt elated. His first kill with a sword.

A woman ran at him, her sword raised. Ryan blocked it easily. Sword-fighting was growing on him. He liked it. The woman blocked his thrust and his sword quivered against hers. With adrenaline pumping through his veins, he shoved the woman back and when she stumbled he beheaded her.

The sound of other swords clanging echoed through the darkness. Ryan slashed and parried until he thought his arm would fall off. The vampires were experienced and he began to feel like the inexperienced vampires in the alley. How could he fight these horrors when they were so difficult to kill?

Suddenly, the fighting stopped. Ryan looked around. Except for the woman called Keenan, all the vamps were dead, their heads rolling along the gutters, their bodies slumped on the pavement. Max and Mignon stood in front of Keenan. With a swipe of his sword, Max chopped off her hand and it flew through the air. Her sword fell to the street. Keenan screamed and turned. She raced down the street so quickly Ryan was amazed. Her feet barely touched the ground.

"I'm going after her," Max announced and he raced down the street.

Mignon stared around at the carnage. "We'll have to do some clean-up before the cops get here."

He surveyed the carnage, rather proud of himself. "Do we have that kind of time?"

"We have to take the swords and dispose of the bodies."

"You mean like carry them off into the night?" Ryan could see himself lugging a headless body and tossing it into the trash dumpster. *That would look good in his report.*

"Not exactly." She lit a match and tossed it on a body. The body incinerated in one enormous flash and was simply gone. No bones, no anything was left, not even a scrap of clothing. A burn mark darkened the pavement.

"Is that environmentally sound?" Ryan asked.

She laughed. "I'm not hurting Mother Nature."

"Why didn't you do that in the morgue?"

"Only works on the older vampires. The younger ones are too," she grimaced, "moist."

The morbid side of his personality was dying to ask her to explain, but then he would have to live with the mental image. He passed. "Give me matches."

"Gather up the swords instead. Burning is *venator* ritual"

"Can I keep one of the swords?" He wanted a souvenir of this fight to remind him that he had triumphed over the evil forces.

"Yes. We call it Rite of the Kill." She nodded as she burned the last body. "Keep it as trophy. I'll make a sweep of the area."

As Ryan stuffed the swords into a sack Mignon handed him, he tried not to think about moist and dry vampires. This was just weirder and weirder. Every minute he worked this case, the freakier it became. He heard a scuffle and what sounded like a garbage can hit the pavement. His gut tightened. "Mignon!"

He waited a few moments for her reply. With the sack of swords under his arm, his own in his hand, he charged around the corner to find Mignon gripped in the arms of a huge, hulking vampire with stringy white hair. Where the hell had that one come from?

Mignon struggled to free herself, but the man lifted her off the ground and her legs dangled in the air. He held her so tight, Mignon gasped. The more she struggled, the harder the vamp clutched her.

Ryan rushed toward them. If he beheaded the guy, he'd cut Mignon, too. He felt for his gun. He might not kill the vamp, but he might distract him enough so that he would drop Mignon.

Ryan pushed his weapon against the base of the man's head and fired. The bullet exploded into the man's neck and he dropped Mignon. She crumpled to the ground. Ryan then took his sword and sliced off the head.

He balanced on his feet and turned, looking for more. Finding none, he bent over Mignon. She sat on the street staring up at him, a gunshot hole gaping in the front of her sweater just below her heart.

"You shot me!" She put her finger through the hole in her sweater.

Ryan frowned. "And you're alive!" How had that happened? The bullet must have angled off the vamp's spine and spiraled into Mignon, exiting through her chest.

She jumped to her feet and held the sweater out to him. "Look at my sweater. This is a Versace original. Do you know how hard it's going to be to repair a bullet hole?"

Ryan stared at her, open-mouthed, as she glared from her ruined sweater to him. Not even a drop of blood stained the charred black edges. "You're alive!"

She held the sweater up in front of her. "Donatella designed this just for me."

"You're one of them, aren't you?" He lifted his sword. "You're a vampire!" All the desire he'd felt for her vanished. He couldn't believe he'd been lusting after a vampire. He felt a strong sense of betrayal. He'd been helping her. He'd believed her story of justice and myth. What a fool he was.

"Wait." She held up a hand, her face calm. "Let me explain."

Sirens sounded in the distance. Ryan glanced down the street. He could see the red and blue flashes of lights approaching. "Dammit, I should have known. I should have known."

"We have to get out of here. Please Ryan, trust me." Her eyes pleaded with him.

He didn't know what to do. Ryan tried to make his mind focus.

She grabbed his hand so quickly he didn't even see her move. He felt himself being dragged down the alley until they came to a building. The alley was blocked off. They had no escape. He felt her loop her arm around his waist and with a bunching of her muscles, she leaped upward, pulling him with her. They landed on the roof of the building just as the first police cruiser turned a corner and screeched to a halt in front of the bar. She wrapped an arm around his neck.

Ryan forced himself to relax. He dropped the sack of swords on the roof.

Mignon tightened her grip on his neck. "Make a sound and I will snap your neck to save my people."

"I am not saying a word." He didn't struggle against her. He knew she was ruthless, and had no idea how that would turn against him.

He still couldn't wrap his thoughts around the fact that she was a vampire. "Are Max and Solomon like you?"

"Yes. Much older and wiser. They don't mix with humans."

"What the hell do you mean by that?"

"They would never have let you into their lives." She sounded almost regretful.

"Mignon, I need to think."

He felt her emotional withdrawal.

More police cruisers screeched to a halt in front of the bar, parking haphazardly. They represented safety, but so did Mignon. He didn't know how he felt about finding out her secret. She was the scarey monster in the closet, the manifestation of a millennia of myths. Finding out that vampires really existed had made him breathless with fear. Finding out Mignon was one of them and that he'd been mentally undressing her from the first moment he'd seen her shook him to the very core of his soul. How had he not known?

Mignon released him. "I think it best that you don't come around again." She backed away from him. "I do not want to kill you, but I will if I must."

No, she wouldn't kill him. But she would make things harder for him.

He rubbed his neck where her hand had gripped him. "Mignon, I—"

She was gone. He looked around, finding no clue where she had gone.

Berlin — 1922

Mignon sat in the darkened theater clutching Max's hand and gazing at the flickering screen and the story unfolding in front of her. "Will you look at that? He's a bald-headed beaver who needs to see a dentist."

She couldn't help being critical. Since Bram had written his book on Vlad the Impaler, the whole world had developed a new interest in vampires. Though the world considered vampires a myth, they couldn't seem to get enough.

"Shh!" Max said as he gazed at the screen, totally mesmerized. Since the first moving pictures had been developed and shown to an intrigued public, Max had been in love. Nothing had so captured his imagination as the idea of stories on the screen for everyone to enjoy. He had even predicted that someone would figure out a way to add sound to the movies and then the actors would be able to talk directly to the viewers. Max loved innovations; he even had a motorcar. Mignon hated the motorcar. It belched smoked and smelled. Give her a horse and carriage any day.

Mignon wasn't certain she liked the movies. They were just unnatural. She liked stage productions with sound, grandeur, and she loved the immediacy. Or give her a good book and she was in heaven. She had to admit, though, that Max was handsome enough that he could be an actor.

Music flooded the theater with a sense of doom as the demon vampire Nosferatu stalked his prey. Mignon half snorted. "He needs a manicure."

Two of her many times great-grandchildren turned around in their seats and shushed her, annoyed expressions on their faces. Mignon pouted. She and Max had rented the whole theater for her family members so they could view the movie. And now they were telling her to be quiet. Obviously, they had forgotten that this was her party.

Mignon shook her head. How could people believe this claptrap? Vampires did not look like demons from some alien world. They walked and talked and moved, totally indistinguishable from mortals.

"My dear," Max whispered, "if you do not behave yourself, I will be forced to take you out of this theater and spank you like the child you are acting as."

Her eyebrows rose in surprise. "You wouldn't dare."

"Try me."

She subsided into silence and decided she'd had enough. She climbed over her grandchildren and swept out into the chilly night air.

The windows of the shops lining the street were lit with Christmas displays. She paused to admire a small tree decorated with jewelry that sparkled and winked at her. Another window showed a delightful Christmas village with miniature trains going round and round on the tracks.

The *Praetorium* had scheduled the commencement rituals for the newest *venators* in Berlin. They would be given their golden wolf rings and inducted into *Ordo Romulus*, the Order of Romulus, and given gold wolf rings to identify them to other *venators*. Mignon, Max and Solomon always attended. Mignon had decided to bring as many of her family members along as could reasonably get away. After all, they had made her a wealthy woman and she believed in sharing her wealth.

She stalked down the street, tamping down her anger. The movie played out in her mind, reminding her of the United States and the disparaging images of black people that she saw. She felt powerless. As strong as she was and as gifted as she was, she couldn't change things. There would always be evil vampires, racism, men who abused women. In two hundred years, the world had changed drastically, yet it was still exactly the same.

Mignon herself had come a long way. She could remember when she'd been afraid of her own shadow, afraid to go out because of the power white men wielded.

She sensed someone behind her and glanced back to find Solomon.

"Why," he asked as he fell into step with her, "does this one film upset you so much?"

"Because it's all lies."

"Bram wrote a whole book about us that was nothing but a lie."

"But it was funny, and we weren't ugly."

Solomon put an arm around her. "Mignon, of all the things I would have thought about you, vanity was not one of them. Why do you care what we look like on screen?"

"Because that creature was not a vampire, but an abomination. Humanity considers us monsters and we can do nothing to change their concept of us because we can't reveal ourselves. Even worse, if humanity did know about us, they would hound us to extinction as they tried to do during the Middle Ages."

"Maybe," Solomon said with a sad smile. He had lived through the vampire hunts of the past. "But we will survive. We always survive."

"Sigmund Freud would say I have never made peace with my past."

Solomon laughed with her. "And he would also say you want to have sex with your father."

She shuddered. "I don't know who my father was."

"Maybe that's Sigmund's point."

She sighed. "Perhaps I'm tired of the journey."

"I have been around a thousand years, and I have yet to tire of life, of humans, of everything that this world has to offer. You have a different path than I have. My life is simple. I have nothing but the hunt. I can fight every fight as though it were my last. That is why I am a good *venator*. But you are the matriarch of a family. You have the weight of the world on your shoulders. You are a good *venator* because you have something sacred to protect."

Mignon glanced up at the sky. A million stars twinkled against the blackness. She wondered if life existed out there as well. "My descendants have a future, and I will do what is necessary to assure them of that."

"In the thousand years of my life, I have learned that humanity wants to share nothing. They want all existence for themselves."

"Then why do we protect them?"

Solomon smiled. "Because we are the strong and that is what we do."

"You are more than wise, Solomon. You are great."

"Little one, you are way too serious and need to take life a little more easily. Drink some beer. Dance the night away. Laugh a little more. Learn to see each night as the promise of a new beginning." He bent down and kissed her lightly on the cheek. "Now, shall we return to the theater?"

"No," she said. "I'm hungry. Let's check out the cabarets and see what we can find."

CHAPTER TEN

Present Day — New Orleans

Ryan knelt in front of the rose bed his aunt had treasured and pulled at the weeds that seemed to never stop growing. The mid-afternoon sun shone down on him, and heat waves shimmered off the bricks of the courtyard.

He'd changed nothing in his aunt's house except his bedroom. Inside, the rest of the furniture was still in the same position as when Aunt Selina had been alive. Though it was getting a little faded and tired looking, Ryan knew he would probably never change anything. His aunt had been his sole caretaker after his father had died in Viet Nam and his mother had abandoned him on the doorstep.

Even though his aunt had been dead for several years, he still missed her. She'd been a no-nonsense type of woman with a wisdom that he had come to rely on. He wondered what she would think of his current situation and the knowledge that vampires weren't just the product of Hollywood imaginations and old stories.

His cell phone rang. For a second he contemplated not answering. Not on a peaceful Saturday far from the horror of the night, the horror of discovering that Mignon wasn't what she'd appeared to be. His mind shied away as he shrugged and answered the phone anyway.

"Lattimore," he said.

"Ryan," Mary replied, "you need to go to a murder scene."

He didn't want to play cop today. Let someone else handle the scene. "Saturday is my day off."

"I'm sorry, but it's a bad one, parents are dead and a little girl is missing. The lead detective asked for you."

Ryan almost groaned. This was one of those times when he wished murder would take a holiday. "Give me the address."

She gave him an address in the Garden District and he pushed himself to his feet and headed into the house for a fast shower.

Thirty minutes later, Ryan parked in front of a small cottage that looked as if it were posing for a postcard. Rambling roses climbed a trellis that led to the backyard. The grass was neatly trimmed, and a wrought iron fence surrounded the property.

Police cruisers were parked in the street. A knot of people stood just outside the yellow crime scene tape that fluttered around the trees in the front yard.

He identified himself to the uniformed officer on duty at the front door. The smell of death hit him as he entered the cottage and stopped to look around.

The living room was a mess, the furniture knocked askew with shards from a broken mirror on the floor next to a chair. Dots of blood trailed along the wall.

"Lattimore," Detective Walker Castle said as Ryan entered the master bedroom. "Thanks for coming. Come take a look. I have reason to believe that these murders are connected to this serial killer case you've been investigating."

All the cops around Castle looked shaken. Ryan walked over to the bodies of a man and a woman. They were pale and motionless on the floor behind the bed. Blood splattered the walls. But there was way too little blood for two full grown humans.

"What makes you think they're connected to my case?" Ryan bent over the bodies.

Most of Ryan's victims had had two neat puncture wounds in the side of the neck, but this woman's throat was gashed open. He didn't want to think that one of Mignon's brethren was responsible, but he could almost feel the vamp vibes coming off the victims.

"The bodies were completely drained of blood," Castle said.

Ryan noticed that Castle was sweating. The day wasn't that warm. "But this doesn't quite fit the victimology of my case." Ryan glanced at the male victim. Like the woman, his throat was an open gash. "Is this all?"

"No." Walker stood up. "Follow me."

Walker led Ryan out of the room, through the house and into the garage. Inside were two parked cars. One of them had the windows open and a body was half in and half out the window. Another body sat in the front passenger seat. Ryan approached cautiously.

He studied the man in the car window. Like the two bodies inside, his throat had been torn out, but it was neater somehow, as though the killer had taken extra time with it. He looked at the face. "Isn't that Ned Packard from sex crimes?"

"Yeah." Castle's voice was flat. "He and his partner are both drained of blood. Like the people in the house. Not an ounce left. And they weren't killed someplace else. They were killed here in the garage."

Ryan controlled his fury. This had to stop. No one killed cops in his city and got a free ride. He forced himself to put aside his personal feelings and deal with the crime scene. "How the hell did they get into the garage?"

"We're assuming the killer drove the car in here to tease us. Take a look at the second guy. His name is Ben Dover."

Ryan took a look at the second man. His throat was intact and the puncture wounds were clearly visible, announcing that a vampire had done the murders. Ryan didn't recognize the second man, but he still felt sadness at his death. "Why was Packard here?"

Castle handed him a mug shot. "Know this mug? His name is Roland Appleton."

Ryan recognized the face. It had been all over the front page of the newspaper for the last five months. Appleton was a registered child molester who'd been caught with thousands of photos of naked children in various suggestive poses in his house—most of the photos were of the children in his neighborhood. "So Appleton's out of jail." Ryan had lost track of things the last couple of days.

Castle wiped his damp forehead with the back of his hand. "Got kicked on a technicality, was released two days ago and Packard and Dover drew the assignment to keep a tail on him."

Ryan felt an uneasiness settle in the pit of his stomach. "And the missing child?"

"She was the main witness at the trial. Looks like he came back to finish the job."

"Any sign of her?" Ryan felt bile at the back of his throat. Had Appleton been turned or had he run into an old friend or two and brought them back to the house? If he'd been turned, Ryan would have a child molesting vampire on his hands. He hoped not. He hoped there was another explanation for the carnage. But he just couldn't wrap his head around it. And the two main witnesses, Packard and Dover, were dead. He couldn't ask them what Appleton had been doing for the last two days. He wondered if they'd made notes. Probably, but from the looks of the bodies, Appleton had searched them, which meant he'd probably taken anything that gave information as to his whereabouts.

Ryan had to find Mignon. No matter what she'd said last night, he needed her help. Everything was off the table now.

"Packard had five kids," Castle said.

Ryan reached out and touched the other man's shoulder. "I have to go. When you have everything processed, I'd like a copy of all the reports."

Castle nodded. He turned back into the house, looking none too eager to return to the crime scene.

Ryan walked outside, not knowing what to say. Who would believe him? The coroner had arrived and his van blocked the driveway. Ryan pulled his cell phone out of his pocket and dialed Mary. She answered on the first ring.

"Mary," he said, "I need you to get me every piece of information on a child molester, Roland Appleton. Where are his favorite hangouts? Who are his friends? This comes straight to me. Understand?"

Mary told him she'd have the info as fast as she could find it and rang off.

Ryan walked to his car. He couldn't do anything for the child's parents or the dead cops, but maybe he could save the little girl. For that, he needed Mignon's help.

Ryan drove to Mignon's home thinking of what he would say. As he parked his car he figured begging her was his best tactic. He knocked on the door. Seconds later, the door opened and Solomon peered out from the shadowed entry. "I need to talk to Mignon." He walked into the house before the big man could close the door. As the door closed behind him, he realized they could have him for a late afternoon snack.

The door banged behind him. "She won't talk to you."

"Look man, I need your help."

Solomon shrugged. "It's your funeral." And he disappeared into the darkened house.

He smelled her perfume before he heard her.

"What do you want?"

"I need your help," Ryan said. "Please."

She stood about three feet away from him, her hands on her hips. "I told you what would happen if you showed up here again, Detective." Her voice held no conviction.

"I remember, but this is important. May I?"

Mignon seemed to hesitate. Then she turned and moved down the hallway. "Follow me."

In the dark living room she sat down on a couch. "What do you want?"

He figured he'd be just cut to the chase. "Two days ago," Ryan said, "a child molester was released from custody. I have reason to believe he's been turned into a vampire. He's kidnaped a child, killed her parents and the two N.O.P.D. cops who were watching him."

"Really?" She put a hand on her hip, her eyes holding a defiant look. "What do you want me to do?"

Damn it. She was going to make him really beg for her help. "It's a little girl. What happens if this freak turns her? He'd have an immortal play toy. I know I messed up last night. But could you put your personal feelings aside and help me? A little girl's life is at stake, and I can't do this alone." He felt a surge of hope, realizing that he'd gotten under her skin. Deep down inside he knew she wasn't heartless where children were concerned.

She gestured him toward the living room. "Give me a minute." She walked up the stairs.

Ryan's phone rang. "What do you have, Mary?"

Mary gave him a rundown on Appleton and what information the department had. Which was quite a bit.

"What about hangouts?" Ryan asked as she completed her report.

"Appleton's grandparents own a farm out toward Vacherie, but they've retired to Miami. His parents own a bed and breakfast near Destrehan. Appleton rents an apartment in Carrolton."

"Give me the addresses." He wrote the addresses down in his notebook.

Mary continued, "I'd check the old farm. Detective Castle has already sent teams out to the other two locations. And we're still trying to coordinate with the sheriff's department over the farm since it's out of our jurisdiction."

"A child's life is at stake, and everyone's getting pissy about territory?"

"That's what I said." Mary's voice was grim. "Castle hasn't even called an Amber Alert yet."

Ryan didn't think an Amber Alert would do any good. Appleton wasn't a run-of-the-mill molester anymore. If he had been changed, he now had all the powers of his new state of vampirism. He would be unstoppable and more people would die.

"Be careful, Ryan." Mary's voice sounded almost wistful, as though she wanted to be back out on the street herself.

"Don't worry, Mary." He disconnected, mentally urging Mignon to hurry.

Mignon entered the living room. She had her bad-ass clothes on now—leather pants and a long sleeved black t-shirt. She held two swords. She handed the katana to him. Ryan held it, reveling in the feel of the blade in his hands. Until this moment, he had not realized how much he liked having the sword, how natural it felt in his hands.

Max and Solomon, looking lethal, entered after her with their own weapons in hand. Ryan repressed a shiver. Now that he knew they were all vampires, he didn't feel the same sense of security that he had before.

"What have you found out?" Mignon asked.

Ryan told her about the farm and the other properties.

"I'll take Lucas as my driver," Max said, "and check out the apartment."

Solomon hefted his sword. "I'll take his parents' house."

Mignon nodded gravely. "That leaves the farm for me and Ryan."

"Why don't all of us go to the farm?" Ryan asked. "My people are already checking out the other locations."

Mignon buttoned her jacket. "If Appleton's a vampire, the police won't be capable of dealing with him." Mignon gripped her sword tightly. "Can you back your car as close to the house as possible, since it's still daylight. I don't want to go up in a puff of smoke."

"Yeah," Ryan said. "But what about Solomon? Doesn't he need a driver?"

"Solomon is a day walker."

Ryan shook his head. "And that means?"

"As long as the sun isn't at the apex, he can go outside. It's his gift."

He still couldn't past the fact that all this crap was nine levels of weird. "His *dos*."

"Yes. Now get the car. I'll explain more later."

Ryan parked under an overhang that shaded the back porch. Mignon, draped in a blanket, pulled open the door and lay down on the floor with the blanket completely covering her.

"Are you comfortable back there?" Ryan asked as he pulled out into the street.

"I always find it a little humiliating to travel this way, but I'll survive if it means saving the child." She shifted around. "This Appleton, do you know for sure if he's been turned?"

"No. But I saw the crime scene. The parents and the two cops were completely drained of blood. If that doesn't say vampire, I don't know what does. If he didn't do it, then some newbie vamp did the murders for him." Ryan turned on the street and noticed that the van was gone. He wondered when the Feds had left and where they'd gone.

"How long ago was he released from prison?"

"Forty-eight hours." Too short a time, Ryan thought. Released from prison and already turned to an alternative life style. Appleton was a man in a hurry.

"And he's kidnaped a child already." Mignon's voice was muffled with the blanket surrounding her face.

"Nine times out of ten," Ryan explained, "guys like Appleton re-offend within twenty-four hours. We usually put a tail on them for the first forty-eight hours. When they re-offend, we're on them and they're back in jail." In and out and in again, just like a turnstile. Child molesters had no idea that cops probably understood them better than they understood themselves.

"But why this little girl?"

"Because," Ryan said, feeling ill at the thought, "she was the one that got away. He attempted to molest her once before. But this kid was smart and gave the cops a good enough description to catch him. She was the main witness at his trial."

Mignon was silent for several moments. "Is this an act of vengeance?" Her voice had an odd quality to it.

"No, it's a sick freak going about his day." Ryan slowed to let a pedestrian, who had ignored his lights and siren, to run across the street. "About last night—"

"Let's not talk about last night. We have other things to worry about."

"Fine." Ryan could let this conversation pass for the moment, but she wasn't going to stall him forever. "We will eventually have to talk."

"Recovering the child is a one time deal. Once she's safe, you will go about your business and I will go about mine."

That might be what she hoped for, but it wasn't what she was going to get. "I doubt that's going to be as easy as you would like."

"Detective, you are an ant on the sidewalk to me. I could step on you and walk away."

Somewhere deep inside he believed she would get rid of him to keep him silent, but he knew it wouldn't be easy for her. He could work with that. "Okay, I have been put in my place, thank you very much, Miss Mignon." He zoomed up the entrance to west Interstate 10, trying not think about what was happening to the little girl. The sense of urgency was so great he found his foot pressing harder and harder on the accelerator.

The sun was a dim sliver of orange on the horizon and Mignon was able to take off the blanket and climb into the front seat with Ryan without having to worry about bursting into flames.

The farm turned out to be a set of abandoned buildings at the end of a long dirt road that felt in the middle of nowhere. Overgrown shrubs lined the pitted road and live oaks, badly in need of trimming, shadowed the buildings. A long barn with rotting timbers and peeling paint sat back from the road. A cottage with broken windows and sagging doors sat to one side of the barn. Various outbuildings dotted the area to the far side of the barn.

She rolled down the window and sniffed the air. The faint whiff of decay came to her nose. No one had lived here for many years, but just under the decay she caught the faint scent of a vampire and blood. The new ones didn't know how to control their scent and this one was so very new she could smell the violence just beneath the surface.

Mignon fought her distaste of both him and his appetites. She tried not to remember her children in the brothel that catered to such appetites and the people she'd killed there so long ago, yet still so fresh in her mind. The images of her children would remain with her until she died.

Ryan stopped the car and they both got out. She stood on a patch of wild grass and looked around.

"What's the plan?" Ryan asked as he hefted his sword.

"I kill the vampire. You find the child." She sniffed the air again, trying to determine if Appleton was alone or had other vampires with him.

"Come on, let's go," Ryan urged, stepping forward and looking too eager.

Never be eager for killing, she thought. People made mistakes. "Wait." She sniffed again, separating the different scents, tracking them through the old house. "There are humans here." She took a step forward. "Four vampires and three humans. And lots of blood." The scent of the human blood brought an ache to her. No matter how often she told herself that pig's blood suited her needs, the allure of human blood never went away. She felt the pull and swallowed.

"What do we do?" Ryan asked as he studied the old house.

Mignon walked up to the sagging front door of the house and paused to listen. She heard the sound of crying and she kicked the door in. The sound carried on the night air as the door sailed down the long narrow hallway.

"So much for subtle." Ryan followed her into the gloomy interior.

Inside, the smell of blood was overpowering. Mignon stepped over trash and broken furniture. Two men wearing camouflage suits lay on the floor dead and bloodless.

Ryan looked down at the men. "This is army issue. Where the hell did they come from?"

"Who knows? They didn't have a chance." She moved down the hall and found another body. The air shimmered around her. She grabbed Ryan's arm. "Someone is dying."

They ran down the hall and flung open a door. A vampire knelt over a human, teeth embedded in his neck. Before the vampire could move, Mignon pulled out her sword and thrust it through the back of the vampire's head at the base of the primitive brain. The vampire fell sideways with a thump. She twisted the sword and severed the head.

Ryan started to help the man on the floor.

"Leave him, he's as good as dead." Mignon planted her foot in the back of the dead vamp and pulled out her sword.

The soldier opened his eyes. "Kill me. I don't want to be one of you."

Mignon bent over him and tried to enchant him. But his eyes remained focused on her. Like Ryan, he seemed immune to her enchantment. Interesting. "Did you drink this one's blood?" She indicated the dead vampire.

"No," the soldier's voice was faint and the light started to fade from his eyes.

Mignon smiled. "What is your name?"

"Bo Janovek."

"As long as you did not drink, you will not turn, Bo Janovek. You die with honor." She covered his eyes as his body relaxed.

After she stood, Mignon led the way out of the room and back into the hallway. She tried to pinpoint where the new vamp was and the child, but the blood smell was overpowering and she could not separate the scents.

Mignon opened doors as she walked down the hall checking each room. The hall led into a large kitchen. She spotted two vampires tormenting a mortal woman who was suspended from ceiling beam by long blood-stained rope. As she dangled, her feet swayed back forth, and blood dripped down her face and arms.

"Carlson!" Ryan pushed past Mignon.

The woman's head snapped up. "Help me."

The vampires whirled around and Mignon leaped at them, her sword flashing. Ryan took on a third vampire crouched in a corner. Mignon swung her sword and connected with a vampire's neck, slicing clean through.

The other vampire danced away from her. "Watch what I can do young one."

Mignon smiled and leaped to the ceiling and hung upside down. The vampire tilted his head back to stare at her open mouthed. Running along the ceiling, she lined her body up perfectly with his. Then pushing off the ceiling, she aimed for the vampire beneath and thrust her sword through his open mouth, puncturing his neck into his primitive brain. She somersaulted and landed on her feet, extracted her sword from his crumpled body and turned.

Ryan had already killed his own vampire and stood watching her, an admiring look on his face. That's a hell of gift, he thought to himself.

"You rock, lady," Ryan said.

Carlson struggled against the ropes tied around her wrists. "Get me down."

Mignon reached up and cut at the rope with the point of her sword. The rope snapped and the woman dropped to the floor. Ryan untied her hands and she sat on the floor rubbing chaffed wrists.

Mignon bent over the woman. "Who are you?"

"Major Ursula Carlson."

Ryan studied her. "You're a commando. I thought you were FBI."

"Surprise, Detective." Carlson dabbed at the blood dripping down her cheek.

Mignon helped the woman to her feet and handed her to Ryan. "Take her to the car." She smiled at the woman. "When this is over, you and I will have a much needed girl talk."

The promise in her voice made Carlson blanch.

"Have you seen a child?" Ryan asked.

"Yeah." Carlson pointed at a door leading out of the kitchen.

"Through there."

"Take the major to the car," Mignon told Ryan.

Ryan nodded and started toward the door, one arm around Carlson while she leaned heavily into him.

Mignon ran to the door and flung it open. Inside, the child molester sat on a chair, a little girl on his lap. She wore a frilly pink dress and her hair had been braided. She looked dazed and frightened. Her eyes flickered at Mignon.

In front of them, a video camera had been set up on a tripod. Mignon could hear the faint whir of the motor.

The man's arm tightened around the child. "Amanda is mine."

Rage filled Mignon. "I am going to rip you apart, piece by piece." Old memories crowded against the fury that filled her. Once more, she was a mother searching brothels for her children. She glanced around the room.

The man put the girl down and stood to face Mignon.

"Go in the closet, Amanda, and wait for me," she told the child in a gentle voice and with a reassuring smile. Amanda nodded, her eyes dazed and unfocused.

"She's mine. She's mine." Appleton grabbed for the girl but she was already walking toward the closet, not looking back.

"You can't best me, suckling. I'm older, wiser, and stronger than you will ever be."

"I'm not afraid of you, bitch."

When the door was closed, Mignon shoved her sword into the hardwood floor. "I going to kill you with my bare hands." She leaped at the man and gripped his throat, her fingers tightening around the moist skin. The man was strong. He twisted away from her. She followed, grabbing his arm and tossing him against the wall. Before he could slide down to the ground, she was on him again. She kneed him in the groin.

"We have rules." She slapped him hard across the face. "We don't harm innocents."

He spat at her. Mignon kicked him in the stomach. "What kind of monster are you?"

He tried to answer, but she punched him in the face. "Silence. I'm going to kill you. But first you're going to suffer."

He whimpered. She smacked him again. "How many children have you harmed in your lifetime?"

Again, he tried to answer, but she slapped his face. "Did you think that becoming one of us would give you untold power to prey on children?"

Tears gathered in the corners of his eyes. He opened his mouth, but Mignon cut him off.

"Children are precious." She punched him again, the memory of her daughter with the old man in the brothel filling her mind. He had been evil. The madame had been evil. "You deserve no mercy." She twisted his arm until the sinews, tendons, and muscles gave way.

A piercing wail filled the small room. He bent over, his wails bouncing off the walls. She kicked him and he flew against the wall and slid down. "Mercy."

"Here is your mercy." Mignon pulled her silver dagger out of her boot, grabbed him by the hair and bent his head down to the ground. She shoved the knife slowly into the back of his skull. She knew he could feel every millimeter of the dagger's progression. If only she could make the pain last an eternity.

His body jerked, but her hold was strong. Finally after she reached the primitive brain, she slid the blade slowly in and the vampire stopped moving.

Mignon stood over him. Damn, she'd killed him too soon. He hadn't suffered enough. She started to kick the body around the room, trying to control her rage.

"Mignon," Ryan said from the door. "I know he's pond scum, but I think he's dead now. Take a deep breath and step back from the body."

She stopped, pain and anger colliding in her head. She wanted to hurt the man still, to make him suffer for her daughter's death.

"Grab the kid," Ryan said, "and let's get the hell out of here."

Mignon opened the door to the closet. The little girl crouched on the dirty floor. Tears tracked down her face. Mignon lifted her up and gently cupped the girl's face in her hands and kissed her. After a few moments, the child's trembling stopped. Her eyes went unfocused and distant. "I'm taking you home. You will remember nothing," Mignon said gently as she stroked the child's cheek. "Now go to sleep."

The child's eyes closed and Mignon swept her up into her arms.

"Damn," Ryan said, "you didn't even break a sweat."

"Does this seem like a moment of levity?" Mignon snarled. "Why aren't you guarding that woman?"

"She ain't going anywhere."

"Get my sword," Mignon ordered. Ryan picked it up, stepping over the dead vampire and then headed out of the room.

Outside in the clean air, Mignon hugged the sleeping child close to her, remembering the night she found her children in a brothel. She stepped around piles of rubbish heading for the car.

The woman, Major Carlson, sat slumped in the front seat, hand-cuffed to the door handle.

At the car, Mignon set the sleeping child on the back seat and stood to stare at the house. "We need to burn the house."

"My men," Carlson said.

Mignon turned to her. "Sleep."

Carlson glared at her. "Your whammy doesn't work on me. You can't burn the house. I want the bodies. They deserve a decent burial."

Mignon shook her head. "You don't know if any of them have been changed. I'm not taking the chance."

"Let me get the dog tags first," Ryan said.

"We don't wear dog tags," Carlson said.

"Then you can send a recon team in later to recover what's left."

Mignon headed back to the house. In seconds, she had a pile of wood burning. Ryan helped her feed the flames. When the walls caught, they stood back to watch as the fire inched its way across the dry wood and along the inside walls. In minutes, the structure was totally encased in flames.

Mignon started back to the car.

"They need to go to a hospital," Ryan said.

Mignon shook her head. "Only the child. The woman has information we need."

Carlson glared at Mignon. "You can't make me talk."

Mignon smiled. "There are ways."

"What the hell are you going to do to her?" Ryan dug into his pocket for the keys.

"She won't be harmed," Mignon said as she sat in the back seat and cradled the child in her arms.

Carlson's face went deathly white as Ryan closed the front door and walked around to the driver's side. He started the car. "Where to?"

"The hospital first." Mignon hugged the child tight. She felt a welling of maternal feelings.

A half hour later, Ryan pulled into the hospital parking lot and parked in a handicapped spot. Mignon opened the door and stepped out, cradling the child in her arms. She walked into the hospital. At the first nurse she found, she handed the sleeping child to her. "This is Amanda Peterson. Take care of her."

When she awoke she would remember nothing.

The nurse accepted the sleeping Amanda. As she turned to call for a doctor, Mignon slipped away and went back to the car and got in. "Home," she ordered Ryan. "The child is being cared for."

"How kind of you," Carlson said in a sarcastic tone, "to save her for later. When she's a little older, then you can feed on her."

Mignon grabbed the woman's hair and pulled her head back. "Do you know what we call people like you?"

Her new enemy said nothing.

Mignon bared her fangs. "Snack food." Mignon had no patience for stupidity. Didn't this arrogant woman understand that she was not in a position to be stupid?

Ryan laughed. "Major, I think she just called you a Twinkie on legs."

Carlson groaned and Mignon released her.

Ryan pulled out of the parking lot. Mignon watched the dark streets. New Orleans was quiet and deceptively peaceful. She thought about Charles and the evil that walked the night. She had to stop him. She didn't know why he was doing what he was doing, but he was upsetting the balance between vampire and mortal. She had to set things right.

CHAPTER ELEVEN

Ursula did the best she could to keep her fear under control. She glanced at the two vampires on either side of her, holding her by her arms. One was tall and dark-skinned with a chiseled face and long braids that flowed over his shoulders. He was handsome in an almost frightening way. From the look of the muscles in his arms and shoulders, he worked out. The other one was a white man with long blond hair and brown eyes.

They helped her out of the car and up the steps to the house, the same house she'd had under surveillance for the last three days.

Just having the vampires' hands on her made her skin crawl. Following the female vampire and Lattimore, they led her through a large country kitchen and down a long hall to a room lined in bookcases and with a desk against one wall.

Lattimore flopped down in a chair. The female vampire took a seat behind the desk and leaned her elbows on the blotter.

"What are you going to do with me?" Ursula asked. A tiny tremor in her voice was the only hint of the fear swirling through her.

The tall, black vampire simply smiled at her as he gestured for her to sit in a leather recliner.

"Max," came a voice from the door, "you know I don't like surprises. But I do like presents." Ursula glanced at the door.

The man who stood there was a vampire who had a look of age about him that told her he had been around a thousand years or more. He approached Ursula and grasped her chin in one hand to tilt her head from side to side. "Very pretty."

"I hope I give you heartburn," Ursula snapped.

The man sighed. "Bravado in the face of such odds. It's an admirable quality."

She shrugged. She didn't want them to see her fear.

The man pulled up a chair and sat down in front of her. "Will you tell me why you are hunting my brethren?"

She lifted her chin. "So we can kill you all."

"Liar." His voice was almost affectionate. "You don't want to kill us. You want to use us. A vampire army controlled by your government."

She felt a spurt of surprise. "How do you know? What are you doing to me?"

"My dear, I'm what my people call *animus capio*." He held her hand.

"What the hell is that?"

His dark eyes held hers. "A soul harvester." The man glanced at the others in the room. "You call our ability to enchant humans the whammy. How very droll."

The female vampire smiled sadly. The two vampire men looked at each other. Ursula glanced at Ryan.

Ryan stared as though trying to decide something, then walked over to her. "Why were you at the farm?"

"To save the kid."

"How did you know about her?"

"Your captain asked for a second pair of eyes on the street and I called my people."

"There's more to that story."

Ursula bit the inside of her lip. "I wanted to help. The child was in danger and I had the ability to save her."

He laughed. "News flash, you got your ass whipped and if I remember correctly, we saved you."

Ursula shrugged. "Does it matter who saved who as long as the little girl is safe?"

Ryan walked away, shaking his head. He slouched down in a chair and crossed an ankle over his knee. He stared at her and she could see that he didn't trust her. Hell, she didn't trust him. He'd sold out to the enemy.

The old vampire drew her attention back to him. "What do you know about vampires, except for what Charles has told you?"

Oh shit! They knew about Charles collaborating with the government. "You know about Charles?"

The old vampire gave a dry laugh. "My dear, your choice of cohorts leaves a lot to be desired."

"What do you mean by that?"

"I can see that Charles has told you about the *Praetorium*—in very unflattering terms. Charles lied."

Ursula felt as though knowledge was being drained out of her, but his fingers held hers tightly She tried to jerk her hand out of his. He was reading her mind.

"You and all like you are nothing but blood-sucking murderers."

He smiled sadly. "Back in the old days, you would have been half right. We exist on blood, but we seldom murder. You are not a stupid woman. If vampires killed the food supply indiscriminately, what we would eat then?"

She'd often wondered the same thing, but she didn't budge on her opinion. Vampires were evil. "You are predators."

The old man laughed. "I have lived four thousand years, child. I have seen your kind try to eradicate the wolf, the bear and everything else that you feared. For no other reason than the fact that you didn't understand."

"You're four thousand years old?"

He nodded. "Why do you want a vampire army?"

She couldn't lie to him. He would know. "Some people are untouchable. Drug dealers. Terrorists. Dictators. Somebody has to make them pay for what they do."

"And once you have taken care of all those little annoyances, what will your government do then? Take over the world?"

Take over the world! Was he mad? Not even the United States government would be so arrogant. "Of course not. There's always someone else ready to take the place of a fallen dictator."

"How true. But how do you plan to control this vampire army?"

"They'll be soldiers. Soldiers follow orders."

The vamps started laughing. Ursula wondered why. What did they know that she didn't?

"Four thousand years," the old vampire said, "and nothing has changed. I have seen men do nothing but destroy themselves. They have built monuments to their vanity, they have wiped out entire cultures. You always have to be the top dog. When does it stop? When will you learn? Do you think we are pawns to be used for such petty purposes in your little wars?"

"I don't get it," Ursula said. "You're stronger and smarter than us. You are the most powerful creatures on earth. How come you haven't tried to take over?"

The old man glowered at her. "We are not the evil beings of your mythology. Politics. Conquest. Petty concerns. Empires have risen and fallen and the brethren have endured. Solomon," he pointed at the black man, "was the son of desert sheik." He gestured toward the white man. "Max, once a gladiator, saw the most powerful government of its time fall into utter ruin. Mignon was a slave. One thing learned when you have immortality is that nothing in the mortal world is permanent. Eventually, this country will fall into chaos. It might be a thousand years from now, but it will happen nonetheless. And I will endure. What you hold dear means nothing to us. You think we are monsters. We are more alike than we will ever be different."

"Okay," Ursula cried, "so you personally aren't so bad. Charles betrayed us. He took our money and gave us only enough information to make us curious enough to want more."

Lattimore started laughing. "You're all bent out of shape because you got played."

Mignon frowned. The old vampire turned to look at Lattimore. "Played?"

"Tricked," Lattimore said. "Conned. Bamboozled. How much money did you give Charles?" he asked Ursula.

"Millions," Ursula found herself saying in conjunction with the old vampire. She glanced at him. He *was* reading her mind.

Lattimore laughed again. "I get it now. It's a hostile takeover."

"What do you mean?" Mignon asked.

"This *Praetorium* thing you have going controls most of the vamps."

The elder vampire nodded.

Lattimore continued. "Charles needs money to become the head vamp."

"How would you know this?" Mignon asked.

"I'm the detective here. I do this for a living. Rule number one is to follow the money. What does Charles want money for except maybe to take over the world, put the vamps in power and keep humans for food? Case closed. We have a motive. I'm good."

Mignon stood and started pacing the room. "But why would Charles change so many people?"

Lattimore grinned. "He needs a posse to help him keep control once he's figured it all out." He glanced at Ursula. "And now I have to figure out you. Old guy, what's the name of her unit?"

The man took Ursula's hand again. "X-Ray unit. Something about commandos. No, Special Forces."

Lattimore nodded. "I've heard of you guys. When I was running around with Special Forces, we heard rumors about this X-Ray unit. Top secret, hush, hush. Let me put on my military thinking cap." He jumped up and approached Ursula. "You want to make a commando squad of vampires to go in and take down the bad guys in this world. That's pretty smart. You have a terrorist training camp in Libya and you need someone to go in bang, bang—they're dead and another terrorist group is annihilated. This plan has potential." He stalked around her.

The vampire Max studied Ursula. "But you haven't implemented it. Why not?"

"The whole idea is still in development."

Lattimore shook his head. "That isn't how the military works."

Ursula didn't have an answer. She felt the old one's sly digging through her memories.

"She doesn't know."

"I'm trying to save lives here," Ursula said.

"So are we. We're here to stop Charles, not to help him."

"Is that why you were fighting him on the bridge?"

Mignon's eyes narrowed. "You were in the helicopter."

"I almost had you."

"When Charles is dead," Mignon said, "you and I will settle our score."

Ursula felt a chill radiate down her back.

The old man said, "Mignon, do not frighten her. She is just a lackey."

Mignon gave the old man an amused smile. "Elder Turi, you never let me have any fun."

"You are so beautiful to look at, I don't want to lose you."

Ursula felt confused. She wasn't expecting this type of interrogation. She'd expected to be food. She hadn't anticipated humor and affection between these vampires.

Elder Turi stood up. "Release her. Mr. Lattimore can take her home or wherever she wants to go." He smiled gently at Ursula. "Thank you for your help."

"I'll take her home," the vampire Solomon said.

Ursula appealed to Lattimore. "I don't want to be alone with him."

Lattimore smiled. "Better off with him than others."

"You're a traitor, Lattimore."

"That's just your opinion." Lattimore produced the key to the handcuffs and released her. "Since your story about being with the FBI is a big fat lie, don't come back to my office butting your ass into my investigation again."

Ursula stood and rubbed her wrists. Solomon opened the door and stood to one side waiting for her. She didn't want to go with him, but she had to admit he was easy to look at.

Solomon politely opened the door to the car for her and she sat down and snapped the seat belt around her. "Where to?" he asked when he sat down next to her and inserted the key into the ignition.

She thought for a moment. "Can you take me back to my car?"

"At the farm, where you found the child?"

"No, I'm not that stupid. I parked a couple miles away and hiked in."

"Then I will take you back to your car."

"Are you really the son of a desert sheik?" she asked when he'd started the car and backed out of the driveway.

"I am the first born of Ben Azi Hamad." He turned onto the street, his large hands handling the steering wheel with ease.

"Then why are you named Solomon? Isn't that a Jewish name?"

"It's a family name." He smiled. "My mother's people were descendants from the Queen of Sheba."

For a moment, Ursula was shocked. "You're related to the biblical Solomon?"

"Yes."

"How old are you?"

"I stopped counting after seven hundred and thirty-four." He stopped for a red light and turned to study her.

"What happened? How did you become a vampire?" She felt weighed down with the heaviness of the history behind his eyes. She should have been afraid of him but she wasn't.

"How is not as important as why."

"I'll bite. Why did you become a vampire?" So much had happened to her in the last few hours that she realized she had lost something inside her. Something that had fueled her fear of the vampires. Now she was simply confused. Mignon had not acted in a way that Ursula had thought she would. She'd rescued the child and treated Amanda with tenderness and compassion.

"To seek revenge," Solomon said.

"Don't leave me hanging now."

The light changed and he stepped on the accelerator. "My uncle slaughtered my family for the power my father held. And Elder Turi found me half dead in the desert and he gave me the gift."

"You think being a vampire is a gift?"

"Yes."

"Explanation, please." Getting stuff out of this man was difficult.

"Why do you want to know? You fear and hate what I am."

How did she answer that? She was half attracted to him and didn't understand why. Elder Turi hadn't hurt her when he'd been reading her mind. They seemed to be decent people, not the monsters she'd been led to believe. Mignon had saved her life. She had comforted the child. Who knew vamps had maternal instincts? "Maybe hate is the wrong word. I just want to understand."

"But you want to exploit the vampires. Why should I make your job easier?"

"We're trying to do something right for the world. My job is to make the world safe."

"Safe for whom?" Solomon asked.

"Decent, hard-working people."

"Does that include me? I'm a decent, hard-working person."

She groped for an answer and realized that the vampires weren't included. "I don't know." And now she had evidence that they weren't as evil as Charles had painted them. Dealing with Charles had been viewed as a necessary evil to get the information they needed.

She had dealt with Charles in a peripheral manner. She hadn't liked him. He had had a distasteful manner about him. Every time he looked at her, or spoke to her, he'd treated her as though she were property. He'd been condescending and arrogant. Yet his every demand had been given to him because he was like the new toy no one else had yet.

"Mortals never do." His voice was sad.

They drove in silence during the long journey to her car. "I'm sorry," she said just before getting out of his car.

"For what?" he asked.

"I don't know." She got into her car and without glancing back at him, started the engine and headed back toward the city.

Instead of returning to her hotel, she headed out to the base. All the way back, she worked out what she would tell the colonel. She didn't know what she believed anymore herself.

"Sir," she said as she entered Colonel Hammett's office.

"Report, Carlson." His tone was almost a snarl.

"I lost my team, but the child is safe."

"Why didn't you call for extraction?"

"There was a lot of confusion, sir, and by the time I got the child out of the house, I discovered that my radio was fried. The house was on fire and I couldn't go back inside for another one." Part truth, part lie.

He seemed to mull over what she'd said, and then he nodded. "Good work, Carlson."

She didn't know why, but she had a feeling she needed to keep some of the facts hidden. The lies spilled from her tongue without a second thought. Without mentioning Lattimore, Solomon, Mignon or the others, she gave the colonel a quick, highly abbreviated, completely fabricated rundown on what had happened. "If not for Lieutenant Jones, I would never have gotten out of that house alive with the child. With everyone down, I felt the only thing to do was set fire to the house and burn everyone since I didn't know who might have been infected."

The colonel gave her a sympathetic look. "Get some sleep. I'll see to the team."

"No, sir. They were my people. I will take care of them."

Hammett smiled in approval. "You're a good soldier, Carlson."

What a crock! He had no idea how confused she was feeling after the unusual events of the night. She'd faced vampires who not only hadn't killed her, but hadn't even considered her food. She wondered if Special Forces knew what the hell they were doing.

"Too bad you burned the house, though."

"Sir, I don't understand."

"If any of your people had been turned, they would have been soldiers loyal to us and we could have used them in our studies."

But they'd been told being turned was the worst thing that could happen to them. "You don't mean that."

"We're looking for a vampire army that is expendable. What better way to study the process than to have our own soldiers turned? We could have learned a lot."

An expendable army? "Do you think vampires would make good soldiers?" She didn't intend to question the colonel, but Elder Turi's laughter was still fresh in her mind.

He shrugged. "I think soldiers would make good vampires."

Oh my God! She felt as if she were sinking. That was not the answer she'd expected from him. "I don't understand."

"If we could figure out a way to have them self-destruct when their missions were done, we'd be unstoppable." He looked delighted at the prospect.

Ursula felt as if the ground had shaken and tossed her down a well. "Self-destruct?"

The colonel smiled, a glittering look in his eyes. "Imagine, drop the teams in, let them do their work, and when they finish, they just cease to be."

"Do you mean die?" Ursula went hollow inside.

"What's the first thing you were taught when you were brought into Special Forces?"

"To be prepared to die for my country." But not to die needlessly.

He cocked a finger at her. "Bingo. So why not have vampires die for the country?"

Ursula felt ill. Vampires might not be the best people around, but they'd been human long before they'd been vampires. "I see your logic, sir." The colonel had just given her top secret information because he thought she could be trusted. She didn't know if she could be.

Vampire soldiers who self-destructed. Ursula had been taught that while the mission was important, nobody was left behind. To turn soldiers and then deliberately have them die seemed so morally wrong. "Thank you for being honest, sir. But I need to see about recovering the bodies of my team."

He gave her a penetrating look. "Our mission is noble, Major. When you return, we're going to have a long talk about your future in Special Forces."

Great! Probably wants me to be a vamp and self-destruct on command. "Thank you, sir." She saluted him and did an about-face and marched out of the office.

She sat in her car for a few minutes, thinking about what the colonel had said. She had worked before in situations where the ends justified the means; she just didn't think being turned into a vampire was what she had in mind for herself. Esepcially a vampire programmed to self-destruct on command.

While she could understand the colonel's point, she felt ill at the casual disregard for life, any life. Yes, vampire soldiers would be unstoppable, but what would happen when they got tired of being soldiers? Or they got tired of killing? Or they went bad? These were things that happened all the time, even under less trying conditions. But to set these guys up to die?

She realized that every mission she'd gone on could have been her last, and she was willing to die for what she believed in. But she didn't want to be thought of as expendable. She mattered. Every soldier mattered.

This was like strapping a bomb on a ten-year-old and expecting him to give his life for a cause he didn't even understand yet. That was wrong. What the colonel intended was wrong. She'd been taught to prepare for death, but not to go out and actively seek it. What could she do to stop all this madness?

Ryan sat at his desk typing. He was so tired his fingers fumbled over the keyboard as he searched through the real estate records. He'd concentrated his search on the warehouse district because most of the incidents with dead bodies had been there. It had occurred to him that if Charles wanted privacy, he would either have to lease a warehouse or own it outright. Ryan found he could trace most of the ownership changes, but the ownership of five warehouses was unclear. He jotted down the addresses with the intention of checking each one out.

Mary entered the squad room. "Did you hear?" She looked excited.

"Hear what? You mean about the little girl?" Did he sound convincing enough?

She sat on the corner of his desk and studied him. "Some woman delivered Amanda to the hospital and then just disappeared again. In fact, no one can even remember what she looked like. Strange, isn't it?"

"There's been a lot of strange going on here lately."

Mary chuckled. "No kidding. Kind of makes you long for the good old days when it was just you and me on the streets, hookin' and bookin' the bad guys. What are you doing?"

"Searching real estate records for changes of ownership in the warehouse district."

"That's my job."

"You have plenty to do. I'm just playing a hunch. If it pans out, I may have my killer."

"Do you know who you're looking for?"

"Yeah! A dude named Charles Rabalais."

For a second she looked startled. Then she glanced at her watch. "Sounds like a boring time for you tonight." She flicked back a stray strand of hair. "If you need me, I can help."

"Thanks. I'm good, I can find my way to Google." Ryan leaned back in his chair. The old swivel chair squeaked.

"Computer stuff is not normally your territory."

"But things change. You've changed. Mary, are you going to tell me what's going on with you? Or keep it a big secret?"

"I'm not the one who goes out and disappears for the night."

He rubbed his eyes. "I'm doing my job?"

"I'm doing mine."

"No, you're not. Give Internal Affairs what they want and move on. You'll get a slap on the wrist and be back on the streets tomorrow."

Her face set in a mulish expression. "You think I'm guilty, too." She crossed her arms, a belligerent glint in her eyes.

Ryan shrugged. "I don't know what to think. You've been secretive, a pain in the ass to work with, and you're acting guilty. Sometimes that's enough to paint a big target on your forehead."

She thrust her chin out defiantly. "I haven't done anything. I'm not one of the bad guys. I've done my job the way it needs to be done. If my methods aren't nice, clean and pretty, I'm not losing any sleep over it. If you feel like I'm not the right partner for you, get another one."

He was thinking about it. Not that he was ready to make the move. He just wanted to get out of the way of the fallout coming her way. "We've been partners for four years. We've put our asses on the line for each other. That's not something to be thrown away. If you need time, fine. But when you're ready to talk—talk. I'm not here to judge you, I just want to help you."

"I'll keep that in mind," she snapped as she slipped off his desk and left without a backward glance.

Ryan couldn't decide what to do about Mary. He felt sad that she wouldn't trust him and relieved that she didn't want him to solve her problems. He had enough of his own. He went back to the search.

Dawn was just breaking when he finally shut down his computer. After a short meeting with Lieutenant Barton to report on what he'd been doing, he walked out into the early morning humidity and stood next to his car, thinking he should go home and get some sleep. He hadn't had any sleep for over twenty-four hours. And if he was going to do anything about the murders, he needed to be sharp and alert.

CHAPTER TWELVE

Just as the sun set, the doorbell rang and Mignon answered it to find Ryan standing on the veranda. He wore tight jeans and a light jacket. She could just see the tell-tale bulge beneath his arm that told her he was carrying a weapon. "I told you not to come back." She wasn't certain if she was pleased to see him or not. Having him in her life was too big a complication. And the only solution to this complication was not to her liking.

He gave her a winsome grin. "You told me a lot of things I'm ignoring. Can I come in? I was hoping you'd just forget what went on between us."

"You mean the part where I'm a vampire and you're not?" she asked. Torn between anger and desire, she wasn't sure how to react.

He half nodded.

She wanted to put the past behind her, but would the price be too high? "That's a typical male reaction."

He laughed. "I'm a typical male. Look, we can have this conversation out here or inside. Do you really want your neighbors to know our business?" He glanced down at the van that had returned to its parking spot.

This time she couldn't stop the smile that spread across her lips. She stood aside and he entered. He smelled clean. His eyes were clear; he'd had a good rest. She stood aside and let him in.

"Where are Max and Solomon?" he asked as he stepped into the entry.

"They just left to patrol along the levee tonight."

"And you?"

"I'm taking the wharves." She led the way into the living room and Ryan sat down in the overstuffed chair he'd come to favor. "How is Amanda? I read in the newspaper that her grandparents are with her."

"She's fine. Doesn't remember a thing. That's quite a whammy you have."

Mignon chuckled, sliding right back into the easy relationship she had with him. "The whammy, that's what Major Carlson called it. I like that term."

"You look tired."

She heard the concern in his voice. "I am. Normally when I have to go after someone, it's not on this large a scale." Mignon began pacing the living room. What was she going to do about Ryan now? About Carlson? About Charles? Why did things have to turn so complicated?

"How did you become a vampire?" Ryan asked.

She stopped her pacing to consider his question. "Are you playing investigator now?"

Ryan shrugged. "I'm curious."

In for a penny in for a pound, she thought. The least she owed him was the whole story. "Charles Rabelais changed me over."

"The man you're after. Is this a revenge thing?"

What was between her and Charles was more than revenge. She didn't even think there was a word for it. "In a way."

He crossed his arms. "Why?"

"He was my master." She looked away, not wanting him to see the shame she knew she could never hide about her past. "I was his slave. His concubine." The mother of his children. "I know children study slavery in school, yet no one living in this country today can envision what it was really like." She half-shuddered at the crowded memories that never seemed to quite go away.

Compassion clouded his brown eyes. "What was it like?"

She didn't know how to handle his understanding. Her first instinct was to run from it. To run from the sympathy he offered. "Everything you read about it in the history books and worse."

"But he made you into a vampire. He must have liked you a lot."

How did one describe Charles? To say he was spoiled or manipulative wasn't enough. Charles was evil personified. "When you're property, you have no choices. Charles could do with me what he wanted." And he'd damned her.

Ryan lifted an eyebrow. "Being a hopped-up, sword-swinging, axe-wielding babe wasn't your career ambition?"

She had been unable to protect her children as a mother should. "Until I knew the powers that vampires had, I thought I was cursed." The first time she had gone to church to explain to the priest what she was, he had recoiled in horror. She had never gone back. "When I discovered what I could do, I knew I could get my children back."

"What happened to your children?"

"One of the rules vampires have adhered to for centuries is to bring no one over who isn't alone in the world. Charles wanted me forever, but as long as I had children he was prevented by the *Praetorium* from changing me. So he sold my children, our children, to a brothel in Charleston."

"He was their father?"

"Yes," she replied. The pain of Charles's betrayal would never end.

"Did you find them?" Ryan asked.

His voice caressed and soothed her. She closed her eyes as a tear slipped down her cheek. "I found them. My daughter was pregnant and the woman in charge still made her take customers." Her lip bottom lip quivered. "When Charles sold my children, I felt rage, but that was nothing compared to the night I found my children." She swiped the tears away.

Ryan's eyes softened. "I'm sorry."

"I killed twenty-seven people that night, but the anger didn't go away. Over two hundred and fifty years have passed, and I still can't rid myself of the rage." Her conscience told her she'd saved eight children who had been worked almost to death in the brothel. Children she'd taken back to Louisiana and raised as her own. The memories of their terrified faces as she'd pulled them out of the brothel remained with her. They hadn't all been slaves. Two of the girls had been white and one of the boys had been from India. They had all looked to her to save them, to keep them safe.

"So that's why you want to destroy Charles." Ryan's voice was gentle.

Her bitter laughter filled the room. "Stop playing therapist. I like you better when you're in your detective guise."

"I've seen some horrible shit in my day, but I never could wrap my head around how someone could hurt children."

"Slaves were livestock. Charles never saw Angeline and Simon as his children. They were nothing more than a profit to add to his treasury." Her body began to shake.

Ryan's hands fisted at his side. "Bastard."

Mignon saw the anger in his eyes burning as bright as the pain in her heart. On some level he understood her reason for becoming a vampire. This made the pain of revealing what she was easier. "Charles wanted me with him for all eternity. With children I couldn't be completely his. My attention would always be divided. At least he didn't kill them. As long as they were alive I knew I would find them." And Charles was right. She had refused to give up.

"Do you drink human blood?" Ryan asked.

Mignon looked at the tips of her boots. Shame washed over her, even though she knew she had done what she needed to do to survive. "I never killed an innocent."

"How do you know?"

Raising her eyes, she met his gaze. "New Orleans was not an innocent city."

"What do you miss most about being mortal?"

What did she miss most? "Bacon, sunrises."

"Me, too."

Mignon press her lips together to stop from giggling. Laughing would only encourage him to continue being fanciful. "Bacon or sunrises?"

"Bacon." Ryan patted his sinfully flat stomach. "A man of my years has to avoid certain things."

She rolled her eyes. "I don't even remember my thirties."

"How old are you?"

How old was she now? Years ago she'd stopped counting birthdays. "Two hundred and eighty-two."

His mouth dropped opened. Then he gave her an appraising look. "You don't look a day over a hundred and twelve."

"You're flirting with me." And she had to admit she liked it. The way he teased her made her warm inside. She hadn't felt that way since she'd been a mortal girl with a mad crush on Jacob, one of the young field hands on the plantation. Part of her still longed for those simple days so long ago.

"For an old broad, you're still pretty hot."

She shrugged. "I'm a baby in vampire years."

"How long do vamps live?"

"Jabari, leader of the *Praetorium*, knew Moses." Jabari and Turi had lived many of the stories that she had read about in the Bible. Not until after her change did she realize how history was kept alive with the brethren. They knew both the truth and the falsehoods of the past.

"Damn," he said, "that's old. Did you know anyone famous?"

A strand of hair fell on her cheek, and he pushed it away. "Frederick Douglass, Winston Churchill, Bram Stoker. Once I met Martin Luther King. He was just a boy, but I enjoyed watching him bloom into the man he became." And grieved deeply when he had died.

"You knew the guy who wrote *Dracula*?"

"Yes." In fact, she still knew him and he was still writing. He now made his living as a romance writer and was very well respected. She thought of all the different literary voices he'd tried over the centuries.

"Bram Stoker must have ticked you guys off."

"Quite the contrary." Bram was a hard-living man who found his vampire existence incredibly fun. "He's one of us. The book killed a lot of rumors about the existence of vampires."

Ryan laughed. "I've always heard that you should write what you know."

She laughed with him, feeling the lightness of the moment and knowing they would probably never have such fun again.

"Snack on anybody famous?"

Why didn't that question surprise her? "I've snacked on a few Klan members."

"Cool. Did you snack on them for fun or in your capacity as a vampire cop?"

"I do love my job. And that was a fringe benefit."

"Does Charles love being a vampire?"

She'd known the conversation would eventually turn back to Charles. "Charles loves power and the fear he generates. When I was still his slave, he never just took what he needed. He would always kill. And he would kill slowly. For him, the fear was as important as the blood."

"And what about you?"

"I learned to control my hunger, taking only what I needed to survive. I left people with no memory of what happened, though their purses were a lot lighter."

A look of pure delight spread across his face. "You were a thief?"

The guilt she'd felt over that sin had long passed. "A very good one. I had eight children to feed."

"Eight kids!" He studied her slim figure, a wicked look in his eyes. "How did you maintain your girlish figure?"

"Only two were my biological children. The rest I rescued from the brothel. But all of those children required a lot of food, clothing, and patience." Those had been good days, living deep in the bayou with the laughter of her children. Many of their descendants still lived in the bayou, and still talked about the fierce black woman who had saved their ancestors from the brothel.

"How did you escape notice?"

"We hid." She had built a shelter with her own hands and tilled the soil as best she could. Until she accrued enough money to live in New Orleans, she had worked hard keeping her family safe. She found herself smiling, remembering her little granddaughter leading a baby gator on a string as if they were going out for a Sunday walk.

Ryan frowned. "Why did you need to hide? You had nothing to fear from mortals."

"Mortals kill what they don't understand. It's best for the brethren to keep a low profile, but from time to time there is unrest, and *venators* take care of the problem."

"You mean some of the brethren don't like playing by the rules. When was the last rebellion?"

"The last time we had a dispute was during the reign of Vlad the Impaler. Max and Bram killed him."

"I'm almost liking Max."

She raised an eyebrow, not believing him. "Almost? He's no threat to you."

"Maybe not, but he looks at you like you're a hot fudge sundae."

Mignon liked the fact that Ryan was jealous. Not that he needed to be. She and Max were ancient history. Literally. "Max and I have a history. He'd taught me to survive as a vampire and then trained me to be a *venator*." From him she learned what being a vampire truly meant and she rediscovered her honor and her sense of self. He'd given her purpose.

"Wow, that would make a terrific movie."

"That would be mundane since one of the brethren is already writing movies in Hollywood. You remember *Vampire Vixens*."

"Yeah, I saw that five times."

"Douglas always had a fertile imagination." She could see that Ryan was impressed.

Ryan was silent for a few seconds. "What are you going to do with Charles when you catch him?"

"Take his head."

"Are you afraid?"

A long time ago, she'd learned to use her fear to her advantage. She would either kill or be killed. That was her job. "Charles has the kind of evil that has always frightened me. Yes, I'm afraid, not just for myself, but also for my family and all mortals. Charles is ruthless."

He pointed his thumb over his shoulder. "So let's get back out there."

She looked him straight in the eyes. "Do you fear me now that you know what I am?"

Ryan shook his head. "I asked your help to get Amanda back."

His eyes did not lie; he didn't fear her. She was relieved. "If you had not suspected that she'd been taken by a vampire, would you have come to me?"

"No." He stood up and approached her, touching her arm. "There are other things about you that make me more nervous than being your next hot meal."

His touch burned her skin. "Such as?"

"For a woman who's been around as long as you, you don't seem to know when a man's trying to put the moves on you."

No matter how much she desired him, she knew that a physical relationship would only lead to trouble. "Whatever you and I are feeling, it's forbidden by the *Praetorium*."

A disbelieving expression crossed his face. "They tell you who you can get busy with?"

"There are rules that keep my kind alive. They're not an attempt to control us. We can't afford to do anything that will alert humans to our presence."

"I've met your kind up close and personal."

"I should have killed you." Her stomach roiled. The very thought terrified her.

"Is that what you do when someone finds out about vampires?"

"I know it seems harsh, but yes. I'm not just talking about my life, but the thousands of vampires who could be at risk. We don't take human life if we don't have to. We have the power to bend most mortals to our wills."

"You couldn't bend me."

Mignon thought he looked just a bit too smug for her well being. "You are a special case."

"Then we should be able to—"

"No, as much as I might want to." She shook her head, knowing that she couldn't let herself be weak for a second. She needed to nip this attraction in the bud before it spiraled out of control. "I've broken enough rules and the new century has barely begun."

He shrugged. "Then what's a few more?"

"I'm trying to keep you alive."

Ryan couldn't deny his feelings any longer. His need for her was burning him up. "You're worth the risk." He planted both hands on the sides of her head. Her soft hair twined around his fingers. Ryan knew he shouldn't be doing this. She'd threatened to kill him. She was dead. Well, sort of. She didn't feel dead. She felt just right.

He kissed her. Her mouth was soft and yielding as it opened beneath his. Half the excitement was not knowing what to expect. He'd expected some resistance, but she pressed against him and moaned.

She felt vulnerable and oh-so-feminine despite her lethal capabilities.

She broke away from him, her face flushed. "Not here," she said with a small chuckle. She took him by the hand and led him from the living room, up the stairs and into her bedroom.

Her bedroom wasn't at all what he expected. A large brass bed was angled from a corner with a netting canopy. The bedspread was a rich red with an exotic pattern in gold and dark blue. For a second he gazed at the mahogany armoire, the two chairs in front of the fireplace which were separated by a leopard print rug, and the dressing table with its assortment of gilt brushes, combs and perfume bottles. No, her bedroom wasn't at all what he'd expected. Not one lethal weapon was in sight.

She closed the door and seemed to wait expectantly. Ryan folded her in his arms and kissed her face, along the line of her cheek, down to her jaw, then to her delicately pointed chin. Then he worked his way down her long supple neck.

She tasted sweet, like nothing he'd ever experienced before. Hell yes, this was worth the risk. He couldn't get enough of her. Her soft womanly scent filled his nostrils. Heat, desire, and need rolled around the scent of jasmine. He couldn't resist the temptation.

She led him to the bed and sat down on the edge. He sat next to her, his hand straying to the bottom of her sweater. He pulled up the edge and splayed his fingers across the smooth skin of her back.

She unbuttoned his shirt and in her haste, she tore a button off. He grinned at her, not caring, knowing they would get to the main event quicker. He lifted her sweater over her head. The black bra she wore didn't surprise him, but how well she filled the lacy cups did. He could almost make out her dusky nipples through the semi-sheer material.

Ryan couldn't catch his breath. Mignon was perfection. She was every centerfold, cheerleader nurse, cowgirl fantasy come to life.

He trembled. Blood rushed from his head down to the hot pit of his stomach. He pushed her down on the bed and shrugged off his shirt. Reaching behind him, he dug into his back pocket for his wallet with its emergency condom kept inside just in case his fantasy scenario came true. As he extracted his wallet and took out the silver-foiled packet, Mignon began to laugh.

"There's no need," she said.

"Vampires don't get knocked up?"

She shook her head. "Never. And anything else we've picked up is pretty much annihilated by our virus."

Ryan tossed the condom packet over his shoulder. "Right on." A lot of time had passed since he had been skin to skin inside a woman. Okay, he could think of one more good reason to like vampire women.

Mignon spread her arms out. "Are you always so chatty before you make love?"

"And here I read that chicks dig talk. I read that in *Cosmo* at the dentist last week."

"I'm not a chick and I haven't been with a man in seventy years. Save the conversation for later."

He drew back, surprised. "Seven zero?"

"Seventy years," she repeated.

"Vampire men aren't too bright, are they?" How could they overlook a woman like this? He kicked off his shoes. "Lights on or off?"

She growled at him.

"I'll take that as a *leave on* sign." He stripped off his pants and when he was naked he dropped to his knees between her thighs. Slowly he reached up and opened the zipper on her black leather pants. She wasn't wearing any panties and he almost passed out. Not even a thong.

Ryan worked off her shoes and then her pants. He just stared at her flat muscled stomach and the perfect globes of her breasts still cupped in the black lace. He took in the V at the juncture of her thighs.

"I'm waiting" she said, her voice trembling.

"Hush, I'm praying."

She sat up. "For what? Guidance? I have a sex manual in here somewhere, but it's probably eighty years old."

He ran his fingers down the slope of her thigh. "You're not wearing panties. Do you have any idea how sexy that is?" If only he'd known that in all this fighting they'd been doing together she'd been pantyless, he would have made his move a lot faster.

Her eyebrows drew together in a bemused frown. "Not really."

"It just screams *easy access*." He sighed. "I'm glad I didn't know that while I had to do my slice and dice thing. I would have been way too distracted."

She reached behind and unfastened the bra, and her breasts sprang free. "Still want to pray? Or are you interested in some play?" She tossed the bra across the room.

He bent over and kissed her navel. "I'm done worshipping."

"Thank God."

"Covered that already."

"Wait." She jumped off the bed and pulled the spread off to reveal red silk sheets. Then she scrambled back to the center. "Ryan."

He could hardly breathe. He was about to make love to the most beautiful woman, make that vampire woman, in the world. Hell, the universe. For a second he couldn't move. "Yes, Mignon?"

She patted the bed next to her. "Before the next Ice Age."

Ryan lay beside her, telling himself he should go slow. After all, she hadn't had sex in seventy years. But his hands and his libido had their own schedule. His heart raced and his palms were damp. He wanted this to be good for her. He leaned over to kiss her.

He cupped her cheek and pushed back her hair. Her mouth opened against his and he felt her hand go to his waist, down his buttock and the back of his thigh. Her low sigh was a good sign.

His hands drifted over her body. He cupped her breast against his palm. No other woman had fit so perfectly, he couldn't belie the softness of her skin. Under his touch he felt her whole body tremble.

She touched his cheek. "Ryan."

He wanted to hold this moment forever, almost as much as he wanted to be next to her naked on this bed.

He brushed his thumb across her hard nipple and fire danced on his skin, he wanted to find the words that would describe this moment, but he realized he wasn't a man to use words eloquently. What he couldn't say, he could show. What he was feeling, he could demonstrate.

Ryan pulled her into his arms. He rained kisses down her face and neck. His hand roamed her body. He wanted to touch every inch of her. Her silky skin entranced him. He couldn't get enough of her.

He ran his fingers over the supple curve of each of her breasts. Her eyes sparkled with passion, desire and just a hint of mischief. She was sexy. And so deadly. He felt as though he were dancing with the devil.

Mignon reached up and touched his mouth with her finger and he sucked the tip. "Make love to me," she said softly.

She had enchanted him. Thoroughly. Completely. He was lost.

Mignon ran her hands down his chest.

His muscles constricted under her touch. Holding himself with one arm, he ran the tips of his fingers over her taunt stomach until he reached the soft curls nestled between her thighs. Her thighs parted and he slipped a finger inside her, finding her warm and wet and ready. He began to stroke the tiny bud, feeling it harden. He put another finger inside her and slowly moved in a slow stroking rhythm. Her body trembled and he heard her moan.

His erection was hard and ready. Heat consumed him. He wanted to dive right in and get to the good part, but if she hadn't been with anyone in seventy years, she probably needed a bit more warm-up. That was okay with him. He was a patient guy who liked to do things right.

Her body wriggled against him. Ryan rested his head in the valley of her lush breasts. He swore he could hear a heartbeat. Maybe that was his imagination, but he didn't care. He took a nipple into his mouth and pulled gently. She arched back and he felt her tense. Oh yeah! This was gonna be so good.

Her internal muscles contracted around his fingers. He increased the tempo of his stroking, wanting her to come hard. Her heels dug into his waist.

Lifting his head, he stared into her dark, passion-glazed eyes. She bit her bottom lip.

"Come on, baby," he whispered, "get crazy for me. That's it. Let go."

Mignon shuddered and a plaintive moan broke from her lips. Her muscles contracted over and over as she reached orgasm and then went limp.

She whispered his name over and over again. He licked her lips and then kissed her. The tips of her breasts grazed his chest, igniting a heat that should have scorched the bed. She had told him that vamps combusted from the inside when exposed to sunlight. What would sex do? He half expected his hands to be scorched from the heat of her body.

She ran her hands over the plane of his back, down along the ridges of his spine and around his hips. She pressed him into the juncture of her thighs.

"Now," she demanded.

Who was he to deny her? Carefully, he positioned himself over her, lowering his body and thrusting until he was inside her.

She gasped. Her welcoming warmth surrounded him. A guttural groan escaped him as he slipped completely inside her. Her entire body shook with the strength of her desire.

Thoughts racing through his mind almost scared him. From the moment she'd told him the truth about herself, things had changed between them. For all her courage and power, Mignon was a vulnerable woman who'd known pain that would have killed the average person. He liked that she'd endured and made the best for herself. He liked that she had protected children.

He was breaking every rule in the cop handbook, but he didn't care. Making love to Mignon was the only thing that mattered. Buried deep inside her, he knew this act would change him forever.

With each push into her body, he came a little closer to heaven and a little deeper into hell. He clutched her hips to hold her still and increased his tempo. Ryan devoured her mouth, tasting their desperation.

Ecstasy and torture mixed and melted together as he moved inside her. She chanted his name in a litany. Fire danced across his skin as he increased the tempo of his thrusts, and her muscles clenched around him. Her body tensed as he drove deeper into her.

When he felt her quiver, her nails biting into his back, he pumped even harder. A cry broke from her and her back arched. Everything he felt surged into his final thrust. Blinding light and ecstasy mingled as pleasure washed over him and sent him on a journey that he would never recover from. For a brief instant the world stopped as the ultimate joy filled him. He couldn't catch his breath.

So this was what it felt like when your world got rocked.

Rural Georgia — 1943

Mignon and Rachel Peterson walked down the hard dirt road, sword practice concluded. Heat and humidity pressed down on them. Sweat ran in rivulets down Mignon's face. The night had not cooled down. Overhead, stars twinkled with such brilliance, they lit the forest to a silvery glow. In the bags slung over their shoulders were their swords. Rachel called the dozen different swords Mignon liked to carry her arsenal. But Mignon insisted Rachel be proficient in them all.

Rachel stopped and tilted her head toward dark trees. "Did you hear that?"

"What?" Mignon's mind had been a million miles away. Her many greats great-grandson was dying of tuberculosis and she was thinking about asking the *Praetorium* to allow her to change him. She could not bear to lose her children. Phillipe was a valuable member of her family. He'd come up with a process for refining pig blood and adapting it for vampire consumption so that it tasted almost as good as human blood. He was a brilliant man and now he was dying. Mignon's heart ached as it did each time one of her descendants passed. Sometimes she felt weighted down by the burden of death while she lived on and on.

"I heard a scream." Rachel stood in the middle of the road and listened. She was Mignon's new *venator*-in-training. VIT as Max liked to call her. One of the European *venators* had died and the *Praetorium* needed a replacement. Mignon had been asked to train Rachel, but had doubts about her. She was a tiny, doll-like blonde woman with sparkling blue eyes and a dainty, curved figure. She came from a tiny town outside Atlanta and was deeply proud of her dairy farm roots. Mignon felt like a giant next to the petite vampire.

Mignon paused to listen harder. She heard the rustlings of the mice in the moldy underbrush, and felt the faint touch of the sluggish breeze in the forest canopy.

The sound came again. "There." Rachel pointed.

This time, Mignon heard the scream, too. "Let's go." She pushed into the underbrush and leaped across a small gully filled with rotting debris.

They pushed through the forest, splashing through pools of foul water. Mignon saw a fire ahead. She headed toward it and stopped at the edge of a large clearing. A dozen people dressed in white robes with white hooded masks covering their faces stood in the middle of the clearing. In the center a man held a torch high to show the cross burning in the grass. On a nearby stump stood a young Negro boy, maybe fifteen years old, maybe younger, his arms tied behind his back and a noose around his slender neck.

Mignon could smell the boy's fear, the men's excitement. She smelled the blood. Her fangs unsheathed. She took a step into the clearing, but Rachel grabbed her arm and pulled her back.

"The *Praetorium* has forbidden us to interfere in the affairs of humans," Rachel said.

Mignon jerked her arm out of Rachel's grip. "This is evil and we fight evil."

"No."

Mignon pushed her away. "Join me or stand aside. But do not stop me."

She stalked across the grassy clearing and into the very center of the waiting men. Her gaze flickered at the young boy. His eyes had rolled back into his head and he could barely stand. Blood dripped from the wounds on his face and arms.

"Gentlemen," Mignon said, "a party and you didn't invite me?"

On the edge of the circle, Rachel stood ready. Mignon smiled at her.

"This ain't yore bidness, nigra gal," one of the men said.

Mignon shrugged. "Yes, it is."

One of the men ran toward her and she sidestepped him, grabbed him by the arm and tossed him over her hip and then broke his arm. The man howled and writhed only inches from the burning grass. For a second, Mignon mentally thanked Max for making her go to Japan to study the martial arts when he realized where her *dos*, her talent lay.

Seeing a flash of metal in the firelight, Rachel sped past Mignon, grabbed the rifle, and with great calm, bent the barrel and handed the rifle back to the surprised man. "I don't want you to accuse me of stealing." The man stared at his rifle and slowly backed up as though trying to disappear into the shadows.

The men in the circle rushed toward her, and Mignon dropped

into a crouch and began to drop them all, kicking their feet out from under them, punching them, and breaking a few bones. When she came back to her senses, a half dozen men lay on the ground groaning and the rest had backed off to stare at her uncertainly.

The leader of the group stood off to one side. He started to clap. "Well done, missy." He stepped toward her. "Now let's see what you can do against a real man."

Mignon nodded and gestured for him to approach.

Rachel stopped her, a hand on her shoulder. "No, this one is mine." She reached toward the man and he almost cringed away. She grabbed him by the neck. Her face took on a dreamy look. "Jonathan Richmond," Rachel said softly. "You live at 472 Magnolia Avenue. You have three children—Andrew, Michael and Ruth. Your wife's name is Naomi."

Richmond groaned. He struggled to get away, but Rachel gripped his neck tighter.

"Now," Rachel continued, "if I even think that you might participate in this type of activity again, I will come to your house and I will slaughter your family one by one and I will force you to watch. I will save Andrew for last because he is your favorite. You will not be able to hide from me. I know your thoughts. I know your past. I know everything about you, including the fact that you have a secret bank account and a mistress in Biloxi. You will go home, and you are going to be a good citizen and a good husband. And I believe you are going to pay for this child's medical bills." She pointed at the young boy on the stump. She gripped Richmond tighter and forced him down to his knees and bent him backward. She let go and the man fell over. He curled into a fetal position, hugging his legs tight to his chest.

Rachel turned to face the men. "All of you," she pointed at them. The men who had been groaning fell silent, their eyes wide with fear. "I know where you live. I know your secrets. And most importantly, I know your weaknesses."

Mignon almost laughed. Never in her wildest dreams would she have thought petite Rachel could be so brutal. Nor would Mignon have known she was an *animus capio*, a soul harvester—the rarest gift among the vampires. She knew only one other.

Rachel waved her hand, "Be good boys, and never forget, I'm watching."

The clearing emptied quickly, the men disappearing as quickly as their wounded bodies would allow. Once the clearing was empty, Mignon approached the boy standing on the stump. Gently, she removed the rope from his neck. He slumped and she put her arms around him.

"Tell me," Mignon said as she soothed him and Rachel untied his hands. "What is your name?"

He drew himself up. "Martin."

"What were you doing so far from your home?" Mignon asked.

"Ma'am, I wanted to go fishing." He pointed toward the woods. "My mama said she had a taste for catfish."

"Don't you know," Mignon said harshly, "that it's not safe for our kind out here?"

"You whipped them pretty good." He rubbed his wrists. He gave Rachel a shy, almost adoring smile.

Rachel dabbed at the blood on his face with the hem of her shirt. "They were outnumbered, Martin."

He grinned. "Yes, ma'am. And thank you."

Rachel grabbed his arm, and then she smiled at him. She nodded and said, "Get on home, Martin, and next time, be more careful. And be a good boy for your mother. I expect to hear great things about you someday."

He looked startled but obediently ran across the clearing and disappeared down a path.

"Now I know why you wanted to be a *venator*," Mignon said to Rachel as she swung her canvas bag back over her shoulder.

Rachel's voice was harsh, "You don't know anything about me."

"I do, Capio. We all have our reasons. Max is a guardian. Solomon is an avenger. I'm a mother. You, my dear, are a reformed sinner."

Rachel laughed. "So tell me more."

"You don't look at people as food, but as victims. You're atoning for years of stealing peoples' thoughts and knowing their lives. Knowing what went wrong, what they loved, what was special about them. A little bit of you must have died every time you fed."

"Before I decided to become a *venator*, I used to feed on the worst of the worst. All I discovered was that monsters are made, rarely born."

"I understand." Mignon picked up her sword bag, glad she didn't have to kill to feed anymore. "One of my children is working on a process for refining pig blood to make it more satisfying."

"I look forward to that day when eating will be a pleasure again. For the first taste of your new form of blood, I will never tell anyone about this night."

"Thank you," Mignon said as they started across the clearing.

"You're welcome," Rachel said with a light laugh. "We done good. I think we should offer our services to the Allies and join the war effort in Europe. I think we could single-handedly end the war."

"That's a thought," Mignon said, thinking about her descendants in the Pacific. If she could offer her services to end the war and bring them home sooner, she would. She would do anything to keep her family safe.

CHAPTER THIRTEEN

Present Day — New Orleans

Long after Ryan left, Mignon relived the closeness of his body and the touch of his hands on her. She couldn't believe she'd broken one of the most sacrosanct rules of the *Praetorium*. *No sex between vampire and human.* She'd never betrayed the brethren. Until now.

Rolling over on her stomach she grabbed her pillow and inhaled the lingering scent of Ryan on her bed linens. Her raging desire for him returned. How could a mortal set her body to flame? The memory of their lovemaking almost made her blush. She had never responded so completely before.

Now she really would have to kill him and she felt deeply saddened. He knew too much about her and the brethren. But how could she take his life when he'd just touched a place in her soul that had been dead for decades? She felt alive with him. She felt whole. Almost at peace.

The door opened and Max entered. He sniffed the air and frowned. "You bedded the mortal." His voice held a touch of disappointment.

She rolled to sit on the edge of the bed, still feeling flushed from the lovemaking. "Are you going to tattle on me?"

"I should take your head. Not only did you have sex with him, you revealed the existence of the brethren. I was beginning to like him and now we must kill him."

She stood. "Not yet."

Max grabbed her by her arms. "Mignon, how could you be so stupid? I thought you knew better."

Max's hands on her body didn't feel the same as Ryan's. He gazed at her and then let her go. He reached for her robe and tossed it at her. "Cover yourself."

She pulled the robe on and belted it tightly around her waist. "He saved my life. That animal in the alley could have crushed me, then taken my head. Ryan killed him."

"So you paid the debt with your body?"

Mignon slapped him. His head snapped back and his eyes went dark with fury. She slapped him again.

Max grabbed her wrist, his fingers clamping around her like a vise. "How am I going to save you this time?"

She struggled to break his hold. "I'm not asking for your protection."

"Elder Turi is in the house. If I can smell the human on you, so can he. If I don't do something, the *Praetorium* will have you executed."

She lifted her chin and stared at him. "I'm not afraid of the true death."

"What about your family?"

For a second she faltered in her resolve. "They will survive."

"You're wrong. You're the only thing that stands between them and Charles. With you gone, the *Praetorium* will order their deaths because they know too much about who and what we are."

Mignon jerked away from him, rubbing her wrist. "Then what will the other vampires do for food? At least my family has found a way to feed us in a more civilized manner. I doubt the *Praetorium* will harm my children." Charles was the one who would kill them. If she did not stop him, he would exact a vengeance greater than anything he'd done before.

"Maybe not, but think about this. The *Praetorium* understands the extraction process. They would simply take over the business, or go back to the way things used to be between vampire and human."

"Isn't that why we're fighting Charles? To stop the horror of before!"

"You look at this as a battle between good and evil. In so many ways, you're still an innocent. This conflict between us and Charles is about power. The *Praetorium* understands that humans have a right to exist, but they will do what they must to preserve the brethren before they will do what they can to protect the humans."

This coming from her oldest friend. "Maximus, when did you become so knowledgeable?"

He didn't speak for a moment. He bowed his head. "I'm still a victim of your charm."

She rolled her eyes. "Liar."

Max chuckled. "Never with you."

He wouldn't kill her, nor would he kill Ryan. At least not today. Mignon kissed him lightly on the cheek. "After all these years, you still have the talent to surprise me."

He rubbed his temples. "Remember that when my head is on the block next to yours."

She smiled at him, knowing he would die before he betrayed her. "Are you giving me permission to love this human?"

"Perhaps I am." His hand dropped to his side. "I know that if I have to choose between you and the *Praetorium*, I will always choose you." He kissed her on the forehead and opened the door to the hall. "I will light a candle for you at evening Mass."

"You're going to church?"

"Except when I am with you, it's the only other place I still remember my humanity." He left, closing the door quietly behind him.

Mignon stared at the door, deeply aware of what Max had just committed himself to. Deeply aware that Max still loved her. He hadn't left her because he didn't love her any more, but because he did. Mignon felt pulled in a dozen different directions. Her loyalty to her family, her loyalty to the *Praetorium*, her feelings for Max and Ryan seemed all jumbled up inside her.

She loved Ryan. For a second she turned that concept around inside her mind. Ryan was a mortal man who would age and wither away if she stayed with him. One whose life would be forfeit if they were ever found out.

Their time together would be short, even assuming she could defend him to the *Praetorium* when they demanded his death. Assuming she could even bear to stay with him. Love with a mortal was too fragile to hold on to for long. In the distant past, other vampires had formed liaisons with mortals that had ended badly, usually with the mortal's death. One vampire had even taken his own life when her human mate had died, so despondent had she been over her lost love. That had been one reason the *Praetorium* had ruled no more affairs with humans.

Mignon could see the pitfalls of loving Ryan. Family was one thing. She was connected to them by blood and history, but bringing a mortal into her life was opening the door to unrelenting grief.

Never in all her two hundred fifty plus years had she felt so confused and vulnerable. Mignon didn't know what to do. Back in the old days, she could have hidden Ryan in the bayous. But with the world growing smaller by the minute, hiding him was no longer an option, even assuming Ryan loved her with the same intensity she did him.

She could change him, but the *Praetorium* had another whole set of strict rules about who could be changed and Mignon had already broken too many rules in the last few days.

She lay back on her bed and stared at the ornately carved plaster ceiling. Maybe if she emptied her mind, a solution would come. She closed her eyes, sought the quiet place in her soul and prayed for a guidance.

Ryan sat at his desk staring at the computer screen. The squad room bustled around him, but he pushed the noise into the back of his mind. He could almost feel the stupid smile on his face, the type of smile that sixteen-year-old boys had after their first bit of nookie.

His world had been rocked, the axis had been rotated, and he was in love with a vampire, a creature of myth and legend, and a bloodsucker who could easily kill him.

A shadow fell across him and Ryan looked up to find Lieutenant Barton standing over him. "So where are you on this case?"

Ryan rubbed his eyes. "I'm stumped, L.T."

"Dead scum I could live with, but dead cops are something else." The lieutenant snapped his fingers. "Have you found me the killer?"

If he only knew, Ryan thought. Think quick, Lattimore. Lie, you're good at it. "Sir, I have this confidential informant who has given me a clue that this might be a satanic, ritualistic, listening-to-Marilyn-Manson cult thing. I don't know how accurate the information might be, but I'm going to check it out."

A glimmer of hope lit Barton's eyes. "Bring in this informant. I want to talk to him."

Great, he'd just dug a bigger hole for himself. "She's not going to want to talk to you. Hell, I can barely get her to talk to me."

"So you're saying these murders are being committed by a group of satan-worshiping cult wackos?" Nielsen frowned.

"It's a strong possibility. You have to trust me on this, Lieutenant. I think I'm close to something, but if I bring everyone in for a chat, I feel I could blow the whole case."

Nielsen glared at him. "Are you going Dirty Harry on me? The last thing I need is a rogue cop."

"Sir, I'm not going rogue. I haven't broken a rule." Not exactly. More like sort of. Except for sleeping with his alleged informant and whacking the heads off a whole lot of folks. He could live with that. "If you've noticed, the body count has decreased." At least on the visible level. Ryan had the feeling that Charles was getting neater, not leaving the bodies around to resuscitate themselves twenty-four hours later.

"And how does that get me a cop killer?" Barton demanded.

"I'm going to get you one." Of course, they'd probably be in pieces, but his boss didn't need to know that part.

Barton rubbed his temples. "I don't need this shit. The mayor insisted I put together a task force. I still have him, the chief, the gaming commission and the chamber of commerce on my tail. No one wants to vacation in a city where heads are rolling around in the streets. I had my ass roasted by Ted Koppel last night. I am not a happy man. If only you would share what you have with Castle. He's certain you're holding out on him."

Ryan was holding out. What could he say? The vampires are coming? "I understand, sir. I'll try to cooperate with Sergeant Castle, but I'm not a task force kind of cop. Remember the Henderson case? You gave me space to work and I brought you a killer."

Barton jabbed a finger at Ryan. "I hate you, Lattimore. I hate you because you're good. And I hate you because you're right. And I hate you because even through this Maalox-induced coma I'm going to fall into any moment now, I know you'll solve this case. With or without Castle. So I'm gonna give you some leeway here. But I swear to God, if you mess this case up, your body won't have enough DNA left to be identified. I will take you out myself." Barton turned on his heel and stomped back to his office.

Ryan almost saluted. He turned back to his computer and tried to look busy while he thought. He'd gone so far over the line professionally and personally, he wondered if he could make the trip back.

Mignon was the most intriguing and interesting woman he'd ever met. To think she was a two-hundred and eighty-year-old vampire blew his mind. She didn't look a day over twenty-five. Yet she knew more about life and love than he would ever begin to know.

Love, that was an odd word coming from him. The only person he'd ever loved was his aunt. She'd molded him into the man he was. What would his aunt say? What she always said, follow your heart. He didn't have time to think about his heart.

He wanted Mignon. He needed Mignon, but he could never be with her. She was immortal, and he wasn't. At one time, she would have looked at him the same way he looked at a cheeseburger. In the back of his head, could he ever really forget that? Hell yes, he'd forgotten that last night, when she'd been naked and thirsty for him, her body responding to his touch. He'd almost forgotten his own name.

God, she was dead. Not dead, exactly, just different. He was a freak. He'd made love to a two-hundred-fifty-year old body. He was a kinky freak. Damn! He was sure he'd broken the law. And she'd responded to him. Hell, he'd brought a two and a half century old woman to climax. Several times. Now that was something to write *Penthouse* magazine about.

He felt turned on again. Just the thought of her slender, luxurious body wrapped around his made him want to leap over the desk and run right back to her house and crawl into her bed and lick his way up her sensuous, undead body. He was lost. His soul was going to hell forever. And he didn't think he cared. Maybe what he needed to do was grab his jacket and get back over to the house to see if last night had been just a fluke.

The sun began to rise by the time the fire was under control. Ursula stood outside the burned farmhouse. When she had returned to the farm with her own team, she'd evicted the county fire department who had been putting out the blaze and the sheriff's department who'd cordoned off the firehouse. Her own people had finished wetting down the structure and then had gone inside to search for the bodies.

The first body bag was brought out. She felt a knifing pain stab her and the word *expendable* popped into her head. Her men had not been expendable. They'd had lives, families, dreams and ambitions. The colonel was wrong. Using existing vamps to do the dirty work was fine with her. But changing over loyal soldiers and making sure they died when they'd completed their mission was immoral.

A second body bag followed the first. Two soldiers tried to hold it carefully, but the corner slipped and the bag slumped to the ground. She heard the click of bones and felt a moment's panic.

She didn't know what to do. She thought about resigning her commission in protest. But that would accomplish nothing. The program would continue without her. She had to talk to someone. She thought about Lattimore, but decided he was not to be trusted. Considering the way he'd looked at Mignon, he was in love with her. Her thoughts moved to Mignon. Though Ursula felt a grudging admiration for the female vampire, she thought the vamp was an act-now-and-ask-questions-later type of person. She didn't know Max well enough to even consider him. Solomon came to mind, but she decided against him.

She needed someone with the kind of wisdom that would give her answers. Elder Turi. She could talk to him. He'd been gentle and understanding. Even though he'd been able to enter her mind and see her thoughts, he hadn't trespassed into private areas.

As the last body bag was loaded into the meat wagon, she knew what she had to do. The problem would be getting into the vamp's house unseen. The surveillance van had been returned to its assigned spot. Even though the team couldn't hear anything going on inside the house, or even tap into the phone network, they could still document who went in and out. The most prominent name on the visitor's roster was Ryan Lattimore.

Ursula parked three blocks away. She'd determined that though the van was in an excellent spot to see a large section of the yard as well as the house, the team had a blind spot. And she used the blind spot to approach the back of the house and knock on the kitchen door.

A tall man opened the door. He resembled Mignon around the eyes and Ursula had the feeling he was related. It occurred to her that Mignon could have had children before she'd been turned. The idea that Mignon had a tie to the mortal world shook Ursula.

"I would like to see Elder Turi," Ursula said.

The man looked her up and down, then nodded and stood aside. "You'll find him down the hall, first door on the left."

Elder Turi sat in a small sitting room that overlooked a deeply shadowed side garden. Orange flowers pushed against the glass. Elder Turi closed the book he had been reading and smiled gently at Ursula. "You wanted to see me, child?"

"Yes. You are old, aren't you? Four thousand years old?"

He chuckled. "You came all this way to check out my age?"

She needed him to be wise and profound and provide her with the answers she required. "I need to talk to someone."

"And my age qualifies me?" He gestured for her to sit across from him. "I'm honored."

She sat down, feeling nervous and almost shy. How did one show a four-thousand-year-old vampire respect? "I have a problem."

"One that I can help you with, perhaps?"

"I don't know. But you are the only person I could think of who might help me sort through my problem."

"I understand." His voice was gentle and unassuming. "Do you wish me to read your mind or not?"

Ursula mulled over what she needed to say. "No mind reading. I want to talk it out." She fell silent as she forced order on her thoughts. "I've come across some information that I think you should know."

He nodded, waiting patiently.

She launched haltingly into what the colonel had revealed to her. As she came to the end, she said, "Changing soldiers into vampires who self-destruct at the end of a mission sounds like murder to me."

Elder Turi was silent for a long time. He stared out the window at the orange flowers. "As a soldier, aren't you willing to forfeit your life for your country?"

"Yes. But I have a choice. I don't think the colonel and those above him will give these men a choice."

"You didn't come here to ask me my opinion on what you should do."

"Dammit, I'm a soldier and make life and death decisions every day. Why isn't this self-destructing soldier concept sitting well with me?" The whole idea felt morally wrong. She'd just lost four good men, and had seen vampires in a new light. They weren't all blood-sucking, murderous fiends.

Mignon and Solomon were caring, compassionate people. She didn't know about Max, but how bad could he be if he hung out with Solomon and Mignon? And Lattimore? Did he hang with Mignon because she wasn't as evil as Ursula had been told? Or did he just lust after her body? The vibes coming off those two were enough to ignite Ursula's underwear. She wondered if they even knew how attracted to each other they were.

Elder Turi nodded slowly. "What do you jeopardize if you attempt to stop this plot?"

"Career, life, future—nothing much."

"You do not play with small stakes, do you?" Suddenly he laughed. "Oh, I think I just made a joke."

Ursula found herself laughing along with him. Jokes, obviously, were a rare thing for Elder Turi. Vampire humor, who knew?

"You could kill your colonel," Elder Turi suggested.

She shook her head. "He's not pulling the strings. Someone else will just take his place. Probably me."

"What about discrediting him in some way?"

"How would I do that? If I go public, you and your whole society will be at risk, assuming I can even find anyone to believe me." And the public would panic over it, or not believe it at all. She'd probably be committed to a straightjacket while the big boys kept on with their vile plans. She felt caught between a rock and a hard place. But a small idea generated. If the colonel weren't around, she would probably be promoted to take his place. What could she do if she were in charge?

She wet her lips before continuing, "If I could get rid of the colonel somehow and get promoted to take his place, would you be willing to help me if I needed a terrorist, a drug dealer, or some gang-bangers taken care of?" She'd said it, the deepest darkest thought in her mind. The only way to get rid of Hammett was to kill him with a little friendly fire. The very idea took her breath away and filled her heart with terror. Would the end justify the means? Her mama would not be proud of her at the moment.

Elder Turi patted her hand. "Child, are you making a moral judgement?"

His touch was like parchment, yet his hand felt almost warm on hers.

"Flying a plane into a building," she said, "shooting up a school yard, or selling drugs to kids is bad enough. But Colonel Hammett and his buddies aren't worried about racial or social injustice, or working for the betterment of the future of mankind. These men are stone-ass killers, and they need to be treated this way. I have no problem killing them. What I have a problem with is using innocent soldiers to do it in a way that destroys the soldiers, too."

Elder Turi looked troubled. "Do you think vampires are without a conscience? My *venator*s are just as troubled by killing one of their own as you are. The deaths on their souls weigh them down. Taking a head is always a last resort."

She'd just added a second moral dilemma to her conflict. She'd never once considered that vampires didn't fit the mold Charles had built for the military. She'd never even considered that they had their own moral code. "Charles Rabelais doesn't have morals. He turned a child molester into a vampire and set that evil free to prey on children. You put down a rabid dog, because there is no cure. Frankly, I'm sorry he's only going to die once. I came to you because I need help. There is only one way to get rid of this plan without exposing you or the military. And that way is getting rid of the colonel. I'm next in line in the chain of command. If I can offer your cooperation to the big brass as an alternative to experimenting on innocent soldiers, maybe they'll listen to me."

"You didn't come to me for advice, child." Elder Turi looked troubled. "You just want me to agree to your plan and absolve you from sin."

"I'm not Catholic."

"Maybe not, but politically you're considering something just short of a coup."

"I can't let the colonel and his handlers continue this way. You're telling me that I'm making moral judgements. What are they doing? They're not asking these soldiers if they want to be turned into vampires just for the purposes of a mission. One man for how many?"

"You are faced with a difficult decision."

She felt a threat of tears in her eyes and she forced them all back. She was a soldier. Soldiers didn't cry. "I'm looking at the big picture here. The colonel was my mentor. Five days ago, if he'd told me then what was being planned, I would have been all gung ho."

"What changed your mind?"

"I saw my men slaughtered in front of me without pity. Then I saw Mignon take that child and comfort her. I didn't want to think of you as people with a conscience, but you do care. In the battle between good and evil you have come down on the good side."

"You don't really know us."

He was right, but she trusted her gut instinct and her instinct told her she could trust him. "I know the important stuff. I was a threat to you and you didn't kill me. Lattimore was a threat and you didn't take him out either." Getting rid of her and Lattimore would have been easy enough—a freak accident, a random shooting. No one would have been the wiser.

"I pity you. You are taking a path that won't be easy. Why not go to your superiors and tell them you've struck a deal with the brethren for their help."

She had the odd feeling that if Colonel Hammett knew she had made contact with the enemy, she could kiss her ass good-bye. If she could have seen her way clear, she might have tried to talk to those above Hammett. "I'm taking the only path available right now." Her words were braver than she felt. Too much was at stake to falter now.

He touched her cheek and his eyes went unfocused. She felt the way she'd felt when he'd first read her mind, but different, as though he were giving her something instead of taking. She accepted his offering even though she had no idea what he'd given her and felt chilled.

"What did you do?" she asked when his hand fell away from her face and his gaze was once again sharp.

"I gave you a gift." He looked grave and tired as he slumped back in his chair.

"What kind of gift?"

"You will know when you need it." He closed his eyes and leaned his head back against the chair. "You need to leave now."

She stood and kissed him on his cheek, surprised that she could do so with such ease. Twenty-four hours ago she would have killed him without a second thought. She slipped out of the room and then out of the house the way she had come. She would wonder later what Elder Turi had given her. Now she had to get back.

Mignon heated her pig blood cocktail in the microwave. The phone rang and she let it ring. After a few seconds, Lucas answered and she listened to the distant rumble of his voice. The only thing she could make out was that he was talking to David and she wondered what David had found out.

After a minute, Lucas stopped talking. The microwave beeped and Mignon took the glass out and sipped at it. Pig blood would never be as satisfying as human blood, but it worked.

After a few more minutes, Lucas entered the kitchen. "David just called."

"What did David have to say?"

"Blunt as always." He poured himself coffee. "David couldn't come up with much of anything. Everything is classified and he's not high enough in the food chain yet to demand a look see. But he did find some information about Major Carlson and Colonel Hammett which linked them to a research station in a fairly remote area in the Blue Ridge mountains."

Mignon finished her blood, rinsed her glass and set it in the dishwasher. "Vampire research?"

Lucas shrugged. "David didn't find that out. He's going to need more time to get the details. This stuff is big time top secret."

Mignon frowned. "Let's assume it's vampire research. Elder Turi says that Major Carlson is deeply conflicted about this disposable vampire army she's found out about."

"Do you think she could get information for us?"

Mignon shook her head. "I don't think this is the time to push her. She's at a major crossroads and Elder Turi feels she should be handled very carefully." Elder Turi had told Mignon about Carlson's visit. Mignon marveled that the woman had been bold enough to enter the house to seek out Elder Turi.

"Where does that leave us with Charles?" Lucas asked.

"Charles is still our primary objective. Though our mission has become more convoluted than even the *Praetorium* thought it would be. For now, we'll just concentrate on Charles and end his threat. Then we'll deal with the military's plans." She could only do one thing at a time and for the moment, neutralizing Charles had to come first.

"We have a lead on Charles Rabelais," Colonel Hammett said.

Ursula sat across from the colonel. "What did you find out?"

"He's been traced to a warehouse near the river." He handed Ursula a report and she read it quickly. "This calls for a full offensive."

Ursula nodded. "But I'm a few quarts low on manpower. Do we have the time to wait for replacements?"

"We have to act immediately."

"Colonel, would you care to join me?" She felt a huge chasm of fear opening under her feet. Once she started on this road, there would be no going back. A chill ran down her spine. Did she know what she was doing? She had to keep in mind what was at stake.

He grinned, looking totally delighted. "And relive my glory days? I haven't seen action since the Gulf War."

Ursula wet her lips. Her throat felt dry and she worried he would read her mind like Elder Turi and see through her invitation to the danger it posed for him. "I would be honored to have you accompany us, sir." She almost wished he'd say no. But he wouldn't. Colonel Hammett was a glory hound. If he could be in the thick of things and look good to his superiors, he'd do whatever it took.

"I would be honored to accept." His voice was eager.

Ursula realized she had been holding her breath, hoping against hope he wouldn't come. But now the die was cast. "Very good, sir." This one decision would cost him his life. "If you'll excuse me, I have to work out our operations plan for tonight."

She rose and left the colonel's office for her own. She closed the door and slumped against it. She'd taken the first step. Whatever Elder Turi had done for her, she could only hope it had something to do with courage.

CHAPTER FOURTEEN

Ryan set his burger bag on the table. He unwrapped a huge hamburger dripping with red juices and topped with a ton of bacon and a thick slab of cheddar cheese. He started to bite into it but stopped. Max, Mignon and Solomon stared at him. Lowering his burger he stared back at them. "What?"

Max eyed the box of fries. "I love french fries."

"Have some. I don't mind." Ryan offered the cardboard container. "We should all carbo-load before heading out tonight. Do vampires carbo-load?"

Mignon grimaced. "Ryan, we don't need regular food."

"Have some bacon anyway." He flipped open the top of the hamburger bun and pulled off a slice of bacon and handed it to her. "I like mine extra-crispy. I want to hear the bacon crunch." He waved the slice at her.

Mignon leaned over, her cleavage showing. She took a bite and a look of delight came over her face. "I'm going to pay for this, but it's heavenly."

Ryan couldn't believe he felt so at ease with them. "And I thought you didn't eat food."

Mignon finished her bacon and delicately licked her fingers. "We can eat, it just doesn't provide us with the proper sustenance, so most of us never bother again."

A city map was spread over the table and alongside it, a list of the addresses Ryan had tracked down through the real estate records. "Too bad," Ryan gestured at the list of warehouses, "we can't just burn the whole city down."

"Then where would all the rats live?" Mignon asked. She wiped a spot of bacon grease from the corner of her lips.

Watching her distracted him for a second. He remembered the

things she'd done to him with that luscious mouth. "I was just trying to think quick and efficiently. I'm ex-military. I was taught to walk in, blow the place to bits and then leave."

Solomon chuckled. "I like to blow things up."

"I knew that about you," Ryan replied.

"Charles is on the run. We've almost stopped him. He's turned no new recruits in the last forty-eight hours, and most of the old recruits are dead. Now it's just a matter of smoking the bear from its lair."

"I had the idea that he would need a quiet, out-of-the-way place, yet still central to the city. I traced every change of ownership in the last six months to either legitimate businesses or long standing residents of the city. But these addresses here have cloudy ownership and the paperwork is hinky and hinky ain't good." Ryan studied the map of the city. "For all of his vampire skills, Charles is a serial killer and his brain operates like one. He goes after a certain kind of victim. He has a certain method. Most of the victims have been within a five mile radius of the warehouse district."

"How did you come up with this?" Mignon asked.

"When I stopped reacting to all the hoodoo voodoo shit and started thinking like a cop again, I realized that Charles has a comfort zone." He slammed a finger down on the map.

Mignon stared at him. "A comfort zone?"

"Obviously you have no serial killer profilers among your brethren. This is textbook serial killer *modus operandi*. If I hadn't been blinded by all this other-worldly, blood-sucking, head-lopping crap, I would have figured this all out sooner." He pointed at the map. "Charles is right here." He took a pen from the table and drew a circle around several adjoining buildings.

"How do you know?" Mignon asked.

"This is the kind of stuff cops are taught at the academy. Don't you watch TV?"

Mignon shook her head. "I've always believed it's a mindless waste of time."

"A world of information." Ryan felt excitement course through him. He was cop man again. This was what he loved to do.

Solomon leaned forward. "Do we blow up these buildings?"

Ryan grinned. "I do like your style."

Mignon held up a hand. "We don't blow up any buildings. There's no guarantee we'll kill Charles. We need a better plan than just blowing everything to hell. We have an hour until sunset."

Ryan studied the map. "What would happen if you missed Charles? If he got away, would he spend the next couple of decades planning for his next action and then start this shit all over again?"

"I don't know," Mignon replied. "I don't think the military is going to wait for another twenty years. And Charles has never been known for his patience. Once he puts something into motion, he's relentless until the end."

"Don't you have a game plan for this?" He couldn't believe the brethren had never planned for a defection from their ranks.

Mignon shook her head. "Except when absolutely necessary, we don't interact with mortals. With the exception of a few we've seen mortals as enemy or prey, but never as buddies."

"Charles seems to have lowered his standards. Isn't he the smart one?"

Max shrugged. "We become incredibly arrogant in our old age."

"And that is where you made your first mistake." Ryan wondered just how many vamps existed. Mortals had the upper edge simply because they outnumbered the brethren. Obviously, Mignon hadn't noticed how outflanked her whole society was. Charles saw mortals as a necessary evil. Why else would he throw in with the military?

Max glanced at the weapons lined up by the door. "It's not like this isn't the first time such a rebellion has happened among the brethren."

"I don't care who you are," Ryan said, "you can't walk around this life thinking you're invincible. Someone bigger and tougher than you are is going to show up at some time and put you on the wrong end of a smackdown."

"When this is over," Max said, "I think I will have to ponder the questions of our future security. Society has changed a great deal in the last thirty years, and obviously the brethren cannot continue to be isolated from the rest of the world."

"I have a feeling the human race won't last if you spend a hundred years too many trying to figure out your place. And then what will you do for food?"

Mignon said sharply, "We don't feed on humans."

"Only," Ryan said, "because you choose not to at this moment in time. What happens if there's mad pig disease?"

Mignon shot him a sharp glance. "Are you trying to be funny?"

"I'm being realistic." But he could see that he'd given her something to think about.

They left the house after dark. Ryan drove to the warehouse district. Mignon followed him in her car. She parked behind him, a block away from the most likely of the warehouses. Three brick warehouses stood side by side, each one an invitation to Charles's nighttime activities.

The first warehouse was locked up tight. Mignon easily broke the lock and they checked inside. The warehouse was huge and empty.

"Clean." Ryan trained his flashlight at the mouse droppings littering the floor. "Let's check the one next door."

The second warehouse was open and though it showed no signs of habitation, Ryan could feel something different about it. He stepped into the cavernous room, his feet crunching on dirt and plastic disks of some kind.

Ryan looked around. "What do you think?" He flashed his light on the empty corners.

Mignon sniffed the air. "Keep looking," she instructed.

He inched his way through the darkness, flashing his light at the walls. A door showed and he opened it to find a pile of dead bodies neatly laid out on the floor. He counted them. Forty men and women lay in a neat row. He recognized the first three faces he saw. All of them were wanted for petty crimes. Another face further on he recognized as being on the FBI's most wanted list. "No wonder there have been no new kills to find. Charles is stacking his army here, waiting for them to hatch."

"I think," she said, "your idea of blowing up this place is a good one."

"It's not like I have any explosives just lying around the house waiting for me to make them into a big bang bomb."

Mignon frowned at him. "We don't need explosives." She pulled a cigarette lighter out of her pocket and tossed it to him. "Just behead them all and start a fire. There's plenty of fuel here."

"Sounds good to me." He walked down the long line of bodies and felt the hair on the back of his neck stand straight up. Something was so strange about all of the bodies racked out as though they were in the morgue.

Mignon started back toward the door.

"Where are you going?"

"You don't need my help. I'm heading over to Jackson Park. Charles will be where there are people."

"Are these going to rise soon? I don't want to be hacking away with no backup."

Mignon studied them. "They won't rise for another twenty-four hours. You can take care of them. I'll take care of Charles."

"Hold on, Mignon."

Mignon stopped and turned around, raising an eyebrow.

"I want to be in the mix, not mopping up."

She grabbed him by the shirt and pulled her toward him. "Stay safe, my love. I'll put you in the mix later." She yanked him to her and planted a hard kiss on his mouth.

After two brief seconds she let him go. His head reeled with desire. "Okay, fine."

Before Ryan could voice another protest, Mignon disappeared into the night, melting into the darkness as though she were a part of it.

Ryan turned back to the bodies and hefted his axe. This was peasant duty. He was a bad-ass. He'd killed himself some vamps, and here he was hacking off heads, stuck in the background. He wanted to be with Mignon, killing, not doing the clean up. He started at the end of the row and started hacking off heads.

"I know you," he said to an inert body. "You're Moe Moe Borelli, small time loan shark and leg breaker. You're an all-around asshole, Borelli." He hacked the head off. "Dammit. The vampire mob. That's funny."

As he finished the row, his cell phone rang. He was tempted to answer the phone with a flip, 'Lattimore's Mortuary. You slice them, we dice them.' But he didn't think the caller would think it funny.

He flipped open the phone. "Yeah."

"This is Mary. I'm over by the port authority. I think I've found your bad guy."

"Mary, you're supposed to be at the station protecting yourself from paper cuts."

"Shut up and get over here."

"Where?"

She gave him an address that was only ten minutes away and disconnected.

Ryan dialed Mignon's phone. Instead of getting her, he got her voice mail and left a message with the address Mary had given him. He disconnected and went about finishing up the next row of soon-to-be vampire criminals. When he was done, he pulled cardboard boxes into a pile near some lumber. He opened the lighter and poured a little fluid over the boxes and the lumber and closed the lighter and then lit the flame. He set the lighter down in a tiny puddle of lighter fluid. He stood back and watched the cardboard catch and then the wood. He backed out the door as a post caught fire and spread up to the roof. He closed the door and ran to his car, feeling a surge of adrenaline. *Okay, Charles, here I come.*

Ryan opened the door to the warehouse. The inside was dark and gloomy, though patches of moonlight lit the trash-strewn floor. He pulled his mag flashlight out of his pocket and flashed the beam over the shadows.

"Mary," he called.

No answer. He had the right address. As he advanced into the empty warehouse, he heard the rustlings of mice and rats in the corners and the rafters.

"Mary," he called again.

"Ryan," she answered in a faint voice. "Over here."

He followed the sound of her voice and found her in a small room with desks pushed against the wall. She stood in the center of the room, a soft light casting deep shadows over her. She wore a black tuxedo suit with a white shirt and stiletto shoes. "Ryan, I'm glad you're here."

"You're all dressed up."

"I have a late dinner date."

She gave him a closed mouth smile that made him go cold with tension. "Okay. Let's get this over with. I don't want you to be late."

"Follow me." She headed toward the back of the room.

"You're not supposed to be here, so you hang back and let me take this guy." He pulled out his sword.

"I won't get in the way." She opened a door that led to a small hallway.

He followed her down the hallway to another door. She opened the door and stood aside. As he stepped into the dark room, the thought that Mary hadn't questioned his sword surfaced. Why hadn't she been surprised? He stepped into the room, trying to ignore the feeling of danger deep in the pit of his stomach. The light went on and he found himself facing a half dozen vampires who closed in on him.

As Ryan glanced back at Mary, he felt a jolt that flung him across the room. He hit the wall hard and slid down, his ears ringing. He grabbed at the sword, but one of the vamps kicked it away.

Mary walked over to him. She opened her mouth and he saw elongated fangs slide out. "Surprise."

She hit him again and the room went black.

Ryan opened his eyes. His head hurt. As he tried to get his bearings, he realized he was tied with ropes and hanging from the rafters of a large, damp and empty room. The heavy rope bit into his wrist and his fingers had lost all feeling. He was also cold. He glanced down and found himself completely naked. He licked his lips and felt a trickle of blood oozing from the corner of his mouth.

This is not good. A shiver started in his belly and radiated outward. The memory of Mary and her fangs left him feeling sick. Mary had been turned into a vamp. At least now he knew her secret.

He looked up to study the ropes, trying to figure a way out. Slowly he started to wiggle his fingers to get the blood pumping back in them. If he could get them to work right, he could get himself free.

The door opened and Ryan forced himself to strop moving. A tall slender man entered the room. Dark blond hair framed his thin, cold face. Ryan had seen this man before, the first night he and Mignon had gone hunting.

"Detective Lattimore," the man said in a formal, oddly-accented voice. "We finally have a chance to talk. Mary has told me so much about you."

"You must be Charles," Ryan said with a bravado he was far from feeling.

Charles simply smiled. "And you are my rival."

"Rival?"

"For the affections of the lovely Mignon."

"This isn't about world domination?"

"That is so mundane," Charles responded. "This is about the affairs of the heart." He pressed one hand to his chest.

"Vampires in love. How droll. So you're stalking her."

"Stalking?" Charles looked puzzled. "I'm wooing her."

Ryan didn't know whether to laugh or not. "Murder and mayhem. That's your way of wooing? That's peculiar. I don't understand why you consider me a rival. I'm no threat to you."

"I suspect you have her heart, but after tonight, you'll be a memory."

Mary entered the room and handed a long, lethal looking whip to Charles. "Can I watch?"

BLOOD LUST

Charles nibbled her ear. "Of course, my darling."

"Mary," Ryan said, "what the hell is wrong with you? You're a cop, sworn to uphold the laws."

"I turned in my resignation tonight. I'm embarking on a new life." She laughed, almost merrily, an eerie light in her eyes.

Ryan detected a faint note of uncertainty in her voice. She might be embarking on a new life, but she wasn't certain she'd made the right decision.

Mary approached Ryan. She looked different. She had a slinky, cat-like manner to her. Her hair was shinier, and her skin had a luminescent glow to it. Being a vampire had refined her prettiness.

She ran a hand over Ryan's chest and down to his groin. "I've always wanted to sleep with you, but you never gave me the time of day."

"You were my partner."

"Yes, we were buddies, weren't we? Good old Mary."

"All that stuff Internal Affairs said about you is true, isn't it. You were on the take."

"I like beautiful things." She touched a necklace about her neck. Diamonds winked against the gold. "Now I have the means to get them."

"What do you want from me?"

She pulled his head toward her and ran her tongue up his throat, his chin, to the corner of his lips. She licked at the blood and then stepped back. "Dinner."

He was going to be her dinner. Not what he had in mind. He kicked out with his legs. Mary punched him in the stomach and he swung away from her. Pain ripped through him as he felt his muscles strain under his own weight.

"My dear," Charles said, "we agreed. For the moment he is bait." He stroked her cheek. "You may have him—later."

Charles unfurled the whip. Ryan gulped. Be a man, he told himself. What was a little pain? Charles smiled as he drew his arm back. Ryan felt the sharp sting of the whip across his shoulder and chest. He bit down to stop from crying out.

Mary clapped her hands. "Harder," she said. "Harder, Charles."

Charles flicked the whip again and Ryan felt the stinging pain across his back. The room tilted on its axis and he couldn't help wondering if he could hold out until the cavalry came.

Mignon prowled the square. Max and Solomon would be joining her shortly . Charles was being elusive. Usually, Mignon could detect small clues to his presence, but not tonight. The square was very different at night with the tourists gone. The vendors and tourists had given way for the night people.

A few women lounged against the wrought iron fence facing Decatur. Whenever a car slowed, they would saunter out of the shadows to show off their wares.

Music blasted from a nearby bar. Across the street toward the French Market, a street band played to late night patrons at Café Du Monde.

Tension stretched Mignon's nerves. She could never remember having been so on edge. The range of Charles' grand plan astonished her. He'd been planning this coup for years. Mignon shuddered at the scope of it. So many vampires running loose in the world would jeopardize humanity. Didn't Charles understand what would happen if he prevailed?

Despite Ryan's flippant remarks, the vampire community needed the humans. They had a symbiotic relationship that would become seriously unbalanced if Charles had his way.

Deep in an alley's shadows, she leaned against a pole and pulled out her cigarettes, then remembered she'd given her lighter to Ryan. She put the cigarettes away reluctantly. The doors to the cathedral swung open and the late night Mass let out.

She reached in her pocket for her cell phone. Ryan should have finished his little job by now. She flipped open the phone and realized she'd turned it off. Damn! She turned the phone on and waited for it to connect to the service. She started to dial again, only to have it ring.

The number that appeared on the display was Ryan's. But when she answered she found Charles on the other end. A shiver went through her.

"My sweet Mignon," Charles said.

"Charles. How did you get Ryan's phone?"

"The old-fashioned way. I took it."

"Where is Ryan?"

"He's hanging around." Charles laughed. "Had I known a killing spree would bring you within my grasp, I would have done this years ago."

"Charles," she said, "stop now, before things get out of hand."

"But I'm having so much fun." He laughed. "Why did you choose a mortal for your lover when you could have had a god?"

"I didn't choose you, you bought me."

"Details. You're always obsessed with details."

"Where are you?"

"Come find me."

"I'm going to enjoy taking your head."

He laughed again. "You can try. Come alone and I might consider letting him go. I can be generous. Consider it a token of my affection. After all, I meant something to you once." He hung up.

Mignon noticed she had voice mail. She dialed into her box and heard Ryan's voice giving her the address. She debated calling Max and Solomon, but they had their own jobs to do, so she called Ursula Carlson. Mignon was going to need help and Carlson was the only person Mignon felt could provide that. She reached Carlson's voice mail and left a message.

Mignon sprang into action, darting across the street toward the parking lot for her car.

Ursula broke her men into teams of two with orders to work from the outside in. First secure the doors and then search inside. She truly hoped Charles was here.

The colonel stood at her side. He looked confident and calm. Ursula wondered what he would think if he knew she intended to kill him tonight. She felt the weight of her untraceable gun against the side of her ankle.

"Kill everyone," Ursula said, "except Charles."

Her men nodded in understanding. They checked their equipment and drew their swords. Then the teams faded into the darkness.

"Colonel," she said, "I would be honored to have you as my partner."

He nodded at her, looking pleased. "I can't wait to see some heads roll. I've been behind the scenes for too many years. A man loses his edge."

"Can't have that, sir," Ursula replied. "You take point, if you would please." She hefted her own sword. The sword was an elegant weapon, she thought as she gripped it tightly and started toward the door she'd assigned for herself. She almost felt Charles inside.

She opened the door and Hammett darted inside the warehouse, covering the corridor. She paused for a moment to grab her gun out of the ankle holder. Her heart raced and her palms were slick with sweat. She sighted on the colonel. Before she could fire, an arm reached out from a doorway and grabbed the colonel to pull him into a dark room. Ursula froze for a millisecond. That wasn't the game plan.

She heard the snap of bone and galvanized into action, racing toward the door. As she approached, the colonel's limp body fell across the threshold and a man stepped over him into the corridor.

"Good evening," Solomon said to Ursula.

"You killed him."

Solomon simply smiled. "Elder Turi told me what you planned."

Ursula shook her head. "This was not your mission."

He touched her on the face. "I could not let you do something you might find immoral. The blemish on your soul would haunt you for the rest of your life."

"I was resigned to doing what needed to be done. Elder Turi didn't trust me."

A sadness filled his eyes. "You have chosen a difficult path, Major.

I don't envy you, but I could help you."

In the back of her head, she knew she was both grateful and humbled. "But the blemish is now on your soul." Assuming he had a soul.

"I have killed many in my life. What's one more?" He shrugged and started down the corridor. "Are you coming? The night is not over."

She started after him while attempting to bottle up her guilt. Hammett was dead and she felt nothing for him.

The warehouse loomed black and sinister. One of the bay doors was open, beckoning to Mignon. Right! Go in the front door and walk into an ambush. Did Charles think she was that stupid? Not even for Ryan would she forget why she was here.

As she studied the warehouse, Charles's presence pounded at her. He was powerful. More powerful than Mignon. Yet he was a young vampire, too. He'd only been turned a few months before he'd turned her. How had he amassed such power?

She decided that the roof offered more possibilities. She jumped up and stood on the edge of the roof staring at the skylights. An old air-conditioning unit sat to one side.

She sniffed the air, catching Ryan's scent mingled with the scent of blood. Was she too late? Had Charles already killed him. Probably not. Charles needed Ryan and would kill him later.

She walked across the roof to a door that opened to a staircase leading down. She eased her way down the steps until she came to another door. She opened the door and found herself on a catwalk suspended high above the warehouse.

She stepped out onto the catwalk. The warehouse interior was dark except for a greenish glow in the center.

"Come, Mignon," Charles coaxed. "I know you are here. I can smell you. I can feel you."

She jumped down from the catwalk and approached the green

glow. Ryan lay to one side, completely naked, his hands secured behind his back with his own handcuffs, and his face pale, but she could see the shallow rise and fall of his chest. He was still alive, but blood covered his body and oozed into a thickening puddle beneath him. His eyes were slitted open over the gag which covered his mouth. His clothes lay in a puddle near him, his gun on top. Fury rose in her.

Charles stood at the edge of the illuminated area holding a bloodied whip in his hand. He'd always reminded her of a beautiful angel—an angel of death.

Mignon felt a stab of revulsion for him. Any feelings she'd once had for him were long gone. Before he'd turned, he'd shown affection for her, but it had been tinged with a cruelty she had never understood, a cruelty that had extended to her children. He'd sold them because he'd wanted her defenseless and alone. But the opposite had happened. He had not anticipated the bond she had with her children and the lengths she would go to find them.

Charles smiled at her. "You always look at me with such hate. Do you know how much your lack of love for me hurts? You still hold the past against me, Mignon. I gave you the greatest gift of all." He flung his hands outward.

"Yes, you did. You gave me my children."

For a second he looked surprised. "No, I gave you immortality."

"You cursed me with immortality. Do you know how hard it was to watch my loved ones age die over and over again?"

He tilted his head curiously, frowning slightly. "But I gave you power."

"You wanted to make me a monster like yourself."

"But being a monster has served me well over the years. As if you have suffered? You are wealthy, eternally beautiful, and powerful. Not even I can resist such a combination."

Mignon shook her head. "None of those things meant anything to me. All that mattered was keeping my family safe and together. You never did know who or what I was. You owned my body, but you never understood what was in my heart."

Charles glanced at Ryan. "Does the detective know? Does he know what's in your heart? When I am finished training him, he will forget all of what is in your heart. I have learned my lessons well. While you and your little *Praetorium* were out trying to protect the world, I learned the secrets of the mind. Anyone, no matter who they are, can be turned to evil." He gestured at Ryan. "Your detective is a killer. An assassin. He spent many years learning the art. He'll be an asset to my cause."

Mignon's heart throbbed with fury. "Why do you want to dissolve the *Praetorium* and make cattle out of mortals?"

"I have no desire to rule the world. Who gives a damn about mortals?"

"Then what was all this for?"

"What I have always wanted. You. Back in my life. Back in my bed."

"This is your idea of courtship?"

Charles glared at her. "You left me. I loved you. I still love you."

Mignon couldn't stop the laughter. "You must be joking. You've turned all these people just to show me how much you love me."

"You needed to see my power. You would never return willingly."

"I'm not coming back at all."

"Not even to save your lover?" He gestured at Ryan. "Join me now. Whether he lives or dies depends on your decision."

Mignon shuddered. Not even for Ryan would she join Charles. If he turned Ryan, she would kill them both, though her heart would hurt forever. "Either way, I lose him."

Charles chuckled. "My dear, you have always been such a moralistic person. Change him, and you'll have him forever. I don't mind if you have a diversion, as long as you always come back to me."

"He doesn't want what we are."

"If you don't change him, you'll watch him wither and die. Make your choice."

She unsheathed her sword. No matter what her feelings were for Ryan, or whatever else she wanted, Charles must die. His own sword seemed to leap into his hand and he backed away from her, crouching, preparing for her onslaught.

They met in the middle of the green light, swords clashing, sparks flying from the edges. The metallic sound reverberated through the warehouse. Shock waves radiated up her arms. She thrust and parried. Charles stepped back, a small smile on his lips that never wavered.

Mignon didn't think she could win against him, but she steeled herself for the conflict. Ryan's life hung in the balance. She could not let him die. She could not let Charles change him, though she doubted that Charles understood Ryan's mind. Deep inside he was an honorable man. Ryan might be a killer, but he killed for reasons that Mignon thought were noble. If he had the evil that Charles thought was there, then he would have already gravitated to Charles.

Charles leaped away from her. She pressed her advantage. Her love for Ryan lent her strength and when they met again, their swords crossing, she deflected his blow and a look of surprise crossed his face. After all this time, she could still surprise Charles.

They danced around each other.

"You are the most beautiful woman I have ever known," Charles said. "Come to me. Join me."

His words bombarded her. "No."

Out of the corner of her eye, she saw Ryan move. He crawled slowly and painfully toward his clothes. Mignon knew she had to keep Charles's attention on her. He tugged at the holster on top of his clothes, trying to free his gun. Then Charles blocked her vision by throwing himself against her with all his strength.

Mignon staggered back. Her whole body shuddered from the shock of his attack and she fell to her knees. He stood over her, a malevolent smile on his face.

Charles raised his sword. "No mercy."

So this is how her life would end, on her knees at the hands of the man who'd made her what she was. Mignon spit at him.

A shot rang out, reverberating through the building. Charles stumbled back, his mouth opening to an O. He turned and stared at Ryan.

Ryan was on his knees, bracing himself as best he could with one hand. The handcuffs lay on the ground, the key next to them. He pointed his gun at Charles. Though the barrel wavered slightly, he fired again and again, each time hitting Charles squarely in the chest.

Charles glared at him. He swung his sword, opening Ryan's body from neck to stomach, baring bone and internal organs. Ryan fell back.

Blood spurted.

Mignon rose to her feet and with a mighty swing, buried her sword in Charles's neck. His head flew up into the air and then slammed down onto the concrete. A look of total surprise filled his eyes. His body sank down to sprawl in the center of the green light.

A side door flew open and a woman sprang into the room. Her hair was wild about her face. She saw Charles lying on the floor and a strange keening erupted from her. She knelt on the floor at Charles' head. "You killed him."

Mignon bit her lip and swung the sword. "Join him."

The woman's body collapsed on Charles.

Mignon turned to Ryan. She flung her sword from her and knelt down in the spreading pool of his blood and gathered him into her arms.

The voices of her people crackled in Ursula's ear-bug as they swept the warehouse clean and made their reports.

She listened to the litany of their reports. Seven vampires in one room. Four in another. Two dozen bodies on the verge of rising in a third room. Her teams swept through each room and left true death behind. The seconds stretched to minutes. Ursula followed Solomon down the corridor, looking for Charles in each room they passed.

When all the teams reported that all the rooms were empty and all the vamps dead, she gave her location and ordered everyone to her.

She heard the sound of gunfire coming from the warehouse next door. Ursula followed the sound with Solomon on her heels. Solomon slammed open a locked door and rushed in.

The room was large and smelled of blood. Ryan Lattimore lay in a pool of blood in the center of the room. Charles's headless body sprawled nearby with a headless female body on top. Ursula recognized Ryan's partner, Mary.

Mignon cradled Ryan Lattimore.

Ursula walked up to them. He would be dead soon. She was surprised to find tears on Mignon's face. "I'm sorry."

Mignon glanced up at her, her face radiating grief. "Your business is done, Major."

Ursula glanced around the room. She nodded at Mignon and started back for the door. She contacted her people and gave them directions to the colonel's body and ordered them back to the base. She reported that Charles was dead and the female vamp had escaped.

As she walked out the door, Solomon stopped her. She glanced at his hand on her arm. "Where do we go from here?"

"I will be in touch."

She nodded, turned and left the room.

Mignon clutched Ryan to her. Silently, she willed him not to die. She felt Solomon standing behind her and knew he shared her grief.

Ryan smiled weakly. "I love you." His voice was a distant whisper as his life signs faded.

"I just found you. I cannot let you die." If he died, she would seek the morning sun and die with him. She could not continue to exist without him.

He smiled at her, his lips growing slack and the light fading in his eyes.

"Ryan," Mignon said, "listen to me. I can turn you and save you. Just say yes. I can turn you."

"Mignon," his voice trailed away.

Solomon touched her shoulder. "Mignon."

She shrugged him away. She could feel the essence of who Ryan was slipping off into the universe. "I can change you. Otherwise, I die with you. I will seek the dawn and join you." Another rule broken, but it wouldn't matter. She'd broken so many. If Ryan agreed, he'd be with her. If not, the *Praetorium* would have no one to blame.

Surprise lit his eyes.

"Say yes."

He nodded his head so slightly she almost missed it. Then she smiled. She bit open the vein in her wrist. "Drink," she crooned. "Drink." Her blood flowed into his mouth. He swallowed. His body shuddered and went slack. His breathing stilled and his eyes lost their light.

Mignon cradled him against her. Her love overwhelmed her. He couldn't die. She wouldn't let him. "Please. Not him. Please. Just this once." Tears pooled in her eyes. Had he swallowed enough? Had she saved him? She would know soon enough.

"Mignon," Solomon said softly.

"Leave us," she ordered. She would sit with Ryan so that he would not be alone when he woke—if he woke.

CHAPTER FIFTEEN

Mignon exhaled a long breath. She wanted to go home, back to the island, back to her little cottage on the beach and her children. Though Simon and Angeline were long gone, their bodies were buried in a small cemetery nearby. She had brought them from New Orleans and kept them where she could visit them.

"Mignon." Elder Jabari stood, his voice thundering from the back of the room where he sat in his velvet chair surrounded by the other members of the *Praetorium*. "What are we to do with you? You revealed our existence to the mortals, you changed a mortal without permission, and you continue to flaunt your family in our faces."

Mignon bowed her head. "What do you expect me to say, Honored One. All is true." She glanced at Ryan sitting in the back of the room, grinning at her as though he enjoyed her discomfort way too much. "Ryan Lattimore earned his right to be among us. He is a hunter of skill and cunning. We can learn much from him. His time in the military will bring us new ways of defending ourselves."

Master Jabari growled. "That is not the point. You usurped the authority of the *Praetorium* by changing him. You must be punished."

Mignon stood her ground. Jabari had always shown her a certain affection. "I know. I'm willing to take what the *Praetorium* will give."

Jabari nodded. "I'm ready to render the decision of the *Praetorium*. Since we cannot control you through normal means, then we sentence you to serve on the *Praetorium* for the next hundred years."

A murmur moved through other members. Master Hans stood up. "That is not punishment. We should have her head."

Elder Turi stood. "The decision has been made. I stand with Master Jabari. And anyone who disagrees with me can meet my sword."

Max also stood and nodded. Mignon knew no one would challenge Max. There wasn't anyone here in this room that Max couldn't kill if he chose to. She blew him a kiss.

Elder Jabari chuckled as he leaned toward Hans. "Trust me. For Mignon, serving with us will be punishment enough. And how else are we to keep an eye on her?"

The murmurs died away. Mignon grinned at Ryan. "I accept. I'll see you at our next meeting." They could have taken her head. Any form of punishment was preferable to that. She had too much to live for now that she had Ryan.

She left the room and Ryan followed. He put an arm around her and pulled her close. "My woman, the politician."

"Remind me in fifty years why I didn't let them take my head."

"Because you have me. I'm worth the aggravation."

She faced him and cradled his face in her hands. She kissed him. "Be careful, dear one. Your swords are not as honed as mine."

He chuckled. "When I get you back to the hotel room, I'm going to show you what I can do with my sword." He pressed against her, his lips soft against hers.

"For the rest of eternity, I hope."

ABOUT THE AUTHOR

The writing team of **J.M. Jeffries**

Jacqueline S. Hamilton is the proud owner of twenty-seven shades of red lipstick. Though she considers herself a happy person, Jackie fights daily with her envy issues. She considers herself an expert in the fine art of being lazy. She would rather lay on the sofa patting her tummy, teaching Miriam's dog how to smoke and lie then do something like write. Jackie is an unrepentant pen thief and is passionately enamored of Steven Spielberg's "Animaniacs". Jackie decided to write romance novels because she can't sing, can't dance, it doesn't involve high math or high heels. She also believes the body God intended to give her was misplaced on Jennifer Lopez. Jackie doesn't exercise because she believes the eleventh commandment is "Thou shall not sweat," which is why she doesn't have a body like Jennifer Lopez.

Miriam Pace is the only woman in the world with her own hand cream collection, which she uses everywhere on her body except her hands. Her greatest beauty secret is lip balm for the elbows. She has the refinement of a Victorian lady, the intelligence of a Nobel Prize Laureate, and—when the stars are straight and the moon is full—the vocabulary of a truck driver. She has been known to level mountain ranges with the lift of an eyebrow. But friends consider her generous, warm and a closet dominatrix. She is affectionately known as the curator of the Pace Zoo. At any time, one can find sheep in her back yard, a German Shepard mix breed dog who if she had a opposable thumb would rule the world, a Queensland heeler who tries to herd everything on two and four feet, kamikaze koi with an attitude, a Bengal cat who prowls the house pretending to be the 'real' thing and a Maine Coon cat who just knows he's the cutest thing on the planet. Acknowledged as the Goddess of All Things, Miriam is the first person everyone turns to when they need a decision. She has been accused of making up Jackie's mind for her, lets Jackie be the Goddess of Whine and indulge in her drama queen moments.

Excerpt from

TAKEN BY YOU

BY

DOROTHY ELIZABETH LOVE

Release Date: October 2005

CHAPTER ONE

It had to be nervousness.

How else could she explain the anxiety she felt as she waited to meet the man who tiptoed around her dreams and didn't know she existed?

Not only was Reese McCoy a stranger to her, but he the famed football player, model and successful businessman. So much rolled into one man. That was probably why her heart was racing.

At Atlanta International airport, Leila stood in the shadows fifty feet away from the gate, scanning the crowd for the face she had seen many times in newspapers and on TV. She hadn't discovered any of the details about his personal life until the previous night when she had discussed him while viewing his pictures in the photo album of her friend Chi. The album was followed by an exciting look through a male pinup calendar. The barely clothed pinups hinted at a story about Reese McCoy that completely enticed and motivated her to reexamine the photo album.

This time around she had noticed that the less publicly known pictures in the album revealed expressions of happiness that seemed to lessen more and more as time passed by. Leila found that somewhat unsettling.

When Reese McCoy finally deplaned the aircraft from Scottsdale, Arizona, he flashed that wonderful smile—one Leila had come to like—at the airline attendant greeting passengers. His black pants and matching shirt nicely emphasized what she knew was an incredibly fit body underneath.

Lord, she thought, tingling, *he's too fine in person.*

Reese suddenly turned that alluring smile toward her. It masked the troubles she had heard he was having. Yet, still, it caused her breath to catch, pant a little. Too bad she had never met him in person before now.

Leila was about to wave to get his attention, but he turned and looked about, searching for someone. Leila knew he was looking for his friend, but wished it could have been her. She also knew that would never be the case. It seemed Reese McCoy had very little time for things outside of business, especially something as bothersome as a serious relationship.

Suddenly, his gaze returned to hers. This time their eyes locked for several moments. A slow, meaningful smile danced across his face. Leila couldn't stop her own mouth from reacting to his contagious smile. When he winked, she realized she was again staring. Did he think that she was just another pretty face on the long list of many that his tempting smile could entice? Embarrassed, she glanced away to refocus on her reason for being there.

Amazingly, in the short time she looked away he closed the distance between them.

Standing a few feet away he said, "Hello, pretty lady."

Probably a practiced line, she thought. He had no idea who she was or why she was there.

"I'm here to pick you up," Leila somehow found the confidence to say without breaking her stare.

He chuckled. "I haven't been to Atlanta in awhile, but come-on lines have certainly gotten bolder. I guess my next question should be, Your place or mine?"

"My place." Leila enjoyed his surprised look. She'd caught him off guard. Maybe he wasn't as practiced as she thought.

"Ohhh... yes," he growled softly, slowly, as his eyes roamed over her body. "I do miss Atlanta."

I think I'm flirting! That boosted her ego as she extended a hand for a shake. "I'm Leila Chamberlain. A friend of both Parker and Chi. Parker will call you about the change in plans, but he asked that I pick you up. He's stuck out of town on business and won't be back until very late. And Chi can't get away from the hospital. So I'm to babysit you until he returns." Leila was well aware that Reese had come to town to serve as Parker's best man.

"Babysit?" Reese chuckled, looking away.

Leila wasn't sure, but it looked as if there were a hint of something akin to regret behind that sienna stare. He recovered quickly. "I should start over," he said, accepting her hand to shake. "Nice to meet you, Leila. It's a pleasure."

Leila laughed then. "Parker thought you would be upset because all your plans for tonight changed at the last minute. He said something about you being a stickler for preplanning. I can't wait to tell him you used the word *pleasure*."

"Mention it's because of his choice of babysitters." Reese adjusted his carryon luggage over his shoulder. "I'll follow your lead."

His sinfully charming grin had returned and that caught her off guard. "I guess we should get your luggage."

"That's one option."

That certainly has a double meaning! She, however, stuck to the agenda. "We have a stop to make. I'm to remind you to get fitted for your tux today. We can go there next if you like."

"Although Chi and Parker's wedding is one of the reasons I'm in town, I have a few business errands to run. I'll get the tux later. I guess I need a rental car now."

223

"No, you don't." She dodged a traveler hurrying toward them. "Parker's Jeep and a key to his home are at my place. I'll take you there."

"You *were* serious about going to your place?" Reese smiled at her.

"I never kid around about inviting a man to my home." Leila stepped onto the down escalator that led to the underground rail system, which carried passengers to terminals. "It's also my place of business." She casually tossed that comment out.

The smirk on Reese's face showed he was possibly considering less than appropriate 'business' options. Or maybe he just found her seriousness to be funny. "Oh, really."

They rode down the escalator in silence, then joined a horde of people waiting for the train. When it arrived, everyone dashed aboard and attempted to find a spot to stand in the already crowded car. Leila moved to hold one of the stationary bars as Reese stood sardined between her and the people behind them. He managed to grasp the bar just above her hand. She could feel the heat of his body touching her back.

"Thanks for coming to pick me up," he said, leaning forward.

"No problem." Leila looked back over her shoulder at him. The mere inches between them sent heated awareness through her. She took in his wide, firm chest and strong, muscular arm, as his spicy cologne enchanted her. The train jarred to a stop at each terminal as it made its way to baggage claim, and each jerk brought Reese closer to Leila. Of course she could have taken a step forward to stop that from happening, but bumping into the tall, lanky man in front of her was not as appealing as bumping into Reese.

"What is Mr. Chamberlain going to say about your entertaining me while my friend's away?" His breath was on her ear.

"My father gave up on advising me years before he died," Leila said. She knew he was attempting to find out more about her personal life. Although single and available, she wasn't quite sure if she wanted to admit that yet.

It tickled her pride knowing she'd done very little to capture his interest, yet clearly she had. Well, if not counting the blatant stares, the flippant invitation to her home, and the unnecessary closeness they were now sharing.

Her senses seemed sharper. She was aware of his heat, aware of his attraction, and aware they would soon be alone together. Intrigued at how his mere presence had fully consumed her thoughts in a rather short period of time, she reflected on the little she knew of Reese. Her reaction to him was purely physical, the worst kind, and she needed to contain it. He was quite stunning in those calendar layout pictures. His barely clothed body posed next to *August* made that month definitely hotter.

What gave her pause was that he was an ex-football player, there-fore probably a playboy. He had lost custody of his son during a bitter divorce, and his ex-wife lived in town. He had buried his only family, an aunt, several years ago and had taken her death hard. The recent downturn of his shipping business had relegated him to a struggling firm.

The train doors opened and they headed to baggage claim. As Reese watched for his suitcases to appear on the luggage conveyor, Leila stole a glance at him. He looked just as rugged and daring as he had in the younger photos, but now the fine lines of wisdom that cradled those eyes suggested experience she wanted to know more about.

His skin coloring reminded her of warm pecan pie, her favorite. She unconsciously licked her lips as she recalled the pictures showing more of that skin. Both he and Parker had posed as calendar models. Parker had done it as a dare. Reese, however, had needed the money and exposure.

In all the pictures she had seen, a smile completely brightened his handsome face. Unlike now. The smile was genuine but the cheerful-ness seemed to have faded somewhat. She liked his faint beard that sur-rounded lips that promised heaven in a mouthful. Instantaneously, her mind drifted to a scene where she was experiencing that mouth, those fine hairs against sensitive parts of her body.

"I would pay big money to know your thoughts," Reese said,

watching her. He looked as though he already knew them.

"I didn't think I would recognize you from the pictures Parker showed me." Leila was proud of how well she came up with a valid reason, even veiled excuse, for blatantly, probably heatedly, staring at him again. "You haven't changed much in the past few years."

His smile disappeared as if memories from the past plagued his thoughts. "Pictures can lie. I'm nothing like that guy anymore."

He was frowning and she blamed herself. *From lust to accusation. I should shut up and just get the man to his vehicle,* Leila scolded herself.

"I just meant…" Leila was about to say, 'You look the same physically,' but it was too late because he had turned to retrieve his bag from the spinning conveyor.

She was sure his statement had nothing to do with physical changes, but more with the circumstances that surrounded his life. She didn't know the details, but Parker had labeled them as "difficult times." Since Parker had also labeled his first fiancée's death, his sister being shot and the accident that almost killed the love of his life, Chi, as "difficult times," Leila figured Reese's life must have been just as trying.

He collected the last of his luggage and followed Leila outside into the warm June afternoon. They went to Leila's car in short-term parking. She easily maneuvered the car out of the airport only to encounter caterpillar slow highway traffic.

"Is this typical for this time of day?" Reese asked a few minutes later, looking at the time.

"Not on I-75. There must be an accident ahead."

"How far away is your place?"

"Without traffic it's about twenty-five minutes."

"This can go on for awhile." Reese reached into his overnight bag to retrieve his cell phone and dialed. "Bill? It's Reese McCoy," he announced when the person answered. "I'm in town, but stuck in traffic. First, the plane was delayed. Now this. Can we delay our meeting until this evening?" Reese listened. "No, no. That's okay. I'll get there as soon as I can. I really need you to see my plan and consider supporting it… Yeah… Bill, it's a solid plan. Don't shoot it down until you have a chance to review it." The longer Reese talked, the flatter his tone got. He hung up and stared at the phone for a few seconds, visibly shaking off a difficult mood.

"I can take you directly to your meeting," Leila offered. "Pick you up and take you to get the Jeep afterwards."

"I'm not sure how long I'll be or where we're headed afterwards." Reese watched the traffic come to a halt. "The sooner I get to Parker's, the sooner I can shower, change and get to the meeting." His look suggested appreciation. "But thanks for offering."

Leila liked the sincerity she saw. "I have a better idea. You can change at my place, it's closer and we need to stop there anyway. I'll get off the highway as soon as I can. Maybe get around this." She turned and leaned back to get a map from her briefcase on the backseat. "I keep a city map with me for moments like this." When Leila looked up, she found Reese had turned toward her, looking down the V of her white blouse.

"Take your time."

"Are you sure? That call sounded important."

"It was. But I'm in no rush to listen to them shoot down my plan. This…," his eyes roamed provocatively up her chest to her eyes, "…delay is taking my mind off it."

His somber look from moments ago had disappeared, replaced with a warm, much more pleasing smile. Visions of teenager years "necking" in the car danced in Leila's head. The inches between them would only take seconds to remove.

She wasn't sure which one of them moved first, but somehow his mouth seemed much closer to hers. Her heart jiggled a little and she found herself breathing heavier. Then something in his eyes called to her.

Sampling him was a fantasy that had crossed her mind several times while looking at pictures of his fantastic body. Now she was sure she was the one to move closer this time.

The honking from the car behind startled her.

"Oh!" She jumped and let out a nervous little laugh. Looking quickly about, she then moved back under the wheel. It took her a few seconds to realize the car was already in gear and all she needed to do was remove her foot from the brake pedal. She felt like a clumsy teenager instead of the professional, sometimes sassy, business owner that she was.

That was a stupid gesture I just made, she said to herself, then turned to Reese. "Traffic is moving."

"Uh huh," he grunted, his smile widening.

Luckily, since she couldn't think of anything else to say, jazz from the car radio filled the air. It bothered her that she'd neither resisted nor gone through with the kiss. A kiss she'd been wanting to experience since the moment she'd dreamt of him. This kind of indecision was another example of why she would always be the lonely maid of honor and never the bride. She could dream about having a man but couldn't pull off impressing one as an experienced flirt.

Remembering the map, she busied herself with searching for a convenient route as she followed the slow-moving traffic.

"How long have you lived here?" Reese asked.

"I moved back about four years ago. It's changed a lot since I was a kid." She studied the map, then looked up at the road ahead. "I think I can get around this by getting off at the next exit."

"I'll leave my comforts in your competent hands."

Leila looked at him. *His comforts.* Was he picking at her for failing to resist him and failing to kiss him? Certainly kissing was a bit much for someone she had just met. She played it safe and pretended to take a greater interest in getting around the heavy traffic. The ride through the busy districts was the perfect distraction.

They arrived at her home, or *partial home*, as Leila called it, about thirty minutes later. They had talked very little en route because Reese spent most of the time on his cell phone discussing shipping matters. The gist of what Leila picked up on was that his cinching an important business deal was imperative to the expansion of his company. Based on Reese's solemn tone, she figured things weren't going well.

Reese noticed the day care sign. "You have a kid we need to pick up from day care?" he asked as she parked the car.

"I live on the floor above it," Leila said, getting out of the car.

"Interesting place to call home." He went to get his luggage out of the trunk. "How come?"

"I own the building. The day care center is my business."

"Very clever." He glanced around at the upscale business location.

The day care was the size of a two-story warehouse with a large playground and expanse of land behind it. Several cars were in the parking lot. A few parents were picking up children. On the playground, several kids played on slides, swings and monkey bars, while others played a game of putt-putt golf. Several kids cheered when another whacked the small ball between the legs of a gigantic sized parrot.

Upstairs, Leila's apartment door opened into an extremely spacious room. She had a flair for the dramatic and had reconfigured the room into sections with cream Roman columns separating the foyer and hallway from the living room. The floors were bleached hardwood with matching paneled walls. Large plants were aplenty. A deep purple, leather sofa sat against the back wall, on the other side of the glass top table, matching chairs faced the sofa.

The unusually high windows on the back wall spanned up to vaulted ceilings and allowed a view of blue skies and green tops of leafy trees. A view she considered her peak at heaven. No one could have imagined that a busy playground, a major road and several businesses were just beyond those walls. It was just like she wanted it to be.

Reese's cellular phone ran again. "Hey, Suzette," he said casually.

The female name got Leila's attention. But she shouldn't be eavesdropping. Or at least, not look as if she were eavesdropping. Leila went to her desk at the far side of the room and opened the top drawer, pretending to be busy as she tuned in to Reese's side of the conversation.

"I'll rearrange my schedule," he was saying. "I don't want to change the plans for this weekend. Okay. Bye."

Leila sensed he was studying her downcast head. She put down the mail she held and reached back inside the top drawer to get a stuffed envelope, which she handed it to him. "These are for you. Jeep keys, Parker's house key, and directions to the tuxedo shop."

"Parker is finally getting married." Reese shook his head. "I still can't believe it."

She angled her head, confused. Leila wasn't sure if she appreciated the comment. "For a best man, you don't sound too supportive."

He looked at her, his expression tame. "Parker deserves to finally find happiness."

For some reason she wanted to be annoyed at Reese. Possibly as a means to dampen her fascination with him, but his sincere look wouldn't allow her to use his comment as a reason. Well, the man did live several states away and, according to Chi, was on the rebound from a terrible divorce. If that wasn't reason enough to sway her interest, then obviously his looking forward to seeing this Suzette person should have been. It wasn't. Leila fought down the urge to flirt, to compete.

She walked around him. "You wanted to shower and change. Let me show you to the bathroom."

Reese stepped inside a bathroom that only an interior designer could have imagined. The high ceiling was painted with clouds and the borders with leafy red and purple roses. It had a Jacuzzi tub, a freestanding glassed-in shower stall, and more Roman columns. The center wall featured a vanity area on one side and a loveseat with bookcase on the other.

"Very nice. I like your taste." Reese set down his luggage.

"Thanks. I live too close to my job. So home had to be an escape for me." Leila opened the closet door and handed him a towel and washcloth. She pointed and said, "Everything else you'll need should be under the sink."

She turned and noticed him unbuttoning his shirt. When he started to casually pull the shirttails from out of his pants, she froze. Not out of panic but out of pleasure. She'd dreamt about seeing that body up close and personal.

Then Reese placed his hands on his hips and the shirt opened even more. "Anything else you want to tell me?" Reese asked.

Again she was staring. His chest was more enticing than the one she'd conjured up in her dream last night. She dragged her eyes up to his. His cocky grin didn't help matters. It was one thing to secretly drool and pant like a cat in heat. Being caught, however, was rather embarrassing.

"I need to go downstairs to check on the day care." Leila found herself struggling to find something other than him to gawk at. Failing, she walked toward the safety of the door.

Unfortunately for her, he stopped her by catching her by the arm as she passed. Leila stepped away from him but he refused to release her.

"What is it?" she whispered.

"There is something else," Reese said, pulling her closer to his inviting body.

She sidestepped. "I've delayed you long enough from your meeting," Leila said to his hand since she wasn't brave enough to look him in the face. He might see just how in need of his touch she was.

The telephone rang. Again she jumped and inwardly cursed because of it. She really needed to gain control of herself. "Let me get that." She looked at the telephone that hung on the bathroom wall by the loveseat behind him. Though parts of the too-large bathroom looked and felt like a den, it was still too intimate a setting for her with Reese there. She decided to take the call elsewhere.

At her desk, Leila found herself breathing heavily when she answered. "Chi! Hi! Your timing couldn't be better... We just got here. Reese was about to jump in the shower..."

"Stop him!" Chi said. "I need to talk to him."

"Oh, okay, hold on." Leila hurried to the bathroom door and called out. "Reese, it's for you!" When he picked up the bathroom telephone, she went to hang up the one on the desk.

As she did, Reese stepped out of the bathroom, the cordless telephone resting on his bare shoulder. He had taken off his shirt and shoes, and his pants were partly unzipped. "I think that's a fantastic idea. I'm sure of it," he said to Chi. "I assume you've already talked to Leila?"

Leila came to stand in the hallway, watching him watch her. His stare was disconcerting. So sexy, so disarming, so distracting. Thankfully, the man would be leaving her home forever once he showered and changed. Moments earlier when he touched her, she'd had the impression he was going to do something quite thrilling. That would have been a mistake for her, in light of the Suzette call, but for some reason she felt disappointed that it hadn't happened.

Luckily, he was leaving and her life would soon return to normal. She could sit back and think about her crazy reactions to him later. Whatever he had just said to Chi, Leila hadn't heard; she was too busy enjoying his near nakedness.

In less than an hour he will be gone, she reminded herself. She exhaled slowly to calm her racing heart.

"Leila," Reese said, "Chi was wondering if you could help with something tonight."

"Sure," she said. "Of course."

"More wedding guests are flying to town."

"Does she need me to pick them up from the airport?" she asked.

"It seems Parker has run out of room for everyone. So Chi was wondering if you wouldn't mind entertaining me tonight...," Reese paused to smile, "by letting me use your bedroom."

Although he was perfectly clear, Leila asked, slightly flustered, "What?"

He removed the distance between them and said again, very slowly, very provocatively, "I want to stay the night with you."

BLOOD LUST

2005 Publication Schedule

January

A Heart's Awakening
Veronica Parker
$9.95
1-58571-143-8

Falling
Natalie Dunbar
$9.95
1-58571-121-7

February

Echoes of Yesterday
Beverly Clark
$9.95
1-58571-131-4

A Love of Her Own
Cheris F. Hodges
$9.95
1-58571-136-5

Higher Ground
Leah Latimer
$19.95
1-58571-157-8

March

Misconceptions
Pamela Leigh Starr
$9.95
1-58571-117-9

I'll Paint a Sun
A.J. Garrotto
$9.95
1-58571-165-9

Peace Be Still
Colette Haywood
$12.95
1-58571-129-2

April

Intentional Mistakes
Michele Sudler
$9.95
1-58571-152-7

Conquering Dr. Wexler's Heart
Kimberley White
$9.95
1-58571-126-8

Song in the Park
Martin Brant
$15.95
1-58571-125-X

May

The Color Line
Lizzette Grayson Carter
$9.95
1-58571-163-2

Unconditional
A.C. Arthur
$9.95
1-58571-142-X

Last Train to Memphis
Elsa Cook
$12.95
1-58571-146-2

June

Angel's Paradise
Janice Angelique
$9.95
1-58571-107-1

Suddenly You
Crystal Hubbard
$9.95
1-58571-158-6

Matters of Life and
    Death
Lesego Malepe, Ph.D.
$15.95
1-58571-124-1

2005 Publication Schedule (continued)

July

Class Reunion
Irma Jenkins/John
  Brown
$12.95
1-58571-123-3

Wild Ravens
Altonya Washington
$9.95
1-58571-164-0

August

Path of Thorns
Annetta P. Lee
$9.95
1-58571-145-4

Timeless Devotion
Bella McFarland
$9.95
1-58571-148-9

Life Is Never As It Seems
J.J. Michael
$12.95
1-58571-153-5

September

Beyond the Rapture
Beverly Clark
$9.95
1-58571-131-4

Blood Lust
J. M. Jeffries
$9.95
1-58571-138-1

Rough on Rats and
  Tough on Cats
Chris Parker
$12.95
1-58571-154-3

October

A Will to Love
Angie Daniels
$9.95
1-58571-141-1

Taken by You
Dorothy Elizabeth Love
$9.95
1-58571-162-4

Soul Eyes
Wayne L. Wilson
$12.95
1-58571-147-0

November

A Drummer's Beat to
  Mend
Kay Swanson
$9.95

Sweet Reprecussions
Kimberley White
$9.95
1-58571-159-4

Red Polka Dot in a
  Worldof Plaid
Varian Johnson
$12.95
1-58571-140-3

December

Hand in Glove
Andrea Jackson
$9.95
1-58571-166-7

Blaze
Barbara Keaton
$9.95

Across
Carol Payne
$12.95
1-58571-149-7

Other Genesis Press, Inc. Titles

Acquisitions	Kimberley White	$8.95
A Dangerous Deception	J.M. Jeffries	$8.95
A Dangerous Love	J.M. Jeffries	$8.95
A Dangerous Obsession	J.M. Jeffries	$8.95
After the Vows	Leslie Esdaile	$10.95
(Summer Anthology)	T.T. Henderson	
	Jacqueline Thomas	
Again My Love	Kayla Perrin	$10.95
Against the Wind	Gwynne Forster	$8.95
A Lark on the Wing	Phyliss Hamilton	$8.95
A Lighter Shade of Brown	Vicki Andrews	$8.95
All I Ask	Barbara Keaton	$8.95
A Love to Cherish	Beverly Clark	$8.95
Ambrosia	T.T. Henderson	$8.95
And Then Came You	Dorothy Elizabeth Love	$8.95
Angel's Paradise	Janice Angelique	$8.95
A Risk of Rain	Dar Tomlinson	$8.95
At Last	Lisa G. Riley	$8.95
Best of Friends	Natalie Dunbar	$8.95
Bound by Love	Beverly Clark	$8.95
Breeze	Robin Hampton Allen	$10.95
Brown Sugar Diaries &	Delores Bundy &	$10.95
Other Sexy Tales	Cole Riley	
By Design	Barbara Keaton	$8.95
Cajun Heat	Charlene Berry	$8.95
Careless Whispers	Rochelle Alers	$8.95
Caught in a Trap	Andre Michelle	$8.95
Chances	Pamela Leigh Starr	$8.95
Dark Embrace	Crystal Wilson Harris	$8.95
Dark Storm Rising	Chinelu Moore	$10.95
Designer Passion	Dar Tomlinson	$8.95
Ebony Butterfly II	Delilah Dawson	$14.95

Erotic Anthology	Assorted	$8.95
Eve's Prescription	Edwina Martin Arnold	$8.95
Everlastin' Love	Gay G. Gunn	$8.95
Fate	Pamela Leigh Starr	$8.95
Forbidden Quest	Dar Tomlinson	$10.95
Fragment in the Sand	Annetta P. Lee	$8.95
From the Ashes	Kathleen Suzanne	$8.95
	Jeanne Sumerix	
Gentle Yearning	Rochelle Alers	$10.95
Glory of Love	Sinclair LeBeau	$10.95
Hart & Soul	Angie Daniels	$8.95
Heartbeat	Stephanie Bedwell-Grime	$8.95
I'll Be Your Shelter	Giselle Carmichael	$8.95
Illusions	Pamela Leigh Starr	$8.95
Indiscretions	Donna Hill	$8.95
Interlude	Donna Hill	$8.95
Intimate Intentions	Angie Daniels	$8.95
Just an Affair	Eugenia O'Neal	$8.95
Kiss or Keep	Debra Phillips	$8.95
Love Always	Mildred E. Riley	$10.95
Love Unveiled	Gloria Greene	$10.95
Love's Deception	Charlene Berry	$10.95
Mae's Promise	Melody Walcott	$8.95
Meant to Be	Jeanne Sumerix	$8.95
Midnight Clear	Leslie Esdaile	$10.95
(Anthology)	Gwynne Forster	
	Carmen Green	
	Monica Jackson	
Midnight Magic	Gwynne Forster	$8.95
Midnight Peril	Vicki Andrews	$10.95
My Buffalo Soldier	Barbara B. K. Reeves	$8.95
Naked Soul	Gwynne Forster	$8.95
No Regrets	Mildred E. Riley	$8.95
Nowhere to Run	Gay G. Gunn	$10.95

Object of His Desire	A. C. Arthur	$8.95
One Day at a Time	Bella McFarland	$8.95
Passion	T.T. Henderson	$10.95
Past Promises	Jahmel West	$8.95
Path of Fire	T.T. Henderson	$8.95
Picture Perfect	Reon Carter	$8.95
Pride & Joi	Gay G. Gunn	$8.95
Quiet Storm	Donna Hill	$8.95
Reckless Surrender	Rochelle Alers	$8.95
Rendezvous with Fate	Jeanne Sumerix	$8.95
Revelations	Cheris F. Hodges	$8.95
Rivers of the Soul	Leslie Esdaile	$8.95
Rooms of the Heart	Donna Hill	$8.95
Shades of Brown	Denise Becker	$8.95
Shades of Desire	Monica White	$8.95
Sin	Crystal Rhodes	$8.95
So Amazing	Sinclair LeBeau	$8.95
Somebody's Someone	Sinclair LeBeau	$8.95
Someone to Love	Alicia Wiggins	$8.95
Soul to Soul	Donna Hill	$8.95
Still Waters Run Deep	Leslie Esdaile	$8.95
Subtle Secrets	Wanda Y. Thomas	$8.95
Sweet Tomorrows	Kimberly White	$8.95
The Color of Trouble	Dyanne Davis	$8.95
The Price of Love	Sinclair LeBeau	$8.95
The Reluctant Captive	Joyce Jackson	$8.95
The Missing Link	Charlyne Dickerson	$8.95
Three Wishes	Seressia Glass	$8.95
Tomorrow's Promise	Leslie Esdaile	$8.95
Truly Inseperable	Wanda Y. Thomas	$8.95
Twist of Fate	Beverly Clark	$8.95
Unbreak My Heart	Dar Tomlinson	$8.95
Unconditional Love	Alicia Wiggins	$8.95
When Dreams A Float	Dorothy Elizabeth Love	$8.95

Whispers in the Night	Dorothy Elizabeth Love	$8.95
Whispers in the Sand	LaFlorya Gauthier	$10.95
Yesterday is Gone	Beverly Clark	$8.95
Yesterday's Dreams, Tomorrow's Promises	Reon Laudat	$8.95
Your Precious Love	Sinclair LeBeau	$8.95

Order Form

Mail to: Genesis Press, Inc.
P.O. Box 101
Columbus, MS 39703

Name _____

Address _____

City/State _____ Zip _____

Telephone _____

Ship to (if different from above)

Name _____

Address _____

City/State _____ Zip _____

Telephone _____

Credit Card Information

Credit Card # _____ ☐ Visa ☐ Mastercard

Expiration Date (mm/yy) _____ ☐ AmEx ☐ Discover

Qty.	Author	Title	Price	Total

Use this order

form, or call

1-888-INDIGO-1

Total for books _____

Shipping and handling:
  $5 first two books,
  $1 each additional book _____

Total S & H _____

Total amount enclosed _____

Mississippi residents add 7% sales tax

Order Form

Mail to: Genesis Press, Inc.
P.O. Box 101
Columbus, MS 39703

Name _____

Address _____

City/State _____ Zip _____

Telephone _____

Ship to (if different from above)

Name _____

Address _____

City/State _____ Zip _____

Telephone _____

Credit Card Information

Credit Card # _____ ☐ Visa ☐ Mastercard

Expiration Date (mm/yy) _____ ☐ AmEx ☐ Discover

Qty.	Author	Title	Price	Total

Use this order form, or call 1-888-INDIGO-1	**Total for books** _____ **Shipping and handling:** **$5 first two books,** **$1 each additional book** _____ **Total S & H** _____ **Total amount enclosed** _____ *Mississippi residents add 7% sales tax*